You're **NOT** My Mommy

BABE TONER

Order this book online at www.trafford.com
or email orders@trafford.com

Most Trafford titles are also available at major online book retailers.

Print information available on the last page.

ISBN: 978-1-4907-8256-0 (sc)
ISBN: 978-1-4907-8258-4 (hc)
ISBN: 978-1-4907-8257-7 (e)

Library of Congress Control Number: 2017907563

Trafford rev. 05/12/2017

 www.trafford.com
North America & international
toll-free: 1 888 232 4444 (USA & Canada)
fax: 812 355 4082

1

Jenny was a real cute girl and everyone wanted to be with her, she was the captain of the cheer leaders and was the most looked at girl at the games. She was very flattered when she was given a compliment especially from the young men. She wanted everyone to like her and the boys who caught on fast how easy she was and she believed anything they told her. They would often call out things to her while she was cheering and kicking her legs higher than any of the other girls and showing her stuff that she thought was cute. There were things that she would eventually have to deal with because with the young stallions when you give them an inch they would want the whole nine yards. She didn't know it but every time she moved around in her skimpy outfit the boys were looking for something that she would show them in the course of her cheering. A smart girl would have stayed her distance but Jenny couldn't.

She loved the popularity and couldn't see where it would end up. The party invitations were coming at her fast, so fast she couldn't turn any down, even though her girlfriends told her not to go to these drink fest's where the boys would get out of control from drinking and practically rape the girls that hesitated to say yes. She just couldn't get over how popular she was. The parties started out dancing, then touching and when she could no longer say no she found herself in the middle of having sex at every party and always with a different partner and that wasn't all they expected from her. If it was that time of the month and she couldn't have sex then they would insist on oral sex. She could see that she wasn't alone having sex with the boys all the girls were doing it to, both ways, anything to make them happy and like them. So she didn't think any more about it. There were times when she didn't insist on the boys wearing protection which was very chancy, of all the things that could happen to her this could prove to be a very big mistake someday.

Her parents were too busy raising her two brothers and two sisters that ranged from twelve down to five. They didn't have time to see that Jenny was on the right course or not, they trusted her to do the right thing. That freed them up to spend more time with the younger children; they never even looked at her report card which would have clearly showed them that she was only just passing. They hoped that she was doing as well as she looked she was. Let's face it Jenny looked very successful and was head and shoulders over the rest of her school mates. There were a lot of women that wished they looked as good as she did. When she got together with her girlfriends they would often talk about some one that got pregnant especially the girl that got pregnant from the black football player. He scored a touchdown that night and she lost the game. They were in shock that this could happen to a girl with all the things there were available to keep that from happening. Jenny said that's where she draws the line; those guys have a history of deserting their women and leaving the poor girl on her own. Jenny knew it wasn't just the black guys; the white guys used college as an excuse as well not to marry or take care of these girls. They heard that the girl that got pregnant from the black football player, her mother took her to Canada for a hysterectomy. None of the boys would have anything to do with her and she faded away with her parents and they eventually moved.

With one more year to go before she graduated from high school, Jenny was a changed girl, she wasn't that much fun for the other girls to be around because she always wanted to be with the boys and party, the sex was really good and couldn't be all that bad if it felt that good. She was consumed by this fast life of drinking and never being with the same guy twice. At home her parents still couldn't see anything on the horizon, believe it or not she was beginning to get a bad reputation from all this drinking and screwing around and it took a while but her phone stopped ringing and her girlfriends were busy with their steady boyfriends. Having sex with one guy was better than having sex with the whole school. Jenny went from the most popular girl in school to the most unpopular girl in school. Even as a cute cheerleader it still didn't help. The cheerleader coach called her in her office one day and said that there are some very disturbing stories going around about her and was she aware of them. She said she wasn't and what kind of stories are you talking about.

"Well to be very frank with you Jenny, one story that I heard is that you are the best fuck in school."

"Jenny gulped and said, "Who could be spreading such vicious lies around school like that about me."

Miss Miller looked at her and said, "It was those ungrateful boys that you turned on that were destroying you. They even told everyone that you would rather do oral sex then screw."

"I don't know what to tell you Miss Miller, but those things are untrue."

"I did a little investigating on my own and talked to five young men that are in your class and are on the football team and every one of them said they had sex with you and everything else was also true. Jenny I can't clean up your name but it's time you crossed your legs and shut your mouth because these boys hold you up as a trophy. You're something to go after because you're easy. You can go to the principal and get me in trouble for the way I spoke to you but I felt that if I came down to your level you would understand it better. You are going to get very sick from one of these sexual perverts or you will get pregnant. Either one of these are not very good for you, there is no way you can't get hurt in this life style your living."

Jenny stood up and thanked Miss Miller for talking to her and as hard as it was to hear what she had to say to her she still appreciates the interest. She knows now that the very people that used her were the very people that ruined her reputation. She went along with the crowd and the crowd deserted her. She was so unpopular no one would even ask her to the senior prom, that destroyed her and everyone in the whole school knew that as well.

The night of the prom she was so down in the dumps so when she received a phone call from Dave one of her old drinking chums who didn't have a date for the prom either asked her if she wanted to take a ride in his new car. As bad as she felt she didn't see any harm in it so she jumped at it and he picked her up at her house. She loved the car and loved the look of the mustang and it smelt so clean. She was very vulnerable to his nice talking or even innocent touching so when he parked it on lover's lane she knew that he wanted more than to take her for a ride and she needed something to give her a boost and he had the tools to do the job. There wasn't much he had to do to lure her into the back seat hell she had those panties off before the engine shut off. She was no stranger to the back seat of a car looking at the different dome lights on her back; she wanted it bad and used this moment as her date for the prom, her private prom. She never once gave it a thought about what Miss Miller talked to her about, this felt too good to be bad.

It was a wonderful evening in spite of not going to the prom Dave was a good lover and he proved it that night. She was so contented even after he dropped her off she was still purring like a kitten. The last week of school Jenny had missed her period which scared her to death. She was so scared that she was sick every morning for one straight week. She heard about these pregnancy test and bought one, it turns out she was pregnant and scared and not having a clue what to do about it. The first thing she did was to call Dave and told him she wanted to see him this evening only this time she met him in the park and ride parking lot and told him that she was pregnant. He told her that he wasn't surprised from what he had heard. Well she called him every name in the book and he told her that she could have told him all this on the phone. She actually thought he would be a little more sensitive after hearing that he was going to be a father. He told her that he was now enrolled in college and couldn't take on any more responsibility at this point in his life.

"Well what about me, I can't take on any more responsibility either."

"You should have thought about that when you decided to turn on all the guys in your senior class."

"You know Dave you are being very insensitive about our problem. You want us girls to go drinking with you and have sex and when something that has happened to me you discard us like we were trash."

"You have been with too many guys to know who the father is of your unwanted child."

"A woman knows who the father is no matter how many guys she's been with. So now I am on my own and can expect no help from you at all."

"That's right, I can't help you. Do you want to have a farewell fling before I leave tonight?"

"I wouldn't have a farewell fling with you if you were the only man left on Earth."

"Now don't be mad at me, I am one of many that have slipped between your legs. It must have been good or you wouldn't have done it."

"Well to be perfectly honest with you, it was good in a reckless kinda way but as usual the woman is left with the damages and the men walk away. Now I have to tell my parents."

"Don't mention my name unless you mention all the other guys that you had sex with."

"Boy you are really scared aren't you? Now you think you can tell me how to tell my parents. You just don't want them to find out about your sex exploits and refuse your responsibility in this matter"

"I am only scared of what a poor pregnant girl will say to her parents so she won't look bad to them. You'll tell them he told me he loved me."

4

"Well theirs no use in carrying on this conversation except to tell you that you have just given up your legal rights to this baby when you denied that it is you. You even called me a whore without actually using that word. That is what hurts the most the name calling."

"I am sorry but you screwed too many guys to be sure it was me, to all the sperm donors around school you were just a sperm bank always open for a deposit."

"I think I am tired of talking to you, so stay out of my life and fuck off."

With that Jenny left for home and wanted to pick the best time to tell her parents about her predicament which wasn't going to be easy after all the freedom they gave her. Jenny is taking all the blame for this which won't help in telling her mother that's she's pregnant. When she got home her mother was up sitting in the kitchen having a cold glass of ice tea, Jenny walked out into the kitchen and right away he mother could see that something was wrong and asked Jenny is she ok.

"I am fine, but I have a problem."

"I know I found your pregnancy kit in the bathroom trash can."

"That's me not being careful and getting caught."

"What did the father have to say about it?"

"Well he called me a whore and I kicked him out of his car."

"Are you a whore?"

"I don't think I am a whore, I did whore around a little."

"Whoring around a little makes you a whore I should have told you that only women bleed and in most cases like this, the men walk away Scot free and in denial about the whole thing. Now you are left with a baby to raise and no one to help you. This man or should I say boy doesn't want to have anything to do with this baby am I right? So make sure he doesn't and can't come back to you later on and make a claim. You would be surprised what people will do later on down the road"

"I know that you can't take on another mouth here to feed so if I could stay until I have the baby I am hoping to find a room with some widow or someone like that and move in."

"How will you support yourself?"

"How do most women support themselves, I'll become a waitress. I am out of school now and I can find a job working tables."

"Carrying a baby around inside and those heavy trays to the tables won't be easy."

"It will be easier then telling dad, won't it?"

"*He already knows about the test kit. I told him I found it in the trash, I don't hide anything from him and he doesn't hide anything from me.*"

"*What did he say?*"

"*He said that he felt sorry for you if you are pregnant. This was something that he never hoped that would happen to you. He saw you as a girl that knew what she was doing and it turns out that you didn't*"

"*That's it.*"

"*He said that you would have to leave and be on your own. He doesn't want the children to see you walking around pregnant and going through all the problems with being pregnant and see you raising a baby out of wed lock.*"

"*That sounds a little old fashion.*"

"*It might be but that's how he feels and that's how we must solve this problem at home. It has to be his way and the highway. I can assure you that he means every word. You broke a trust and he feels you can't be trusted anymore.*"

The next day Jenny went out looking for a waitress job and found one at the diner, the owner kept asking her to stay and help him with the books after she gets off. She could clearly see that he wanted sex so she quit and was out looking again. She was hired where ever she went because of her looks. She either had to put up with the ass pinching and patting or quit again. She quit because this was how it all started back when. She knows it all starts out as a simple brush by and moves up to a boobe crunch and so on. Her mother finally asked her why are there so many jobs and she told her straight out that it was the owner or the manager or even the employees that want me to go to bed with them. It's every job so far, what am I going to do. Her mother told her not to give in; they will only use you again.

Jenny heard of a receptionist job at one of the car dealers and was hired on the spot. Being pregnant made her look pretty as ever and was going to be a big asset to the dealer ship. The salesman would bring her coffee and donuts every morning and being pregnant she would love to eat the donuts and leave the coffee alone. There were numerous requests for dates but she turned every one down for good reasons. The salesmen were nice about it and respected her decision not to date. Once she turned someone down she would offend the ones she turned down if she would say yes to someone. She needed the job and she had to save all of her pay just to stay a head of the cost of living on her own. Her parents weren't going to help her. Her mother asked Jenny if she wanted a baby shower and without hesitation she told her no. She could detect from her mother's voice that she didn't want to give Jenny a shower.

Jenny looked back on the last couple of years of her life and was amazed to see that getting pregnant, was enough to turn away her parents and the kids at school that she thought were her friends. They all deserted her in her hour of need. She couldn't understand how all these wonderful times turn into such an unforgiving circumstance. With her parents blaming her how about her blaming her parents for not sitting her down and telling her about all the birds and sob's. I think there's a good case here to defend Jenny a little.

Being five months pregnant now she is definitely showing it, there wasn't any doubt she was pregnant. You know those car salesmen respected her for having the baby and not having an abortion. She tried to wear the best of clothes and would go to the goodwill store and look over their clothes hoping to find something nice; she needed to save what she could for the rough days ahead. She never asked her mother why are they making themselves so distant from her so one evening it was just Jenny and her mom and Jenny asked her mom why are you and dad so distant. Her mother told her because you broke the trust we had in you while you were going around taking care of everyone else but you're self and now you are depending on us more and more each day. We are not happy with you and your situation and we want you to start finding a place to live.

"That sounds very bad."

"We think so. As soon as you have the baby we want you to be out of here own your own."

"I don't think I want to have the baby and then leave, I think I should leave now. You have made it perfectly clear how you feel and I cannot live here under those circumstances."

The next day at work Jenny saw a 3x5 card on the bulletin board saying room for rent she knew the salesman and approached him about the room. He told her that he had two other guys sharing the other rooms in the house. There were four bedrooms and two bathrooms that would be shared among three men. She had her concerns about her privately and the bathroom sharing schedule. Bill the guy with the house told Jenny that she would be on her own that he wasn't a baby sitter. Now that should have scared Jenny but she wanted to get out of her house as soon as possible. Her parents didn't even care. She took the room and had to ask the guys living there to help her move some of her belongings. They all chipped in and moved her in less than three hours her parents never said goodbye and now if Jenny didn't know she does now, there wasn't any love for her in that house.

Jenny didn't know that there wasn't going to be too much love in her new house. The three men were down right crude. They would walk out of the bath room after a shower naked, not flush the toilets. Bringing in their girlfriends and have sex with them with the doors open, they were constantly using profanity and watch porno movies on TV and never clean up after themselves. They would be uncooperative whenever they could. They would walk in on Jenny when she was showering or on the toilet. The list goes on finally Jenny asked bill if he would talk to the guys about all the things that were going on at the house that were really bad. He told her he would, but didn't. Now here's a poor young girl pregnant relying on Bill who was a nice guy at work and Dr Hyde at home, she was trying to get through this horrible time. She needed to find a suitable environment to bring up a child.

One evening while Jenny was showering and the bathroom door was locked Bill let himself in and tried to rape her. She screamed the house down and no one came to her aid, not one of them. The next day she went to the dealership manager and told them about Bill and the perverts that live with him and what they were doing to her the whole time she lived there and how Bill tried to rape her last evening. She was told that it was out of their hands and there wasn't anything they could do about it. They told her to call the police and press charges.

She did meet with the police and she told them everything that Bill tried to do to her and they told her that they needed some evidence or all they could do is to bring him down to the station and scare him. Jenny thought that would be good. The next time she saw him he was livid and told her he had just spent three hours at the police station answering questions about the other night that she lured him in to the bathroom and changed her mind before anything happened. She told him he was sick and now that she complained about him to the police they have a record of my complaint about him and God help you if someone else should make a complaint like hers. He told her to get out of his house and she told him she has already left. She reminded him that it wasn't a house it was a dump and the people living were what you would find in a dump, trash.

There was an ad in the paper for a room to rent, she went and met the lady and they hit it off real good. Jenny told her that her baby was due any day now and the old lady told Jenny that having a baby around the house would be fun. Jenny couldn't work anymore so she would watch TV with the old lady until her water broke and the old lady said it was time to go. They had made arrangements with the cab company that she would need a ride to the hospital to have her baby. They promised her they could pick her up in five minutes after the call. The old lady was upset with Jenny's parents over the way they treated her over this pregnancy and took the easy way out.

Jenny was learning a lot from the old lady and she wanted to help Jenny through this child birth and back on her feet. Sure enough the pains were starting to come at first far apart and finally the pain was getting harder to get used to. The old lady called the cab co. as planned and sure enough the cab was there in less than five minutes. The old lady said she was going with Jenny to the hospital seeing as how this was her first child and she was all by herself. That old lady was a big help to Jenny through the initial stages of delivery, in the room she looked in all the draws just being nosy by doing this she knew where everything was so when she heard someone call out for jell or anything else she would show them what draw everything was in.

It seems as though the baby was too big to come through Jenny's birth canal and was stuck there, they called in the clinic doctor and he suggested that she should have a C Section. The old lady told them to do it and Jenny gave her approval. The old lady stayed with her even in the delivery room holding her hand. It wasn't very long before she gave birth to a 6 lb. 12 oz. little boy. Jenny started crying that this was over with and now she could get on with being a good mother. The nurse asked her for a name and she said she liked Jerome and the nurse asked her to spell it she answered Jerome and the last name would be the same as yours seeing as though you're not married. Jenny nodded yes and was starting to get sleepy. They wheeled her and Jerome out of the delivery room and into the room that was assigned to her. The old lady spotted a nice arm chair and sat in it just to rest her legs and feet from standing so long. Jenny looked over at the old lady and saw her asleep and snoring a little as well. It wasn't long before the baby was in his little incubator and Jenny was sound asleep.

The nurse put the lights out except for a little night light near the door this was going to be a day to remember August 21ˢᵗ. 1970 for the rest of her life and Jerome's first day for the rest of his life. Even though all three of them slept good, little Jerome wanted something to eat every three hours. She had made a decision to nurse him for a while; she didn't want Jerome to deform her. She had heard of some women's boobs sagging and would be in serious need of a brazier when the baby was finished nursing

The cab company was called to come and take her home and when she got there the old lady had her room all fixed up for her and a beautiful basinet for Jerome to sleep in. Jenny started crying again and was thanking the old lady for being so nice to her. The old lady confessed to Jenny that she wanted to do for her what she couldn't do for her own daughter who was killed in an auto accident out in California before she could see her and her new born baby. Jenny gave her a big hug and told her she was sorry. The old lady told her that she wanted to help her with the baby and when she was ready to go back to work she would watch after Jerome for her. Jenny told her that it was awfully nice of her to want to do that for her but it might be a little too hard on her.

"Nonsense girl I want to do this."

"Will you let me know if this will be a problem for you?"

"Of course I will I would never let anything get in the way of doing what is good for Jerome."

"I never expected anything like this Mrs. Topkis."

"I want to do this so give an old lady a break."

"Ok enough said."

"Now honey do you plan on taking the baby for your family to see?"

"I don't have any plans to ever go to them."

"I don't blame you for feeling that way, after what they did to you."

"Can you imagine deserting your daughter in her hour of need? You're a complete stranger and you have showed me more love then they have ever showed me. I have two brothers and sisters who will become strangers to me."

"They will have to answer to someone about what they have done to you."

"That someone is not even in their thoughts, if they thought they had to answer to someone they might think differently."

The old lady told Jenny not to go to work for a while, Jerome will need you. These are very important times in his life. While he was inside of you, your voice was the only voice he heard for nine months. We have to make sure he knows you're around all the time. She told her that you don't have to pay any rent until you go back to work. Jenny broke down again and hugged Mrs. Topkis for the longest time. When Jerome was a month old he started to smile at Jenny and Mrs. Topkis when they spoke to him. Jerome was starting to look like a beautiful baby boy. Jenny was good looking and she must have passed it along to Jerome The old lady thought it might be a good idea to shorten Jerome's name you know like a nick name. Jenny said like Rome and the old lady said that was what she meant. She told Jenny that she loved it, so from now on we will call him Rome that sounds a little less stuffy, the other children would have had a field day with Jerome.

One day while the old lady was sitting with Rome she called Jenny over to sit with her.

"The other day when I went out for a few hours, I went to my lawyer's office because I don't have any family anymore I left my entire estate to you and Rome."

"Mrs. Topkis you shouldn't have done that, you hardly know me."

"I know you enough to know that's what I wanted to do. You will not need anything ever again."

"I am in shock that you would do this."

"Don't be, I didn't have anyone to leave my estate to and I didn't want the State to get it. You will be getting a letter from my lawyer explaining everything to you. He wants you to fill out a questionnaire and return it to him as soon as possible."

"What does your lawyer think of all this?"

"He goes along with what I want or I'll be getting a new lawyer."

"Mrs. Topkis you can be tough when you want to be."

"Yes it's something I learned from my deceased husband of thirty nine years."

"I am sorry about that."

"If there is one thing that I want you to remember Jenny and that is, a fool and their money are soon parted."

"I do understand what you just said Mrs. Topkis."

Jenny went to bed that evening realizing how lucky she was to have met the old lady. She realized that she will probably have more money than her parents will ever have from a woman that she would have never met if it wasn't for the baby. Then she thought her parents didn't want her to have the baby and to leave their home, making it doubly hard for Jenny to survive. I guess things happen for the best and meeting Mrs. Topkis was the best.

*J*enny was very comfortable with Mrs. Topkis looking after Rome and she would go out and shop or pick up something at one of the stores. She thought that it is time to get back to work after being at home for nine months now; Mrs. Topkis wanted it that way. She decided to go to an employment agency, be tested and see what positions were open for her. They sent her for an interview with a large ins. Co. for a position as a receptionist and typist. It wasn't that far from the house and at first impression it looked like a good place to work. After the interview they wanted to hire her right on the spot. She was pretty and fit perfect for the position. They knew that she was going to be the first person the visitor would see and she would leave a good impression with them. Jenny was happy they even offered her hospitalization coverage after a thirty day waiting period. She was thrilled at this offer because she needed it for the baby and herself. She couldn't wait to get home and tell Mrs. Topkis the good news.

Jenny let herself in the house and Mrs. Topkis was asleep in the chair and Rome was in his bed fast asleep. Jenny thought that it was unusual for her to be sleeping in the middle of the day. The old lady awoke and said she must have fallen asleep, Jenny told her that it happens to the best of us. But was a little worried that this could happen at a less desirable time and there could be a problem. Nothing more was said of it and it went away. Jenny went out to get a few things to wear for the start of her new job, they offered her a clothing allowance that was going to be a big help for her. Jenny could feel that they expected a lot from her, how much is a lot will soon surface and she will know exactly where she stood.

She had to report to her immediate supervisor Mrs. Faller whom Jenny found out that all the girls called her Mrs. Failure. She treated Jenny alright but was real cold and not easy to get close to. The first day was important for her to get through because Mrs. Failure gave her a litany of instructions that were aimed at her to be very careful of the men that might want to hang around her desk and flirt. Mrs. Failure told Jenny to run them off or she will. Jenny did remind Mrs. Failure that she was here to do her job and with a baby at home she didn't have time for any flirting sessions. The man hater approved of Jenny's remarks and left.

Jenny had too many contacts with the boys at school not to recognize them for what their worth. Mrs. Topkis has eased any pressure that Jenny might have had with dealing with the pressures from the men at her place of employment and being afraid of being fired because of advancements made to her by people in positions that could affect her job. She felt independent and could work more relaxed. The firm was getting a better Jenny because of it.

There were an awful lot of people that came by her location each day and most everyone wanted or needed to stop and talk to Jenny. There was a young man that came by her desk every day and brought her something such as coffee or donuts and Jenny would always tell him that she wasn't allowed to accept anything like this because it was strictly forbidden by Human Resources. One day he asked her to go out and she told him that it was strictly forbidden for her to go out with anyone from work. He flared back that they can't tell you what to do after work

"Well weather they can or not I have only been here a few weeks and I plan on doing whatever makes them happy."

"Even if it keeps you from meeting someone like me."

"That is exactly what it does; it keeps me from meeting someone like you."

"What's that supposed to mean."

"It means that I am not interested in you and don't want to break the company guide lines that will keep me in my much needed job."

"Why do you need this job so much?"

"Because I have a baby at home and I don't need to date another one."

With that he turned around and left and was never to be seen again. Jenny had come a long way and can now say goodbye to any man, something that she couldn't do before. She was on probation the first ninety days and was scheduled for a performance review the next day. When she sat in front of Mrs. Failure she was looking over some review papers for the longest time. Jenny thought she should have been more prepared and have her review read over before she came for the interview. Finally she lifted her eyes and said I can't find anything wrong here except we would like to see more typing from you. Jenny told her that she usually answers at least two hundred plus phone calls and at least fifty to a hundred face to face inquiries or walk up every *day. She told Mrs. Failure that if the load continues they will have to find someone that can assist her in her job, such as phone relief or typing relief in order for her to do her job.*

"Really, and if you don't get any relief young lady what then will you do?"

"Then I won't give you any notice and not show up for work some morning when I find a new job."

"Well that is a very brazen thing to do, don't we do enough for you."

"Don't think I am not grateful, but you are giving me the impression that you're the boss and we have to dance to your music and you're not taking any advice from us employees, such as me."

"I am not sure that I approve of your attitude young lady."

"Mrs. Faller all I am trying to do is to prevent this receptionist job from falling apart and whoever is reviewing the breakdown, if there should be one and there will be one if I can't take on the overload. You will be called before the powers to be and answer to them why you didn't see this coming. Will you tell them that you ignored advice from the people that were experiencing these problems? They would look at my review and you would be terminated immediately. You never let me see my review you just wanted me to sign it and give it back, it has to be good because I am good at this job."

"O you're good at this job and very good at telling me what to do."

"I am just trying to help."

"Ok you go back to work and I will see what we can do here for you."

"Thank you."

It was only four days that Mrs. Failure came out to Jenny's desk and told Jenny that she didn't have to type anymore and they want to bring in an escort that can take the visitor to the location that they need to be at or help out with some of the phone calls. Jenny assured her that this would work and solve the problem out here in the lobby. This might be one of the first times that Mrs. Failure has been successfully been put in her place and someone live to talk about it. Usually anyone crossing her path is let go immediately. Jenny knew she had her by the short hairs and didn't have any recourse but to do the right thing.

Mrs. Topkis is telling Jenny that Rome is trying to walk and he is having so much fun walking along the furniture and just laughing out at himself trying to walk and fall down and quickly get up again. Jenny could see that the old lady has become very attached to Rome and that he has become the main focus in her life. Romey just loves her to death and it has turned out to be a very close relationship. Mrs. Topkis takes him out for a ride in his stroller, just around the block, just for him to breathe the fresh air and brings him right back home. Jenny knows that she has fallen into something special and will never want to destroy this life experience ever.

Mrs. Topkis talks to Rome every day and he looks at her and tilts his head when he thinks he is hearing something that he has heard before. He is so cute and she knows he will be talking soon. Now when Jenny gets home from work she wants to talk to Rome too so he is being well tutored and it will show up in Pre School. Jenny thought he would be a head of most of the children thanks to Mrs. Topkis. Jenny has bought Rome a children's computer on his second birthday for him to play with and a keyboard for him to play with as well. This is a new learning tool that could advance a child far into the future of what is out there for children to do. He has taken to it real well and sits at it with Mrs. Topkis every day and his mother in the evening after work.

With all the attention that Rome was getting he was becoming very smart and could understand most everything that was said to him keeping it on a child's level of intelligence. Jenny asked Mrs. Topkis if she would mind if they got Rome a little dog that doesn't shed hair. She thought that would be great and with that Jenny went down to the humane kennels and found a little shiatsu. He took to Jenny when she was looking at him and thought Rome will love this little fuzz ball. Rome will have a ball with him and will be able to make friends with someone or something outside the family and was house broken to boot. She called Mrs. Topkis and told her what she has done and she told Jenny to bring him home they would be waiting.

Well when Jenny came home with the dog and opened the front door and said your dog is here and put the dog down he ran to Rome right away. Rome could hardly contain himself he just sat on the floor and held the pup on his lap and played with him for the longest time. Finally the pup looked for something soft to lie down on and fell asleep from exhaustion. They made up a place for the pup to sleep in, Mrs. Topkis had a cage from a dog she had years ago, so they used it and filled it with pillows and some dog toys and the dog was gone for the evening.

Jenny noticed when she was giving Rome his bath that his pink birth mark was getting redder behind his right ear. It was heart shaped and was the size of a nickel. Her brother Paul also had a birthmark behind his right ear the size of a nickel she thought that things like this get passed around from generation to generation. Mrs. Topkis liked the name Penny for the dog and so did Jenny and Rome liked it also. Penny and Rome were inseparable they spent the whole day with each other. When Rome took his nap the dog took one with him. When Rome took his bath the dog took one with him. There was a strong bond between them that could never be broken. Penny would have given his life if it would save Rome's life, they did everything together.

Things at work were going good for Jenny; she has turned into a very pretty woman that turned a lot of heads. She would love to read from the Beatrix Potter books stories or the rabbit and ducks and geese until Rome was totally consumed with his new little friends Peter Rabbit, Puddle Duck and the rabbits Christmas party. They were more than just stories they were real to him with his imagination. It was almost a nightly ritual; Rome would soon go fast asleep with his friend Penny at his side. It would bring tears to Jenny's eyes just to see this played out every night. She would soon find herself on her knees every evening thanking God for having her son Rome and having met Mrs. Topkis. Now that Penny is here she thanked God for him as well.

This has turned into a loving family, one of which most people would love to experience. Mrs. Topkis now sees Jenny as her daughter they both have given their all to each other and Jenny loves to call her mom and means it when she says it. The old lady has never experienced this kind of love before and wanted to hold on to it as long as it would last. They both didn't have a family and found each other by chance and no one could ever come between them.

Christmas morning was the best experience the two women have ever experienced with Rome at center stage. Rome loved every gift and showed it to his mother and Mrs. Topkis. Penny would play with the wrapping paper or the boxes and they all would laugh and really feel what Christmas was all about, to be with your love ones and give a piece of yourself to them. Rome was grateful for any gift he got; it was a pleasure watching him open his Christmas gifts. Christmas breakfast was Jenny's favorite and Mrs. Topkis was getting the turkey ready for dinner, she showed Jenny how to prepare it so she could make Christmas dinner someday and make it like hers. She told Jenny it was handed down from generations in her family and now she was the last, the only one left to carry on a tradition that will die out unless Jenny will pick up the torch and carry on. She assured Mrs. Topkis she wouldn't let her down, that she would carry on the tradition of the Topkis family.

She told Jenny that she was married to a Topkis but the family name was O'Riordan from Co. Cork Ireland. Jenny said to Mrs. Topkis your Irish then, yes I am and very proud of it. I am going to give you a book on the family history for safe keeping; it goes back a couple hundred years. Maybe someday *you can go over and visit and see what you can dig up. Records are easy to find in Ireland, you can trace the whole family tree in a few days. She told Mrs. Topkis she would love to visit Ireland and look up some of her relations.*

There's nothing to report on Jenny's love life because she doesn't have a love life because she doesn't want a love life. She's perfectly happy where she is right now, she is consumed with her son and Mrs. Topkis who is busy teaching her everything any mother or woman could ever user in their lives, from cooking to sewing to banking all the way down to how to fire a pistol. The old lady was an expert on the firing range with her 9 mm Glock 19 and her two 15 round clips. She told Jenny that her fire arms instructor was the best she has ever met, his name was Carl Pace and when you want some instructions you get up with Carl, if he can't shoot um he'll knife um. If Jenny was by herself she would go to him right away.

It was time for her review again and it was the best she has ever had, but no money just a lot of compliments. Jenny asked for a pay raise and she was told that she was at the top of her pay scale as a receptionist. Jenny told her that she will start looking for another job where she can make more money with a different company. Jenny stood up and told Mrs. Failure she doesn't want to talk anymore because this is just a lot of bull shit and you ought to be ashamed of your self telling someone that has a review like mine that there isn't any more money to be earned. You took all the hope out of my life and expect me to go on with the job like nothing's wrong. Did they teach you that in school or is it company policy to demoralize the employee. Well this bitch jumped up and told Jenny that she has never been so insulted like this in her whole career here with the company.

"That's probably because you never tried to get away with this obvious deep dislike for me and mix them up in your everyday dealings with me. I am the best employee you have and I demand a meeting with the regional manager right now and I am not leaving your office until you take me to him along with my present and past reviews."

"You don't dictate to us what you want."

"Right now I don't know about us I only know about you and this is between me and you."

"The regional manager is out of the office until Friday which is a few days away."

"Ok I see him on my own."

"You have to follow the chain of command, or you will be terminated."

"I dare you to terminate me, I'll have you in front of the labor relations board faster than you can spell it, I am grossly underpaid here and I want a salary review. I can see how you piss off people that you come in contact with."

"You have a foul mouth young lady."

"Piss and bitch is not foul mouth, you need to learn something besides sneaking your smokes in the ladies room when you think no one is looking."

"Ok if you're not foul mouthed, then you have a bad attitude."

"It doesn't show up in my reviews."

"No but it does with me."

"Maybe it's because you really don't know how to handle someone that has some intelligence or confidence and won't allow you to ride rough herd over them."

"You're still at the top of your pay scale no matter what you say."

"Five dollars an hour is not at the top of anyone's pay scale in fact our pay comes from the service fee you charge your customers for each payment they make. You don't have to use any of the company's money for salaries and you say I am at the top of my pay scale. The customer is paying my salary and probably doesn't know it."

"Tell me Jenny is there anything around here that you like?"

"There is as long as you don't have any connection with it."

With that Mrs. Failure left the room and Jenny went back to her desk and went back to doing what she does best and that is to smile and help anyone she will come in contact with. She knows that she probably said too much and was going to make sure that no one was ever going to do her over in the work place again. It was only a few days later that she was told to report to the claim dept. and take claims reports from the customers that call them in. She had heard about this job and knew it wasn't for her, so she quit right on the spot with no notice and was out the door in a matter of minutes with her pay check. She knew that Mrs. Topkis would understand and wouldn't blame her for quitting.

She called the employment agency and told them what happened to her at the ins. office and they told her to come in for another interview. She showed up as sharp as a tack, she looked like something out of the fashion magazines. The lady doing the interview knew what Jenny was talking about when she told her of the way they over loaded her with work that two people would have a hard time doing and then froze her pay to boot.

They want Jenny to go on an interview with another Ins. Co. that was looking for a female to train and license and work as an agent in their large sales department selling policies to people that walk in and adding policies to their portfolio. Jenny was real excited about the opportunity and could see that she could make a lot of money. She showed up early and went right into the interview that lasted for over an hour. They asked her to take a 120 question test that was about a lot of things but not that hard. They wanted her to finish so her average would be better based on 120 and not the number she would finish less than 120. She didn't quite finish but did get 112 questions answered and she scored very well.

She finished the test and was asked if she would mind taking another interview where she was asked if she could sell someone an Ins. Policy. Her reply was if you show me or train me I should be able to do it. They told her that her looks wouldn't hurt her at all; in fact they thought she should be very successful at being an Ins. Agent. They offered her a position as a sales trainee until she gets licensed. She would work from 8:30 to 5:30 Monday through Friday and some Saturdays from 9:00 to 1:00 when needed, with a four hour cut one off the days during the week that she would work on Saturdays.

She could study at the office four hours and work with an agent the other four hours. She would take payments, answer the phones finish up with the customers for the agent when need be. It isn't any surprise to hear that she was the most popular woman in the office. All the agents wanted to have their turn to work with her. They were seen every morning looking at the work bulletin board to see who Jenny was assigned to each day. She was stunning and single and that made the boys how'll, they really couldn't help it. The word soon went out that Jenny has a little boy and she doesn't date anyone from work. That eventually calmed down the wolves and made the working atmosphere much better.

She looked forward to her classes every day and was doing very well; there were four test, property, casualty, life and health. She would sit for two at a time and before she would be tested the Ins. Co. would test her to see where she stood as far as passing goes with their test first. Every now and then one of the agents would be assigned to sit with her and quiz her to see if she is able to handle all of the info there is to learn and in every case she was more advanced than some of the other trainers before her. Jenny was there now for three months and Mrs. Topkis was very proud of Jenny that she was going to become an ins. Agent. The ins co said she was ready for her property and casualty test next week and she was very nervous taking it but when she opened the test paper it was like being at work, it was that easy.

She was notified that she passed five days later and she would soon sit for her life and health test that week that she had studied for longer than her property and casualty test. She passed with flying colors and would have to sit for an interview to see how she felt about being on her own in her own office making all the decisions that she would have to make in order to write a policy. She worked with an agent four hours a day now so being on her own would not be hard and besides if she needed any help the agents would jump at it to help her. She was all smiles when her first customer was sent back to her, it was a man and she sold him auto ins. Apartment ins. and an AAA membership. This was her first customer and she was very impressive.

Mrs. Topkis was spending a lot of time with Romey when Jenny was at work and Jenny would tell her how much she appreciated all the things she was doing for Rome. She told Jenny that he is so easy to teach she don't know what it is but he is smart and wants all the knowledge he can get. Mrs. Topkis was treating Rome like a son and loved him very much; you might say that she was consumed with him. Jenny thought he had two mothers one in the morning and one at night.

Jenny was starting to make some good money; they were paying her 15% commission on her property and casualties sales and 35% on her life sales and 25% on her health sales. The nice part of the job was that she would earn renewals of 10% and the company would own the accounts. She was selling for only six months and was earning a monthly check for four and five thousand dollars sometimes after taxes. She would bank most of it because she didn't need much to live on. Jenny took care of all the expenses at the house and Mrs. Topkis wouldn't take any rent because she couldn't not after getting attached to Rome.

Mrs. Topkis's health was very important to Jenny and she would take her to all of her doctor's visits she wanted to feel comfortable with her watching Rome and that she was in good physical condition. Jenny knew she didn't sleep good through the night and asked the doctor how they could improve that. He prescribed some mild non addictive sleeping pill for her to take at bed time and should get her through most of the night. Mrs. Topkis was happy to know that she could sleep through most of the evening. Jenny really felt bad that she could only spend a few hours with Rome in the evening while Mrs. Topkis had him for nine hours every day. Jenny made up for it on the weekends, the three of them went to the park and to the movies and out for lunch or dinner sometimes whenever the weather was good enough. Rome knew he was out in public and never once acted up and through a hissy fit.

Rome was really speaking very clear and was the perfect gentleman, thanks to the two women in his life. He loved to sit and watch Mr. Rogers; he was so engrossed that he couldn't hear a bomb go off. It was fun just watching him watching Mr. Rogers. His buddy Penny would sit with him through the whole program, it was heartwarming to see this. Penny would put his head across his lap and put his head between his two out stretched paws. Mrs. Topkis would often be moved to tears seeing the two of them together. They reeked with innocence, why couldn't this stay like this forever. I guess the answer is because life moves on and there are things that interrupt our lives and only leave those cherished moments as memories.

Jenny was setting more records at work with her sales and she was being recommended by her customers to their friends to make an appointment and meet this woman. She was always happy and they didn't know it but she was cautious. She never told anyone where she lived or who she lived with. That was important to be careful seeing as how every customer was a stranger. She knew that she and the old lady had no defenses except to shoot someone with the gun that the old lady had and that wasn't going to be easy for two innocent women to do.

Rome has only been in the company of those two women and has been sheltered all of his life, Jenny knows that he needs the company of other children so they take him to the park every day if the weather permits. They could easily see that he enjoyed it and looked forward to it. He would run to the places where the other children played, and would stay there for a couple of hours. The whole time he would be out of his mind with excitement, there were a lot of times that the old lady would take him to the park while Jenny was at work. Jenny felt safe with that arrangement and trusted that the old lady was watching him at all times. The Park was on the nice side of town where the children were less aggressive and the parents were too.

Jenny's last review she was asked if she would like to go into management and she told her immediate supervisor that she would have to think about it but for now she is better off where she is in sales. She has a little boy at home to think about and that would be her first priority. Her supervisor understood and told her let's see what happens down the road things can change quickly. Jenny was glad that the review went well and that the company appreciates her hard work. This one day when Jenny arrived at home the old lady was asleep in her favorite chair and Rome was asleep on the floor. Jenny thought that falling asleep at 6:00 was not good anything could have gone wrong when a four year old is left unattended for a short period of time.

Jenny gently awoke the old lady and asked her how she felt.

"I am sorry I must have fallen asleep."

"We are lucky that Rome has fallen asleep as well."

"Jenny you are so right, I don't even remember getting sleepy I am just out like a light."

"Why don't you stop taking him to the park when I am at work, we can do it together on the weekends, how's that?

"That is probably the best thing to do under these circumstances. I wouldn't want to fall asleep there to leave him unattended."

"You know I love you very much and you know I wouldn't do anything to hurt your feelings."

"I know that Jenny, I can't be looking after a young boy and fall asleep on the job."

"Thank you for your understanding Mrs. Topkis I love you too much to hurt you."

"I feel the same way about you too, you are deep into my life and that is where I want you two to be."

"You have always said the nicest things to me."

"I mean every word of it too, so from now on we'll go to the park together, the three of us."

"What do you want to do for dinner Mrs. Topkis? Do you want to go out for a fast bite to eat? I think Rome will be up to it, don't you?"

"I do too, let's go."

They went to a nice little Italian restaurant in the shopping center called Vincent's; they have the best soup and pizza in town. The waitresses are the best around; they just loved Rome and would make a fuss over him when we were seated. They almost could read your mind and would have the drinks on the table in a matter of seconds. Rome just loved the pizza and he could easily eat one big slice. They could never finish the pizza so they boxed it and took it home and had it the next day. The next day was Saturday and they all slept in and caught up on some lost sleep. When Jenny awoke she could smell the sausage and eggs and quickly ran down to the kitchen where Mrs. Topkis was cooking away, she loved cooking breakfast and she thought that was the better meal for the day. Rome was wide awake and eager to have his favorite meal that would get him started in the right direction and he didn't even know it.

Mrs. Topkis thought what a waste of life that Jenny didn't have a man to share her life with like she was sharing with her. Jenny wanted to raise Rome a little more and was very reliant on the old lady for her help with Rome. She couldn't back her out of her life to please someone else like a boyfriend. He would have to be something special and she hasn't come across that guy yet. She wasn't looking and didn't have any room in her life for another person. Mrs. Topkis would never mention anything to Jenny because she knew that Rome came first and not some hit artist that made her think that he loved her just to get in her pants. Jenny was far too smart for that bull crap; she has heard all the sweet talking these guys can put out, that won't get them to first base with her. She was beautiful, but with a child and that would eliminate a lot of men. It seemed like these guys thought they weren't going to marry in to an already started family, bringing up a child that was not there's. I can assure you that would have not deterred her if she met someone that had a kid.

Rome's fifth birthday was great the two women wanted him to have the nicest party they could throw for him, they invited a few of his friends in the neighborhood and they had a ball. Jenny took some pictures and the old lady stayed close to Rome and would give him anything he would want. He opened up his gifts and loved his big wheel that the old lady got for him, they had a few things to put together like the wheels and he was good to go. When they sang happy birthday and it came time to blow out the candles he was ready with a big blow. He blew so hard the candles tilted a little from the wind. Jenny was at work this one day that Rome was begging the old lady to take him to the park; she told him that it would be better if they wait for mommy and they could all go. He looked at her with those sad eyes and said, "I want to go with you mom mom." Well that just tore her up and she told him that it could only be for a short visit.

It was only a short walk to the park and Rome walked right next to her all the way. There weren't that many kids there and Rome joined up with a couple of kids and were playing on the monkey bars. Mrs. Topkis had fallen asleep on the park bench and when she woke up she couldn't see Rome anywhere so she stood up and screamed out this blood gurgling Rome where are you? There was no Rome and she kept screaming out Rome where are you and again there was no Rome. She was beginning to attract attention when one of the ladies that knew her came over to her and asked her what was wrong. She told her she can't find Rome he's missing.

The lady pulled a contraption out of her pocketbook and put it to her ear she had called the police to come quickly there was a small boy missing from the Park on Washington St. It wasn't long before there were three police cars that showed up and they all ran to her and so did all the parents with their *children come over too. Mrs. Topkis was out of her mind with fear for her little friend. The police asked everyone if they saw the little boy. There were a few women that said they saw him playing on the monkey bars and one woman said she saw him walking in back of the bathrooms and disappeared. The police officer wanted to know how the boy was dressed; the old lady told them he had on sneakers a clean pair of jeans and a blue and white short sleeve shirt.*

The news media heard it on the police radio and came a running, this was going to be national news. The old lady asked the woman if she could call the little boy's mother so she could talk to her. The phone was ringing when she handed it to her and Jenny's voice was on the other end saying hello. The old lady told her that Rome begged her to take him to the park; she told him it would only be for a minute. She told her that she fell asleep and when I woke up he was gone. The scream of no on the other end of the phone was enough to send the old lady into shock, she was now useless to the police. The police put a ring of police officers in a ten block radius hoping they would keep the kidnappers inside the circle.

Jenny could see the helicopters flying over the park hoping to scare something up and look for someone with a small boy. There was nothing. The police saw a woman running in the park screaming for her son Rome. She was screaming as loud as anyone could scream; it was scary to see her. It was going to take someone special to calm her down and the police dept. didn't have anyone to do that. The police were going door to door and they even let out the police academy class to assist in this kidnapping this was big time, every radio station for twenty miles had a reporter there. Jenny was holding the old lady trying to comfort her and she didn't hear anything, she was just blaming herself for this tragedy Jenny would scream out for Rome and start to tremble all over before it became obvious that they needed medical attention. The fire emergency ambulance came and they were both carried away on a stretcher and taken to the memorial hospital for medical treatment.

Someone was seen running through the park screaming out that they saw the little boy being pulled along the street and put on the bus that stopped at 18th St. The police called and want the driver that was on duty for that bus route 11 at the time Rome was kidnapped to be available for some questioning right away. A police car was dispatched to pick him up at the bus depot and bring him to the park right away. They could hear the police car coming from blocks away because of the sirens. He was hustled to the car where the officer in charge was and they told him that they have reason to believe that some woman was seen dragging a little boy on to his bus at 18th St.

"Is that true Mr. Hughes?"

"Yes it is."

Is this an everyday occurrence, Mr. Hughes?"

"Well no it isn't."

"So why didn't you stop this unusual behavior."

"Because I see this crap every day."

"You mean that you see kidnappings every day."

"No I don't see kidnappings every day, I see kids acting up with their parents every day."

"Was this child crying?"

"Yes he was, very much so."

"Very much so, and that still didn't bother you enough to step in and question the mother?"

"No it didn't, like I said I have seen it all before."

"Tell me Mr. Hughes was this little boy putting up a struggle or saying anything that you could hear."

"Yes he was but I didn't pay any attention to it."

"What was he saying?"

"He kept screaming out to his mother that you're not his mommy."

"No, I don't believe that. I don't believe that you drove away with all of this happening in front of you. Do you have any children Mr. Hughes?"

"No I don't, I am single."

"Describe this woman to me."

All the police officers reached for their note pads and were ready to write down the description he was about to give of her.

"She was around forty years of age some gray starting to show up in her hair and her teeth were dirty like some poor peoples are. She had on an over stretched sweater that was beginning to fade the blue color that it once had, in other words it was old and had small holes in it. She wore a pair of over worn jeans that were really starting to wear out and an old pair of sneakers that had some tar on them."

"How do you know it was tar?"

"I could smell it."

"Hum fresh tar. Where did you leave her off?"

"I left her off at the end of the line on 43rd St."

They immediately dispatched two police cars there to find the driver or talk to anyone that might have seen this woman and small boy. They talked to the fellow in the tobacco store and he said he called a cab for a lady of that description.

"What cab co. was it?"

"It was the yellow cab co."

They put two policemen on that and found the driver of the cab and said he drove her all around and she got out after an hour on 29ᵗʰ St. She hailed down a bus and went out to the edge of town the opposite of where the police were looking. Little Rome was exhausted from crying and being drug around from one place to another until finally she found the place that was home to her. The house was in bad shape and needed a paint job and the shrubbery needed some trimming. The shingles on the roof were beginning to curl; in general it looked abandoned and had shades with holes in them on all the windows. One house to the left was boarded up and the other house to the right was lived in by an old couple that stayed to themselves and that made it ideal for the kidnapper to keep this crying boy not be heard by anyone.

She kept telling him that he was upsetting mommy and all he would say was you're not my mommy. She put him in bed and tied him to the bed post and brushed the roaches away as best she could, she would have to look for them all evening to keep him from being bitten. She wasn't willing to do that so Rome had to lay there crying out for his mommy and have flashbacks of his mommy and the old lady he called mom mom. The boy was felling hopeless and that he would never see them again. It made him cry the whole time he was awake and he would be woken from the roaches biting him and he didn't have a free hand to swat them.

When the kidnapper unlocked the bedroom door she came in the room and saw the little boy asleep and noticed the roach bites on his arms and immediately concluded that if they should get infected it would be all over for her. So now she had to do something about the bites and the roaches if she is going to keep the boy. The boy she always wanted but never had, she wasn't attractive to anyone and therefore she didn't have any physical contact with any men. She was going to have to go out and buy some roach spray and some over the counter insect bites ointment and band aids to keep these bites clean. There was a drug store down the street and she decided to go there for what she needed. She wanted to change her clothes first so if someone had seen her she would now be wearing something different.

She told Rome that she was going to the store and mommy would be back soon, Rome immediately countered by saying that you're not my mommy and with that she slapped him hard across the face that left the imprint of her hand and would later on swell up like a welt. This was the first time he had ever been hit and was in shock that someone could be so mean. She warned him before she left that she would be gone for only a few minutes and she would have to tie him up to the wooden chair and he better not draw any attention to himself. He asked the woman if she could call his mommy to come and get him. She lunged at him and said I am your mommy and don't you ever forget it.

Betty the kidnapper walked to the drug store and asked the pharmacist what was good for insect bites? He recommended Neosporin so she bought two tubes and two boxes of band aids and four cans of roach spray. This has to work or she will have to move and that might prove to be a very serious problem. She got back to the house and found Rome slumped over in the chair and sobbing in his sleep, she told to shut up or he was going to get another beating. She untied him and told him that mommy was going to fix his bites when he told her again that she was not his mommy when she heard that again she slapped him across the other side of his face, now he has two swollen cheeks with welts on them. She doesn't know the damage a full swing to the face with an open hand can do to a small child.

She didn't clean up the bites that good and squeezed the ointment on to the weeping bites and covered them with a band aid. The little boy was taken from his mom mom, he was drug all over town by some mentally deranged woman bitten all night by roaches that run around at free will and gets slapped so hard that his face is swollen. It would have to take the toughest child to survive this torture and Rome had led the sheltered life and if things don't improve he will not survive this new life. While she is covering up the bites she could see what slapping has done to Rome's face he was swollen so bad that his eyes were beginning to swell shut. She knows that she cannot slap him in the face anymore or she could seriously hurt him. She never thought to give him a bath or clean him up because she doesn't clean herself up and she doesn't clean up her house. The kitchen was the worst with all the dirty dishes thrown in the sink and the food dried on the sink and counter tops. The smell of decay was everywhere.

4

*J*enny was under heavy sedation in the hospitals psychiatric ward calling out for her baby boy and sobbing all of her woken day. The police can't even talk to her and will soon have to break into the house for some pictures of the boy and check for phone messages that might shed some light on this terrible crime. The old lady is in a deep coma and doesn't have much of a chance for recovery. The police finally were given the ok to enter the house and look for something that will help them in this national coverage of this horrendous kidnapping of a five year old boy in broad daylight in front of other people. There was nothing in the house and it was shut down with crime scene tape everywhere, do not enter was the word and do not cross this line were everywhere.

Betty had taken the roach spray and sprayed all over the house, she even cleaned up the kitchen so the roaches wouldn't have a place to dine. There was a lot to do before it could be slightly safe from being eaten alive at night. Betty asked Rome to come to mommy she wanted to see his bites and he told her again that she was not his mommy. She stood and made a fist and knocked him to the floor with a heavy blow to his back up near his shoulder area. He moaned for the longest time and when she stood him up she could see that she hurt him because he could hardly stand erect. At the rate she is hitting him she is going to seriously hurt him and there won't be any medical help for him if that should happen. Rome will either have to stop correcting her about the mommy issue or she will have to stop hitting him, either way one of them has to stop.

This woman has no radio, no TV, no telephone, and only a few lights that work. There is no air conditioning and probably the heater doesn't work. I forgot to mention that there wasn't any running water. She doesn't draw any attention to herself and the old couple next door doesn't hear anything that would alarm them. So what happens when the sun goes down, she sits *in a chair and stares at the wall over the fireplace. All she eats is can food or some fruit, no cooking what so ever. She gets a check every month from the state along with food stamps, this is just enough to get by on.*

There are people from all over the world wanting to help Jenny out of this predicament the money was pouring in at $10,000.00 a day. She didn't have any family and the old lady didn't have any family. So this was going to be very hard to do anything with until Jenny gets better. The fall was approaching and the nights were cooler. Rome would tell Betty that he was cold at night and she told him if he doesn't start calling her mommy he would freeze to death. With his face still swollen he asked mommy if he could have a blanket to keep warm with. She barked at him telling him that she was his mommy and not to forget it. This business that I am not your mommy was hurtful to me, ok she told him and he said yes mommy. In three days she had broken him and he now calls her mommy.

The nights were the worst for Rome because he would cry himself to sleep and have flash backs of his mother's pretty face and how nice mom mom was to him. He might call Betty mommy but he still remembers who his mommy is and misses her very much. A lot of times they would read him stories from the Beatrix Potter collection and now he is being tied to the bed post and beaten, he hasn't seen the sun for five days now and his eyes won't aculeate to it quickly and he will need to be held on to at first just to be able to walk. Betty isn't going to take Rome out until his face clears up and he won't run away from her. This isn't gone to happen over night

With no heat and when it will get to freezing temperature they will have to go to a homeless shelter relief center so they can survive the freezing nights.

Rome was getting fewer roach bites every night and yet Betty doesn't seem to be getting any bites. Rome's face was almost cleared up and the nights were brutal between crying for his mommy and all most freezing to death it's a wonder he hasn't died. He is still able to still see his mommy in his mines eye. He misses her very badly and is broken hatred that he might never see her again. Sometimes Betty can hear him crying and she would get out of bed and threaten him with a beating if he doesn't stop crying. He couldn't stop crying but he was able to not cry so loud.

His wrist and ankles were starting to show signs of being tied up. The dirty rope was leaving dark rings and it was starting to wear the skin behind his wrist. Now Betty had to make a decision whether to continue to tie him up or not. Tying him up all the time will eventually cause dirty cuts and infection. Rome's teeth were starting to look bad so she bought him a tooth brush and made him brush his teeth twice a day, no tooth aches and no dentist to ask a lot of questions. Now having Rome she had to think a head of what some things would do and cause her some serious problems that could be avoided with just a little care. She knows if she gets caught it would be a life sentence without parole.

Jenny was being looked after twenty four hours a day and after one week she is beginning to show some improvement. She spoke to the nurse this morning and asked her if she knew Mrs. Topkis. The nurse said she would look into it for her. She came back in a few hours and said that she is in a deep coma and could use a friend like you to come and talk to her. Jenny sat up in bed and asked if someone could take her to see her. The nurse told Jenny that she would have to be wheeled there because she didn't have enough strength to walk there. Jenny wanted to know how far away was it and the nurse told her it was on another floor and in another wing of the hospital. She wanted to know how she was going to talk to Mrs. Topkis if she was in a coma. The nurse assured her that she will be able to hear you; weather she will wake up will be something else. People come out of comas all the time mostly when they hear a voice they haven't heard in years or someone very close to them. It's worth a shot, you don't have anything to loose.

Jenny was wheeled to the bed side of her friend and the best mother she ever had, it was hard to see her lying there with no sign of life so she reached for her hand and it was warm to the touch so she gripped it firmly and said Mrs. Topkis it's Jenny, just then her eyes opened and she told Jenny she was sorry for Rome's loss closed her eyes and died with Jenny holding her hand. Jenny broke down crying saying that she is losing everybody, what is going on? Why is God punishing me by taking my son and the only mother I ever had. No one said anything to her they just wheeled her away after she left go of Mrs. Topkis's hand.

Jenny wanted to be able to go to her funeral and knew she had to get physically better fast and make the funeral arrangements for her. Her lawyer contacted Jenny and told her he was ready to assist her with the expenses of the funeral and the cost of her grave. Jenny was able to get out of the hospital the next afternoon and immediately start setting up Mrs. Topkis's funeral with the Mealeys funeral home. The only people at the funeral were Jenny and Mrs. Topkis's lawyer. There could have been hundreds of people there and Jenny would have never known it. She was deep in agony of the loss of her only mother and the pain wouldn't go away. Jenny got her a beautiful stone that read here lies one of god's most lovable children mom mom. Jenny cried all the way home and the old ladies lawyer stayed with her the whole time.

Ken sat at the kitchen table with Jenny the old Ladies lawyer and he told her that the house was hers and she left all of her wealth to you as well. She had all of her money in three accounts that totaled $3,100,000.00. Jenny looked up from the table and said she had no idea about all this money. Ken told her that he knew she didn't and it was best she didn't. You both were the best of friends and she considered you her daughter and your son her child as well. Jenny broke down crying again and would cry all night. Ken let himself out and left her a note that he will make all the changes with the banks and the house deed and would be in touch with her in a week. He left his card with the note and his phone number underlined so she wouldn't overlook the phone number. He loved that old lady and would do anything for her and by helping Jenny would be like helping the old lady.

Jenny would sit around waiting for the phone to ring and it never did, she would walk down to the park and sit on different benches and look for a woman that would fit the description of the kidnapper. There wasn't anyone remotely close to that description, but she wouldn't give up. Jenny drove down to her office and walked in and the first person she saw was her immediate supervisor. She ran to Jenny and hugged her for a long time and told her how sorry she was about her son's disappearance. Jenny thanked her and they walked back to her office and Mrs. Booth closed the door. Jenny told her that she doesn't know how she was going to carry on, not only did I lose my son but I lost Mrs. Topkis the woman I lived with that took care of Rome and I.

"O no I am sorry again about this Jenny."

"She was very good to my son and me, she considered us her family."

"O my, what a shock this is."

"Every day is a challenge to get one foot a head of the other one."

"Have you decided what you want to do about coming back to work?"

"I have thought about it sometimes and I don't know what I want to do. I feel so heavily consumed with this loss that I can hardly function."

"If you don't feel like you can come back to work at this time I can sign you up for a leave of absence for six months that might help you over this trying time. I don't want your license to expire because you will have to be working in order to renew them and you don't want to go through all that testing again."

"Your right I really wouldn't."

"I held on to your last two pay checks for you and she handed them to her in an envelope."

"Jenny told Mrs. Booth that she would take her up on that leave of absence and see if she can get her life back in order."

"I am glad that you want to do that Jenny because you were the best sales person we had and we want you to come back if you can. You know Jenny some of your sales records have still intact. You know with that pretty face no one could refuse you for anything."

"Thank you Mrs. Booth for saying that, I guess I better be going I have some things to do at my lawyer's office."

"I hope everything is well there for you."

"The lady that I lived with left me her house and her estate when she passed away. She hung on for the longest time but died with me holding her hand. She was in a coma and heard my voice and came out of it for a split second to say she was sorry."

"What was she sorry for?"

"We had an agreement that she wouldn't take Rome to the park without me being their too."

"O Jenny this is such a sad story, our hearts go out to you.

Jenny stood up and said good bye to Mrs. Booth and walked out of the building to her car. She sat there looking at the two checks that were for a total of $28,000.00 she wanted to put them into her checking account. The next thing she wanted to do was to apply for a CDW permit (Concealed Deadly weapon) and be able to protect herself now that she is all alone and has a lot of money in her accounts to be concerned about. Seeing as how she was a victim of a kidnapping in broad daylight she only had to appear in front of an officer from the DA's office and would be issued a permit to carry right away. The usual process is a lot longer.

I would say now that Jenny is carrying a weapon God help the person that tries to hurt her. It wasn't going to be good for them. Her mind would always drift back to Rome that was having a real hard time with Betty who wanted a son but didn't have any motherly instincts. The swelling in his face has subsided and the roach bites were healing but they would leave a little purple mark where the bite was. His hair was a lot longer than Jenny would have it. Except for the birth mark behind his right ear you might just walk past him and not recognize him at all. He didn't have that much contact with other people so it would be safe to say that no one would recognize him.

Betty bought a few books and started to teach him how to read, even though he was smart he was having hard time learning because of the shock he was still in. Betty knew he would attract a lot of attention if he couldn't read or looked dirty She told him his name was Joe Brown but she would call him Sonny and his reply was yes mommy. She told him that was better. Rome was losing the thoughts from his other life and was now slowly engulfed in his new life with Betty. Sonny's worst time was at bed time where he couldn't stop crying missing his mommy and all the love that she and Mrs. Topkis had given him.

Betty had to spray every night so Sonny wouldn't get bit while he slept. It's been a month now and Betty wanted to make a test walk with Sonny to see if he can be trusted not to say anything. They walked down to the drug store and walked around and left. She walked along the street with him not being noticed by anyone and arrived at the front of the shack that she inherited some years ago. The inside was dirtier than the outside, if that was possible, with Betty it was. You could take one look at Sonny and you could tell he wasn't happy at all. He didn't want to get hit anymore so he went along with what she wanted and felt comfortable with her now.

Betty knew that it wouldn't take much for her to get caught by the police. Sonny's picture was everywhere; it was on all the milk cartons, bulletin boards and magazines that were given away for free. He was probably the most sought after person in that town and Jenny kept up with her advertisements looking for her son. She had gotten herself a Glock 19 and two clips that held 15 rounds of hollow point's bullets. Her crusade was relentless it has only been three months now that she has lost Rome but to her it was a lifetime. The worst thing was that she didn't know whether he was dead or alive and in her mind that was harder to live with. Jenny wasn't one to give up on something especially her son. She still had hope that he was still alive and times where she had no hope he was alive. It just tore her apart not knowing either.

You read about this in the newspaper but you never think that it would ever happen to you, it was always someone else until one day that someone else became you. Jenny had deep symphony for people that lost family members in wars or even shot on the street especially the drive by shootings of the little children shot by stray bullets from the guns of the gang members that could take a life without giving it another thought.

Jenny would often be seen in the malls handing out pictures or pamphlets asking the same question, have you seen this little boy. She would go from store to store in the city and ask them to let her put her pamphlets in their outside store windows. No one refused her and her pamphlets were everywhere. She even managed to get herself on the radio and a couple of news interviews for television. She was consumed with her relentless search for Rome.

Betty wanted to make sure that if she ever left Sonny alone he wouldn't run away she was hoping that she had erased any memory of his mother that he still has. Even though he could see this pretty woman's face in his eyes when he closes them at night Betty was becoming mommy to him. He relied on her for a lot of things but that didn't stop her from being mean to him she would often call him names like you're a retard and you're dumb, you're ugly. All of this every day didn't help Sonny he began to be touched by those nasty names she would call him. She would often poke him on the shoulder to show her dominance over him and if that didn't hurt enough she would pull his side burns until he would cry. There was never a day that he wasn't in pain, either verbally or physically.

Sonny had nothing to do all day; there wasn't any electricity so he would look at the books that she got him with the help of the light coming through the window because when the sun went down the house got very dark. He rarely knew what Betty was doing because she was quiet and would often sit and look out the window but not up close so no one could see her. There was only an occasional car that would go by and that was the highlight of the day. The police never came by they had better things to do. No one has ever come to the door for any reason since Sonny was there.

Sonny wanted to know why the lamps didn't work because it was dark and scary every night. She quickly told him to shut up and mind his own business. He asked her why was it so cold at night, that's when she pulled his ears until it made him cry. She told him not to ask any more questions or she would slap his face and he knows how that would feel. Betty had spurts when she would help Sonny out with his books and if she didn't help him it was because the books were useless. There was something gnawing away at her that kept her unhappy and have tremendous mood swings that weren't good for Sonny. It was becoming obvious that Sonny considered Betty his mommy and sole provider.

His real mommy was being eaten up with grief all day long and wasn't getting any psychological help for it. She would often try to picture him at his age now and could only see him how he was at the time of his abduction; he never ages in her eyes. Jenny would meet with volunteers every weekend and they would plan strategies on how to get the word out. She never got personally close to them and would keep them at arm's length from getting close to her. She doesn't really know if she could get close to any man again. She even finds it hard to make a fuss over any baby that she might come in contact with.

It's been four months now since Rome has been gone, the last time Jenny checked in at the police department a few days ago they told her they are at a dead end and with no new leads coming in the case is just sitting in a in box just waiting for something to happen. Jenny reminded the officer in charge that there was enough description of the lady kidnapping Rome to send the police on a manhunt in the area where people look like that and dress like that. Door to door if you have to, but don't let this case die because no work is being done on it. The officer told Jenny that there isn't a day that goes by that we are following up on leads phoned in or we develop. We will not give up on this case as long as I am still around here.

"I keep getting this feeling that this boy is in some run down area."

"He could also be in another state."

"Maybe not because she didn't look like she could afford to go anywhere."

"We are always looking at anyone walking with a small child along the street. She wouldn't dare go out in public with that boy, because she would be caught. We don't think she has a car because of her get away with a cab and bus. You can rest assured that we will always be vigilant."

"It's so easy to fall asleep lieutenant, every lead is worth checking out."

"You are so correct."

Jenny left the police station not feeling too well, with the feeling that the police and FBI could be doing more. It was probably unfair but that was how she felt. Betty was going to take Sonny out just for a few minutes to see how he was going to react being outside. She didn't hold his hand because he was too old for that; it would have been a dead giveaway. When she went into the drug store the pharmacist called her over and said he didn't know she had a child. She told him that he was with his father in Ohio until he passed away a few months ago. Sonny just stood there and looked as dirty as she did, but the pharmacist didn't buy it but let it go.

While on their continuous search for Rome the detective stopped at the pharmacy where Betty frequents and were curious to know if there was a middle aged woman in here in the past three months with a strange five year old boy. The pharmacist face turned beet red and the detective asked him what was wrong. He told him that one of his customers came in the other day with a very suspicious young boy. He told the detective that she told him that the boy was with his father that passed away three months ago.

"Holy shit, I will have to call this in and I will need a ton of police cars for back up."

"What's wrong with what I said?"

"You maybe just described the woman that kidnapped that little boy three months ago. Do you know where she lives?"

"I don't have her address but she lives next to that boarded up house down the street about three blocks from here."

The police officer ran to his car and called in an officer needs help dispatch to the address where the pharmacy was. It sounded like the end of the world, there must have ten cars that showed up. There was even a phone call put into Jenny alerting her that maybe they have found where her son was being held. She left the house in a rage and had to drive almost nine blocks to the pharmacy where all the police cars were. Everyone was there now even the Mayor just showed up and Jenny got out of the car screaming. She was immediately grabbed and told that if she doesn't stop screaming she would be placed in a police car and not be able to come with them to the house where her son might be. She told him Please don't think that he's there and he corrected himself and said where he might be. She promised them she would be quiet from now on.

The streets were getting congested with reporters TV news men the fire department. The plan was that they would fan out and walk slowly and wait to hear what the three scouts up a head had to say about the location of the house and give the rest of them directions where the house was. This was a huge undertaking and it had to be pulled off by not tipping their hand to the kidnapper. The scouts finally called in and said that they located the house at 311 Somers St. The scout said it doesn't look like it was being lived in. Jenny's heart was beating very wildly and could hardly walk; thank God she had a female police officer helping her. The police went at their work very methodical and had no intentions of messing this up.

The police lieutenant took hold of his mike and called out that the woman living in the house at 311 Somers st is to come outside now. There was nothing, so the men around back were ordered to close in but not to enter until they were ordered to. The sun was going down now and there were trucks with spot lights on that lit up that house like it was daylight. There was gun fire from the second floor and the back at ground level. The lieutenant asked them to hold their fire until you can see who you're shooting at. There *was plenty of fire power coming from that house and the lieutenant knew they couldn't keep it up. There was a white flag being waved out one of the second story windows and a voice saying we surrender. They were told to come out with their hands up now, it only took a few minutes and out they came.*

They were thrown to the ground all three of them and cuffed.

"Where is the lady and the kid?"

"We don't know about any lady and a kid."

"We know she lives there, don't lie to us. What did you do with them?"

"I told you we don't know anything about a lady and a kid. This house was vacant and we decided to hold up in it for a while until it was safe for us to leave."

"You're the three that robbed the bank this morning on Main Street."

"I didn't think that it would have drawn all this attention robing a stinking bank."

The lieutenant sent the detectives in to give the place a once over and it wasn't long before they found some clothes that a five year would wear. Jenny was called in and she identified those items found that belonged to her son. They only found two beds or what was a poor excuse for a bed. There were dead roaches everywhere and four empty roach spray bottles thrown around. One of the bed sheets had blood all over them and the detective said that it was probably where the boy slept. By now Jenny had the shakes and couldn't control herself, she shook like she was outside in the freezing snowstorm. After Betty talked to the pharmacist he must have spooked her and she decided to take a few things and leave quickly. The detective put two policemen on the job for calling the cab companies and seeing if there were any pickups at this house in the last four hours. It turns out that there weren't any pickups for a woman and young boy all day.

The lieutenant surmised that she is walking and called the dispatcher to have all vehicles start patrolling the streets and be on the lookout for a middle aged woman and a five year old boy. Jenny was feeling so bad she couldn't take any more of this disappointment she had to go home and just cry it out, now that she knows that Rome is living a horrible life with a horrible woman. She kept trying to understand why anyone would want to kidnap a little boy and not take care of him. He and the old lady was all she had and she has lost both of them. She is hoping that she is on the run now and can't draw any attention to herself and get caught.

5

*J*enny had an appointment with Mrs. Booth at the AAA Ins. office and got there right on time. Mrs. Booth welcomed her with a hug and told her how much she missed her. Jenny should have said thank you but instead she seemed to be in a daze and she mumbled something that Mrs. Booth left alone. Jenny looked at Mrs. Booth and said holding back the tears and told her that she couldn't come back to work because she can't get over the loss of her son and is busy looking for him. She won't rest until she finds him. Mrs. Booth told Jenny that she understood and was real sorry and she meant it. Jenny said she would stay in touch with everyone and she had some great memories here and deeply appreciated the opportunity that she was given to work for her and the Ins. Co. She said she would never forget them. Jenny stood and slightly staggered and grabbed the desk to get her composure and walk off down the hallway to the parking lot where her car was parked.

Jenny knew that if she couldn't work she must really be out of it. All she wants to do is to watch the local news shows on TV and wait for the phone to ring telling her that they have found her son. She couldn't figure out how she got away from all those police cars, with her not having a car to get around in.

Betty had ran out of the house when they got home from the pharmacy she knew the cops would be at her place soon so she ran out leaving most of her rags and bring her little address book. She walked for a good ten blocks until she felt safe to catch a #13 bus. When she was in prison three years ago she had met a girl there that told her when she gets out to come to her she's out of town and to stay with her. When she was seated she looked into the address book and checked the address again. She remembered the girl who was in prison with her name Judy she told her when you take the #13 bus from town it will stop right in front of my house. Betty was hoping that Judy still lived *there and hoped she would let her stay with her like she said she would when they were cell mates in prison.*

The bus driver called out the next stop and that was Betty and Sonny's notice to get off at this stop. They got off and were smothered with a dust storm caused by the bus exhaust blowing all the dirt around. Betty warned Sonny that he better not do anything that would cause her friend Judy to turn them away because if he does they will be sleeping out in the woods tonight. She grabbed Sonny's collar and practically chocked him with pulling the collar tight against his neck. He wasn't putting up a struggle Betty was just giving Sonny a message of what was in store for him if he should cause her any trouble.

They stepped on to the porch and she rang the doorbell Betty could hear footsteps coming closer to the door. It opened abruptly and there was her friend Judy with a cigarette in her mouth she immediately recognized Betty and reached out for her and they gave each other a hug. She stepped back and asked Betty who have you brought with you?

"He's what's left of my last marriage."

"You didn't tell me you had a kid."

"I wanted to but at the time I almost didn't feel like I did."

"Well come on in stranger and tell me what you have been up to."

"I've been staying out of prison, that's for sure. In fact I only just got off of probation six months ago."

"Good I guess you're tired of them snooping around your house all the time."

"They always wanted to know who my friends were and where do I go with them. All that crap just to keep you straight. I bet if I told them that I was going to church regularly they would want to talk to the preacher or come and see me there."

"Do you go to church Judy."

"Not if I can help it."

"Tell me about your boyfriends."

"What boyfriends, I can hardly get one to look at me. I can go to the bar down the street at night and get picked up for a quickie if I want to run the risk of getting the clap, or aids."

"Can't you make them use a rubber?"

"They don't want to, they tell me that they don't like to go swimming with an over coat on.

"Tell me about your boy?"

"He's five and a half and I am home schooling him, he's real slow at it but I am persistent."

"You know he looks like that kid that was kidnapped six months ago."

"I wish somebody would kidnap him."

"Now Betty he looks like a nice little boy."

"He is after I beat the shit out of him. That brings him right back in line. Betty looked at Sonny and asked him "Isn't that right Sonny."

"Yes mommy."

"So his name is sonny."

"I call him that because it's easier for me to remember."

"What's his real name?"

"His father called him Joe Brown."

"That's easy to remember."

"I guess your right; it's the memories that I 'am trying to forget."

"What brings you out to this neck of the woods?"

"Well Judy we always told each other the truth and the truth is I need a place to stay for a while."

"How long is a while?"

"Probably around six months."

Judy looked at her and said, "I could use some money for this, after all Betty I don't have a lot of money."

"I need to change my address for my welfare money and the money will soon follow."

"How much do you want me to pay you?"

"I think $30.00 a week is very fair."

"I agree and as soon as my check comes in I'll pay you."

"That sounds good enough for me."

"What about sonny, will he be a problem?"

"No not at all and if he does please tell me and I'll straighten it out in a hurry."

"Ok Betty you can stay, you need to get this boy some smarts or he isn't going to make it."

"Your right and I am going to get some books of learning and bring him up to the level that he should be at."

"Judy took a liking to sonny and would help him with his reading and writing."

After a few months Sonny had really taken a liking to Judy and they were always together. Betty didn't care because that was one thing less that she had to worry about. Knowing if she got caught she would be in jail for the rest of her life. Things were going on real smoothly at Judy's place and it was coming up on six months that Betty said she needed to get herself together. Judy never said anything to Betty about what's next because she was really hooked on Sonny. They would kiss and hug every night at bed time and Betty could have cared less. Sonny needed this affection in the worse way and it looks like Judy did as well. The boy had clean sheets every night and no cockroaches to bite him.

Judy could see that Sonny was a good kid and had to wonder about what Betty told her that if anything should happen to her do not call the cops because I took sonny away from his father and I lied about him dieing. So please don't call anyone if I am gone as far as she was concerned I am his mother and he is your son, because I am giving him to you. Betty asked Judy if she minded if she went down to the bar this night and Judy told her to go for it. You might get lucky. Judy saw her cleaned up and thought she would still have a problem because it was hard to polish a terd.

She actually walked to the bar with just twenty dollars in her jeans pocket and no ID. That was all she had and some unlucky sob was in for a bad evening picking her up. She was ready to put out even if it meant doing it on the pool table in the back of the bar. This scruffy guy asked her if she wanted to fuck and she said she might for a price.

"What's the price to fuck you? Or do you want to pay me for the pleasure."

As hard as it was she did smile a little and told him twenty dollars up front. He handed her two ten dollar bills and walked out of the bar together towards his Elcamino. That was the last any one ever saw her again. When she didn't come home Judy thought she was shacked up with someone and would be coming home soon. It never happened and after a few days Judy figured she wasn't coming home and when her next welfare check stub came she figured she met the wrong guy and like a lot of prostitutes murdered the body is never found. Sonny didn't miss her at all and Judy could plainly see that he didn't miss her. She remembers what Betty told her about making any inquiries that sonny was missing from his father and Judy would go to jail for kidnapping Sonny. Being an ex con she didn't have a chance. She did what her heart told her to do and that was to take care of Sonny as long as she could.

It's a year now and Jenny is no different, she is still a mess. She has so many clubs going on that she can hardly keep up with them. She is consumed with Rome and where he might be. The police keep her up to date on the kidnapping woman and told Jenny that she has disappeared off the Earth. They have worked on her case every day and the Capt. is taking everyone off and leaving only one detective that has other cases to investigate. Jenny knows now that her case is being moved back on the burner to keep warm and not as hot as it once was anymore. This was a wakeup call for Jenny and would have to deal with it or fall by the waste side with the rest of the unsolved cases that are mounting in large numbers.

For the first time Jenny had the thought of meeting someone and having another baby and put some life back in her life the few times she dated she always talked about Rome and how much she missed him. The date couldn't get a word in the conversation and none of her dates amounted to anything. She went for an interview at the artificial insemination clinic and wanted to see if she would qualify for an insertion and get pregnant. She was nervous showing up for her interview and whatever else that she has to do to get pregnant. It took three meetings of IQ test, physical exams and see if she would be a suitable recipient of artificial insemination there were a lot of test. She was now down to the pictures of the sperm donors and her IQ and the donors to have the best possible child that they could give her.

She went back for her final visit at the clinic and she made her final selection and was told that the entire cost for the insertion and all the test that were performed on her would cost $31,000.00 payable on or before the insertion. She would be guaranteed a healthy baby or they would try again. She wrote them a check and had an appointment for the next day to implant the sperm that would make her pregnant. The procedure went easy and Jenny was on her way home in a few hours. She was like a different person knowing that she is carrying a baby from a complete stranger and he would be the father of her child. She would never know it and that was fine with her because the last father didn't know it either.

A big clue for Jenny weather she is pregnant or not was if she misses her upcoming period. The anticipation was nerve racking to her. She knows she will be a good mother and she knows not to compare the new baby to Rome because it would make life more complicated. She was going to have this baby and treat it like the second one, just like the way she explained it to the people at the clinic. Everyone agreed that was the only healthy thing to do, the past is gone and it is time to move on with her new life. She has enough money to have a wonderful life and live off the interest with no problem. If a man comes along then so be it and if one doesn't then she will have a family of her own and get involved in her child's life as much as she can without crowding. It was good to see Jenny coming out of her shell and moving on to more things than just mourning her life away.

She will know in a few more days if she missed her period and now it turns out that she has. She went and got the testing kit and she was pregnant. She called the clinic and they said they would see her in thirty days and she could use their facilities or go and find her own medical doctors. She would have to make up her mind soon because the clinic has their standards that have to be met before they take on a delivery. Jenny would have to pay for any medical attention that she receives at the clinic plus her monthly check ups and for the delivery. Jenny just wants a healthy baby and she can do the rest, she doesn't know if she could handle an unhealthy baby

Judy has turned into a loving mother she has given up on ever seeing Betty again, she thinks that she either mouthed off to the wrong guy and was taken for a ride and murdered. She wasn't about to look into finding her because of what was missing from the story she told Judy about Sonny. He was a wonderful child and she wants to make sure that she home schools him to the best of her ability. She knows that he can be somebody if he is applies himself in the right direction. Being six is a great age for him because he can excel in all of his studies. He has showed Judy that he responds to her loving attention and has made Judy's life worth wile now. While she's teaching Sonny his lesions she is learning herself. You might say that what she is doing for Sonny is what she was missing in her life. She knew that Sonny was missing out in playing with other children; she wanted to wait a little longer before she introduces him into a new part of his life.

Judy tests him all the time and his scores show her that he is retaining all of his lesions. She is happy that he is such a good student. She bought him a new computer and he is beginning to master it at age six. She doesn't allow him to play games on it, he is supposed to use it for his lesions and to write materials on word that is his favorite thing to do. To this day Sonny has never asked Judy where Betty is, she thought she broke him. But it clearly shows that she didn't, Sonny is the kind that you can kill with kindness. She knew that the birth mark behind his right ear could easily be used to identify him, so she let his hair just cover his ears and hide the birth mark. He called her mommy and that brought tears to Judy's eyes that he considered her his mommy. This was a wonderful child to call her mommy. She doesn't know where Betty is but she hopes she continue to stay away.

Judy knew that Betty didn't take care of Sonny he was a dirty mess when she saw him for the first time and has taken almost six months to clean him up and make him look as good as he does now. His hair is a little darker and that makes Judy feel better that someone could say something that was different from what Betty had told her. She will never give him up and hopes that it won't ever come to that. She just didn't trust Betty to have told her the truth. She wanted to teach Sonny through the summer with some advanced courses in computers and math or arithmetic, she knows that would excel him into a higher percentile. She is very proud of Sonny and how fast he learns.

There wasn't anyone in her life that cared about her having a child and if she had to explain Sonny to anyone she would tell them that he is her son from a previous marriage. The husband had custody and with his passing away she took him back. Now he's hers for life.

Jenny's little dog Penny has never been the same and really misses Rome, he sleeps on Rome's bed every night. She hopes he will show the new baby the same love like he has shown Rome. She feels that he will and give his love all over again. Jenny really feels good about her pregnancy and can see that she is beginning to feel a lot better now. She is using the clinic for their services and they will stay with her through the whole delivery. She doesn't have anyone that could do that; she will need someone even if it's holding her hand. They told her that the second baby usually comes a little quicker. So when it's time please stay close because he can drop out of you in a matter of minutes. She has heard that before and will take heed.

It doesn't take a genius to see that there is something missing from Jenny's life, she needs some adult company and is not willing to lower her standards to find one. She feels that if she isn't searching, she will find someone someday and is willing to wait. She has far too much money to be desperate; she wants to invest some of it but not much. She doesn't want to lose any money on stocks that she has no control over. She feels very secure now and wants her new life with her new child to be successful.

Judy wants to let Sonny mix with other children but she is scared of the nosey mothers prying until they find out that she is a convicted felon, so she does everything short of keeping Sonny away from other children and takes him to the park to stretch his legs. She noticed that he could throw the little football a country mile. He loved to play any game that involved throwing a ball. Judy hasn't had a man for a while and doesn't want to go down to the local watering hole to get laid. Betty did it and never returned and she knows that the creeps that hang out down there are capable of killing women that are hard to trace. Betty was not traceable and if they find her Skelton someday she will never be identified. They would need her finger prints. It's easy to see that single women with children don't have much of a chance in this man's world.

Judy kept busy shushing off the call of the wild those little demons that get you in trouble sometimes. She wanted to have a fling some evening and shake this Horney feeling. Sonny was too young to leave alone and she didn't know a faster way to go to jail then to leave a child alone just to have a fling down at the Crystal bar. She just sucked it up and kept busy around the house and with Sonny all day. She did all she could to keep Sonny safe and healthy, not going to school with other children is a big help, that was where all the child hood sickness comes from one child giving it to the other.

Judy is worried so much about Sonny that she was getting run down herself and has developed a cough at first she didn't think much about it but when she could hardly walk around the house and it all she do to get out of bed in the morning it was time to see the doctor. They caught the bus outside her door and went the opposite direction from where Sonny came from to the other town twelve miles away. The wait to see the doctor was almost four hours and they were both hungry and looked at all the magazines to pass the time away. Finally she was called and asked Sonny if he could stay there until she returned and he said he could.

The doctor was not that nice; He listened to her heart and asked her if she had heart trouble in her family and her reply was as far as she knew she didn't. He told her that her heart seems to be failing from what it should be for a woman your age.

"How could that be, I am strong and tough."

"You might be strong and tough but something tougher then you has settled in your heart and will eventually do you in. I want to give you a few tests and see if what I think could be true. I want you to set up an appointment for a stress test and I will be able to see your heart better with the equipment that I will use inside of you. I will be looking at your vessels that come from your heart to look for clogging and things like that. I can treat those things easy. There are some things that I can't treat and that is heart failure, no one can treat that.

Judy went out to see the receptionist about the stress test and the next opening was in two weeks. She didn't have much choice. It was nice of the doctor to give her some medicine samples that would help the blood go quicker to her heart. They will hold her till she came back for her stress test. Those two *weeks were awful and Sonny didn't get any schooling from Judy he had to do things on his own he didn't mind because he felt he was helping out. He could clearly see that Judy was really struggling to get around. The morning she had her appointment she had to walk to the bus stop and wait it seemed like forever but was only five minutes. The ride was nice for Judy she loved to rest from the thirty minute ride to the doctor's office.*

They were waiting for her when they came in to the office; they treated her with respect knowing she didn't have any money to pay for this procedure. They also made a fuss over Sonny who looked like a displaced person sitting there in the office. Sonny would have to be part of any plans that Judy will have in store for her after this stress test today. They decided not to give her the treadmill test after looking over what the doctor had to say about his examination of her a few weeks past. She did have to take the test where she had to lay on her back elevated and reach back and hold on to this bar that opened up her chest cavity and allowed them to see in better with their X ray equipment. It wasn't easy especially for a woman that was having congestible heart failure.

Now it was time to see the doctor with the results of the stress test. The first thing he wanted to know from Judy was has she had a virus around a month ago or so. She thought for a moment and said, "Come to think of it I did have a cold and it wrecked me because that was when I first started to get tired and had a hard time getting around."

"What has happened to you was that you caught a Virus and instead of it leaving you in four or five days, yours stayed around and settled in your heart and is in the process of killing you if we don't do something about it."

"What can I do?"

"Not much but to take it easy and not exert yourself around your home, you probably won't be able to do house work, some cooking and no shopping. We might have to put your son into a foster home until you recover."

"I really don't won't to do that if I can help it."

"I can understand your feelings and it's not easy for me to recommend it to you but we are running out of things to do that will solve your health problem."

"I want to keep my son for as long as I can."

"You will need someone to come in two or three days a week to do some house work. There is an agency that I know that will do this free to you."

"Tell me doctor what is going to happen to me."

"I want to be perfectly honest with you and not tell you that everything is going to be fine because it isn't. A virus has settled in your heart and has all but destroyed it. You will need a heart transplant.

"Doctor I don't have any money for that."

"I know that and that is why I have submitted your name to the university hospital hoping that they will have a donor that matches your body type and there will be less of a chance for a rejection."

"What does that mean Rejection?"

"Rejection means if we can't find a donor that matches your DNA make up then your body has a way of killing off any foreign replacements to protect itself from these things that it thinks are going to do it in. By rejecting the new heart if it's not a good match it will kill it off and it will kill you."

"It sounds like you have your hands full."

"We do, we can treat you with medicine and overcome this rejection for a while but it will win in the end. Let's face it you don't have the money to pay for this so it will be close to impossible to find a donor to give you a heart replacement free when they can get hundreds of thousands of dollars for one. I am sorry I am just the messenger; this is the worse part of the job having to tell someone the bad news. No one can teach you how to do it; you just have to do it and get on with things. I know you have a little boy and he will need taking care of and if you can't take care of him anymore then he will have to be put into a foster home."

"Who will determine that?"

"You are going to have a case worker assigned to you and they will determine that."

"Look as bad as it sounds, if you can't take care of him and he isn't capable of taking care of himself then he will have to be put away until you recover."

"If I don't recover?"

"Then he will stay in the program until he is able to earn an income and be out on his own. Our system doesn't allow little boys to become homeless"

The doctor could see that Judy was drifting away and he could tell that this was too much information for her to handle all at once. The receptionist gave her some more sample pills and told her she would see her in a month. In the meantime Judy had to be lucky that they find a donor that fits her makeup and there aren't any paying customers a head of her and that she would be next for the nonpaying transplant list. Hitting the lottery might be easier. The ride home was tough because Judy had to tell Sonny that she might have to go in the hospital for a heart transplant and he would have to live with a family for a while until she get better. He cried for some time because he never had anyone treat him better than she did. That other woman would beat him for nothing and he would take a while before his injuries got better. He asked Judy a lot of questions and she assured him that the new people would take care of him like she did and she would come for him when she got better. Sonny believed her and still didn't like it.

You *know Judy loved that boy to death and would be at death's door before*
she gave him up. That was where she was right now and had to make a call
to the doctor's office and tell the nurse that she could no longer take care of her
little boy and the nurse knew exactly what to do. The next day there was a
representative from the children's welfare and foster care unit to talk to Judy
and Sonny about what was going to happen. Sonny was crying and told Judy
that he didn't want to go with this lady. Judy was crying her heart out and
told Sunny that it was for his own good and he would be well taken care of
and she would be able to write him letters and talk to him on the phone in
due time. That made him feel a little better Judy gave him a card that had
her name, address and phone number and social security number and her
date of birth. On the bottom was her full name Judy Cole. Judy knew that
was enough information for him to find her if he was looking.

The case worker told Sonny to give his mother a big huge because they
were going to his temporary home that was a long ways away. Sonny kept
stalling the case worker until she took his hand and pulled him away. It
wasn't a pretty sight to see him broken hearted once again. She put him in her
car with his little carrying bag and his school papers and computer. The case
worker had to tell the new foster care parents that Sonny was home schooled
and would probably be in the second or third grade. He was seven years old
now and was growing fast. He had no way of knowing that he was going to
be a brother. His mind was very confusing about all the different mommies he
has had and it looked like he was going to get some more. The case worker was
like Jekyll and Hide when they got in the car she called him names and told
him that he would change when he got to his next home. Those children there
aren't going to put up with his baby ways.

Sonny didn't pay any attention to her and let her rattle on. She got mad
because Sonny didn't have anything to say to her so she pulled his hair real

hard until he cried. What was the reasoning for this behavior was a mystery and would be unacceptable under any circumstances. Here we have a heart broken child who finally got some love and now he's back to the mistreatment and mental torture that he thought had gone away. Sonny couldn't help but think what was in store for him at this new house. He would soon find out.

Jenny was doing good with her pregnancy and was three months from having her baby; she did everything they asked her to do. No smoking, no drinking, no drugs, no coffee or tea, they didn't want anything that could affect the baby's growth. She still had a lot of Rome's things and would use his blankets and things like that but would box his clothes and put them in a safe place for keeping. Rome has been gone almost two years now and there was still hope but not much left that she would ever see him again. Jenny needed something good to happen to her and was looking forward to having this baby. It would only be her and the baby and that was fine with her and the medical unit that inseminated her. She trusted them very much and they were going to be a big help to her.

Jenny was still a very beautiful girl and it was a mystery how some good man didn't wiggle his way into her life. As much as she didn't want it a smart man with tact could have captured her heart and swept her off her feet and could have given her all the babies she wanted and could try every night if he had too. She kept the men at arm's length and they could see that she couldn't be bothered. There were a lot of men that thought she was cold, they couldn't get close enough to see that she was heartbroken and would have to be treated with very gentle hands to capture her heart. She was independently wealthy and that made for an independent woman with no man to rely on for a lot of women that was a dream.

On her next checkup they told her that everything was looking good and she should have a normal delivery but to be careful this baby is your second and could want to arrive without notice. She knew what they meant and had no intentions of putting herself in jeopardy. She wanted this baby and paid a lot of money to have it. She would walk a little around the street to keep her in shape; she still managed to keep her cheerleader shape because of her age. Hell she's only 24 and isn't ready to look like a person retired that he doesn't feel like doing anything. She's walking around two miles a day and it shows because she didn't pour on the pounds needlessly and then struggle to get them off. There are some evenings the baby is kicking like hell and some nights it isn't. Jenny would rub creams all over her middle torso just to ease off the stretch marks. It works and she wouldn't miss an evening.

Her little dog Penny is really excited about Jenny being pregnant and acts like he knows it's coming soon. Now penny will have someone to sleep with again, it will be a sight to see. Jenny would often let penny lay on her lap and there were times he could feel the baby kick. Could this dog be so smart that he would know that Jenny is carrying a baby in her stomach? If she had to answer that question she would have to say yes he knows something. Jenny still didn't know what to call the baby if it were a boy; she liked John but probably would settle on Robert. Now if it were a girl on the other hand she was really torn between Joan and Christine and was leaning towards Christine and liked Chris for short. She knows how important it is in choosing the right name for her baby because that is the name it will live with for the rest of their life.

She has things laid out and ready to go and come home too. She's just waiting on the baby's entry into her life and be loved and spoiled for the rest of their life. She is well stocked up on things that this baby would need. She even had a full tank of gas in her car and a baby doctor that will come in and give the baby a physical within twenty four hours of its birth. He could be tied up somewhere but would untangle himself and get to her as fast as he can. She trusted him and knew he was a man of his word. His office was in walking distance of her house and liked that very much.

This one day there was a message on her answering machine to call her mother if she was the right person they were trying to get up with. What kind of a message was this to leave on her answering machine? She never gave it another thought and erased it after she listened to it. She never even wrote down the phone number that she left; she wasn't interested in getting up with her mother, maybe her brothers or sisters but not her parents. They turned her away when she needed them the most; she thought that her child would still be with her if she lived at home. She knew that things happen for the best and had accepted that in her circumstances. Jenny was just waiting for the baby to let her know it wanted out. It was early in the evening of the next day that Jenny knew she was going to be a mommy again.

Jenny called the clinic and told them what was happening to her and they said they will come and get her, just sit and they will be there quickly to pick her up and bring her down to the clinic for her delivery. The pain was getting a little worse. The doorbell rang and there was the girl that she worked with for months. Jenny had a carrying bag for a change of clothes for her and some clothes for her to bring the baby home in. Mary took the bag from her and held on to Jenny going down the steps until she got her to the car door *and held on to her as she got in. It was only a five minute ride to the clinic, where they would be all over her like a ton of stone. They weren't about to let anything happen to her or the baby, so they were cautious in everything they did.*

They put an IV in her and asked her to walk the halls with Mary for a while, when out of nowhere her water broke and the time was getting short. She had dilated almost three centimeters that told them she will be having the baby soon. They weren't going to get too alarmed until she was at least six centimeters. The doctor would check her all the time especially when the pain was real bad. He asked her how she felt and she told him she wanted this over soon. He checked her again and told her it won't be long. The nurses started crowding in the room and she just did a test push and out came the baby. It was a little girl and they placed her on her chest and the baby was exceptionally clean, her eyes were open and she wanted something to suckle on. The doctor couldn't get over how she went right to her mother and started feeding on mom's precious milk. They notified Jenny's baby doctor and he was there in less than an hour.

The nurse wanted to know the baby's name and Jenny said it was Christine. She named it after the old lady, she loved her very much and considered her to be the only mother she had or would ever own up to ever having. She would be allowed to take Christine home in three days and was looking forward to doing just that. The morning of her check out she had a car waiting for her and the driver was Mary who knew exactly where Jenny lived. Mary reminded Jenny that they are willing to help Jenny out if she should ever need their help, she was told to just call us and we will do the rest.

Jenny was happy to be home with the baby and had everything set up and in the right place neat and tucked away. The first night Chris was good she only woke up twice and after a good suckle she went right back to sleep allowing Jenny to go right back to sleep. This went on for a few weeks and now Chris was sleeping longer and now sleeping through the night. This was great for Jenny because she hadn't had a full night sleep in a couple of weeks. She had a phone call from Ruth Jenny's old boss and asked how she was doing. Jenny told her that she had a little girl whom she called Christine, Chris for short. Ruth thought that was great and asked her if she was ok? Jenny told her she was fine and was starting to get used to being retired at age twenty five. Ruth cried out you lucky bugger and said she had a long time before she would retire. They must have talked for a half hour and Ruth told Jenny that she would call her again.

The next morning the phone rang and Jenny picked it up quickly and the voice on the other end asked Jenny was that her and Jenny half recognized the voice and heard it say that it's your mother. There was silence for the longest time.

"Why are you calling me?"

"I wanted to see how you were doing."

"I am doing just fine without you."

"Now Jenny don't be bitter towards us all, it was your father that didn't want you to live at home not me. We miss you so much that we are torn apart at home here without you and we want to see you. You are my first child and I don't want to give you up."

"Don't you remember, you gave me up shall I put it the best way I know how to tell you how I feel. You abandoned me when I needed my family the most you lost your motherly instincts and abandoned me. I had no money or a place to live and you asked me to leave and by me leaving it was going to be better for my brothers and sisters. I don't know if you believed that or not, but I didn't. It was shameful of you to do that to your helpless daughter, pregnant with nowhere to go. I hope my brothers and sisters get treated better than that. I am far better off then you could ever hope you could be."

"Jenny I had no choice or I would have had to leave."

"You are married to the wrong man because no good parent abandons their pregnant eighteen year old child to the streets and waits over five years to get up with them. You made the easy decision and if you would have left with the children you wouldn't have to be calling me today. You made the wrong decision. I hope all those times you spread your legs for him it was worth it. You asked me if I was a whore. Now it's my turn to ask you if you're a whore."

"Jenny you are right, I have no excuse and no matter how much I blame your father it's still my fault for going along with his ways. I guess me giving in all the time kept the marriage together."

"How could you go against your motherly instincts and tell him if she leaves, you all will leave. You let this crazy man's plans that were money influenced destroy you and everything a woman stands for. Shame on you and I am not going to take any relief off you by saying I understand and it's not your fault and all that. It was your fault and this shame you will have to carry for the rest of your life."

"I am not going to ease your self-inflicted pain."

"Now Jenny your being too harsh on me, your brothers and sisters miss you as well."

"Again that's your problem what the kids think. You told those kids a lie and tell them what happened and they all will tell you that you were wrong."

"Tell me about the baby, he must be big by now."

"Jenny told her that she will never discuss the baby with her because you weren't interested then and you're only being nosey now."

"Jenny you sound very bitter and you sound like a stranger to me."

"I plan on being a stranger to you and I will never call you nor will I ever take another phone call from you ever again. I am changing my number to unlisted and don't ever try to get up with me again whether it be through the mail or the phone or in person. If someone dies so be it, I don't care even if you die. If you should ever try again I will have you put on a restraining order that I will enforce to the limit. I don't want you in my life and I surely don't want to be in your life, if you call what you're doing a life. This will be the last time that I ever want to talk to you again. I am even changing my last name so I won't have to identify with your name again."

Jenny hung up and immediately called the phone company and wanted her phone number changed to an unlisted number and never to be given out to anyone (ever.) Then she started the process of changing her last name from Moore to Harris which was going to be a big pain but she wanted to do it so she went through the annoyances of making the name change, that's what determination can do. After hearing her story about her parents no one could blame her. She wasn't going to wait for marriage to do it, just in case she doesn't get married. She would still have to carry the name up until then.

She thought about her mother calling her and all that and not once did she feel anything for her or even miss her. She didn't even like talking to her and wished she would have never called. The mother is guilt ridden and wanted to hear from Jenny that it was ok. Jenny made sure that she didn't tell her how well off the old lady left her, or they would have been all over her like a swarm of bees. Little Chris is a month old and is doing great, she looks right into Jenny's eyes when she talks to her and can give Jenny the impression that she is happy with the little smile she can give her.

Jenny had an appointment with the baby doctor and he gave Chris the once over and pronounced her very healthy and all of her faculties working and are in good shape. Jenny had no desire to meet the donor and had all the privacy she wanted. She would read at least two books a week and was getting good on a lot of subjects. She could hold her own on any subject that could come up in a conversation. Even though it was a long time away she was considering home schooling and in a few years have a radio devise implant put in Chris's shoulder in case she ever is lost or stolen.

The case worker pulled up to Sonny's new home and it didn't look that nice with all the shrubbery overgrown everywhere. Sonny was worried about what the case worker said to him in the car that the other children weren't going to put up with his baby ways. It made him very nervous. They got out of her car and the case worker wouldn't help Sonny carry anything in the house to meet his new foster parent. The case worker showed that she didn't care about Sonny or his feelings the way she would talk to him. The foster mother wasn't any better asking Sonny if he has all of his belongings with him. He told her that he had a few more things in the car and he wanted to go and get them.

The case worker told him to hurry up she didn't have all day. All he had left to bring in was his computer and his home school books. The foster mother told the case worker in front of Sonny that he would be going to the same school as the other children go to and he would go everyday sick or not. He struggled bringing the things from the car into the house. The case worker didn't even introduce Sonny to his new foster mother she had to ask him what his name was. He told her sonny and she said he could call her mother. That made Sonny very nervous; she insisted that he call her mother right there in front of the case worker. Sonny wouldn't do it and the foster mother was furious. The case worker could see that Sonny was going to be a problem to this woman and left in a hurry.

The case worker wasn't gone five minutes and told Sonny to follow her to his bed room that he is sharing with two other children, both older than him. Finally Sonny got everything up to the room the foster mother told him she didn't want any trouble out of him or he will pay heavily for it. She grabbed him by his shirt and told him that the children call he mother and he is to do the same. He looked her in the face and told her you're not my mother. She whirled him around and grabbed him by the hair, a whole hand full and had him lifted off the floor screaming at him to call her mother or spend the rest of the day in his room, just sitting on his bed.

He never looked at her and she could see that he wasn't going to be around her much longer. She would lie to the case worker if need be and get him taken away if she can't break him. Sonny sat on the bed for the longest time and finally he could hear voices coming from down stairs. It wasn't long before his bedroom door opened and in walked two of the biggest rough necks that Sonny has ever seen. They told him to stand up and they got right in his face and were screaming at him words that Sonny had never heard before. The foster mother could clearly hear the children taunting him and daring him to start a fight. It got so bad she had to come up to the bed room and join the gang bang against Sonny. She told Sonny that he wasn't going to have any dinner tonight because of his fighting with the other two children.

If he was stuck in the bed room he decided to change into his pajamas and look at some of his home schooling books. It made him very tired and would often drift off to sleep and wake up nervous from what was going to be a bad time going to get to sleep. His two roommates came into the bedroom and opened the window and lit up two cigarettes and would blow the smoke out the window until they were finished. The foster mother came into the bedroom and smelled the cigarette smoke and asked the two thugs who was smoking in this house. No one said anything so she started looking for a pack of cigarettes and found the pack under Sonny's pillow she grabbed him by the hair and drug him out in the hall way and down the stairs over to the kitchen sink and squirted some liquid soap in his mouth and told him to swallow it. It made him sick all evening and with him throwing up on an empty stomach was bad and dangerous for him.

The two thugs were very happy that he didn't squeal on them so one of them went down stairs and got him something to eat. He needed that or he would have gotten very sick. The foster father stuck his head in the door and told Sonny that he was sorry that he had gotten off on the wrong foot with his mother. That was all he had to say and left as fast as he came. Sonny had made a couple of friends now by not squealing on the two thugs. It must have been three weeks before the foster mother took Sonny to the school for enrollment. They were both asked to go into the enrollment office and speak with the person in charge of enrollment.

They were asked to have a seat and while the enrollment officer looked over Sonny's papers she asked her why she took so long before she would enroll Sonny in the school.

"It's only been three weeks, I was busy."

"Well we are not that busy that we can't file a complaint against you to the foster care program director, because you are not worthy to take care of this child and get paid good taxpayer money to do it."

"This was the first time I could get here."

"I've been watching you and you are a disgrace to the program. I can promise you that you will lose all of the children under your care if I have anything to do about it."

The woman looked at Sonny and asked him if she hits him and his reply was no but she hasn't feed him dinner since he has been there. That was all she wanted to hear and she stood up and called for help from some of her assistants and asked them to call the police right away. Sonny could see that this woman was on his side and loved it. One of the women brought Sonny back something to eat from the cafeteria and Sonny devoured it so they went and got him something else and he devoured it as well. He was given a bottle of apple juice to drink.

The police came along with the foster care case workers and wanted to hear what she did to him. He told them everything that she did to him for no reason, how she would lift him off the floor by grabbing a hand full of his hair and lifting and dragging him all over the house. She didn't give me any supper at night because I wouldn't call her mother. This pissed off everyone in the room and asked her to stand up and told her to put her hands behind her back and she was arrested for excessive child abuse. The child foster people wanted to go back to the home with Sonny and get his belongings. When they got there he asked one of the case workers if they would help him bring down his belongings because the other case lady wouldn't help him. Well the look on their faces was in disbelief.

These case workers could see now that they are going to have to go back after a child is assigned to a residence and interview the child to see if there is any abuse and maybe do this every three months. The police took the foster mother out of the school and placed her in the patrol car and drove her straight to the county lock up where she will be arraigned and charged, fingerprinted and put in a cell until her court appearance and bail whichever came first. The public defender had his hands full defending her. Sonny didn't have to appear they had his testimony that was given in front of witnesses and that was all they needed to convict her. It was all done in one day; she was sentenced to ninety days and two years' probation and never allowed to foster children again. It was all over the news, no pictures of Sonny but the foster mother had all the publicity anyone could ever want. The foster parent program was happy that this case got so much publicity because it might eliminate some of these bad mothers from the program.

7

*T*hey found Sonny a home where there was another child and he was the child of the new foster parent. His name was Brook he was very selfish and not a lot of fun. Sonny would have to rely on the new kids that he would meet at school to have any fun. Sonny would sleep in a different room then Brook did. His new foster mother Mrs. Barbara Martin didn't waste any time in getting Sonny in school, he was put in the second grade and almost the third. The second grade would be better for him because of his maturity level. They could see that he was smart and very courteous. Brook was always trying to get Sonny in trouble with her mother and the mother could see what was going on. It made for a tension filled household. Brook didn't want to share her parents with anyone especially some kid who didn't have any parents. Brook would have to learn that we are all a heartbeat away from a catastrophe, some day we will be the other guy.

It was hard for Mrs. Martin to praise Sonny because of Brook; he would become disruptive and was always competing with Sonny for some attention. Sonny wasn't competing, he was just happy to be alive. Let's face it she didn't have the personality that Sonny had. Sonny felt real comfortable with the Martin's in spite of Brook. He had settled into his school and his new friends. They were bussed to and from school. He called the foster mother Mrs. Martin and that was all that was expected. He had his first interview with the case worker and everything was ok. Sonny had nothing but nice things to say about the Martin's. He did complain about Brook stealing his homework and sometimes showing up at school with his homework missing from his folders. All of his pencils were broken and some pages missing from his school books. The case worker said she would talk to Mrs. Martin right away about it. She told the case worker that she was aware of the jealously that her daughter was having towards Sonny but didn't know that it had gone this far. The case worker told Mrs. Martin that if it doesn't improve they will have to take

Sonny out of the house and she will be removed from the eligible homes to foster children Mrs. Martin was knocked back on her heels when she heard this. She had to get it settled or op out of the program. Everyone appeared to be happy and the case worker had to file her report in forty eight hours or there was going to be hell to pay.

The Martin had made some plans to go away on vacation to south Myrtle Beach for a week and Sonny was excited to go away to the ocean in august. Sonny never saw the ocean and Mrs. Martin had to get permission from the foster home care people to take Sonny out of the state. She also had to file a full disclosure statement where they were going, phone numbers and all that. Brook had told Sonny that she didn't like him and was going to see to it that he would be kicked out of his house when they returned home from vacation. The drive from Baltimore was long they left at 7 am and it probably took eight hours with stops for gas and some drive through food. Brook tormented Sonny through the whole trip. He spilt his drink on him and wouldn't let him have any ketchup for his fries. If there was any way that Brook could show her hatred he did it. On the way to the bathroom at one of their stops Brook threw water on sonny from the sink and Sonny had had enough and punched him in the mouth and caused a nose bleed. Brook ran to his mother and told her what Sonny had done to him for no reason. Sonny came out of the bathroom and you could clearly see that Sonny had water thrown all over him Mrs. Martin Grabbed Brook and pulled his hair and slapped his face. He cried from the pain and Mr. Martin roughed her up as well. Now Brook was in his sulking mood for the rest of the journey. They finally arrived at 4 pm and instead of the two of them showing any happiness it was somber and quiet. Sonny asked Mrs. Martin if he could go down to the ocean and she said to go with brook and he said he would rather not, he didn't feel safe around her.

Here we are on vacation and we are having a serious problem thought Mrs. Martin. When Mrs. Martin said they could all go together, Brook threw a fit so the father took her in the bath room and gave her something to throw a fit over. This made Brook worse because she saw that his parents were taking the side of this kid that he didn't like. She couldn't see that she was the trouble maker. Later on that evening the martin's had a talk before they went to bed and they concluded that their daughter was rebelling against Sonny being in his house and he had to share them with him. Brook did everything that an eight year old could do to destroy their vacation. It was horrible and they cut their vacation short and headed home. They lost money that they didn't have *to loose, they pre warned Brook that if they had to leave early she would pay a terrible price when he got home.*

The both knew what they had to do when they got home and that was to call the case worker and tell them that Sonny would have to be placed somewhere else. Barbara knew that there wasn't one moment that their daughter didn't disrupt their vacation to the point that they had to leave early. Barbara put a call into the case worker right away and told her how her daughter was treating Sonny and how Sonny had to hit her daughter over a water throwing incident and would have to physically defend himself over this relentless bombardment of tormenting. She apologized to the case worker for having to cut Sonny's stay with them short. The case worker thought it would be appropriate for her to apologize to Sonny for being the recipient of all this abuse.

She said she would. Now behind the scenes the foster care program had to get Sonny out of the house knowing what they know now. They looked into Sonny staying at the children's home south of Baltimore that was already overflowing with children. They didn't have any choice but to place him there. The home was for children ranging from 4 to 17 it was out of the way of the big city influence and would be perfect for sonny. Before they would take him to the home someone had to tell him that Judy passed away. The case worker that was assigned to him was given the job to tell Sonny. She sat with him in the car and before they left for the home she told him. Sonny took the news pretty good and the case worker held him for a few minutes and it was over. He got his composure and sat up straight and the case worker left for the home.

He saw the street sign where she turned down on and it read Moors Lane, a name that he will never forget. He feels that he is a burden on everyone and nobody wants him, he kept it to himself that was a lot of negatives to store inside a little boy. As the case worker slowed to the circle driveway in the front of the house, they still had a lot of steps to climb to the big porch that wrapped around the white house that had the paint peeling from the wooden siding. There were two white doors that had two wooden screens doors that looked like they were heavily used by the children. The only children around were the children that were too young to go to school. They sat on the steps and the rockers on the porch, they would just lounge around with nothing to do because the home didn't have anyone that was qualified to teach these children something, it was the old story there wasn't any money for that.

The case worker had come across three plaques of three young men that were killed in the Korean War they grew up at the home. It made the case worker cry to see this small memorial that was dedicated to these three homeless children that joined the Marines and gave their lives to our country and if not for those plaques no one would have ever heard of them. How sad it was to feel this terrible pain knowing that they might have had no one to cry for them. I guess it would be fair to say that they never knew the American dream. She hoped that Sonny doesn't experience the same life ending experience that those other three boys did.

The case worker saw a bench outside what looked like an office and stuck her head in and was immediately told to come in. There was a nice elderly woman that welcomed her to the Moors home and started looking at Sonny and said what a nice little boy he is. There are a lot of children here for what's his name?

"Sonny Brown is what he'll answer to."

"That's a nice name and it will be easy for the children to learn. There are about seventy children here and they all have the same thing in common, they don't have any parents that were willing to care for them or that were alive. Either way they were alone and needed all the love we could give them. There isn't any abuse here we love these children and we will care for them when they are running a fever and they are throwing up and wetting the bed. They consider us their parents and I don't ever want to let them down."

"That was a remarkable way that you put it, usually people in our professions have a tendency to be cold and standoffish. We are victims of our jobs."

"We don't have to be, it's easier to not have feelings then it is to have feelings. What happens to these children here under our custody will stay with them for the rest of their lives."

"I am very impressed with what you had to say and I will be one of your supporters, you can count on it."

Sonny had strolled out on the porch and was sitting with a couple of little girls and they were asking him where his mommy was, it was so sad for this case worker to see this and feel these little children hurting for their mommies and wanted to know if Sonny knew where his mommy was. He finally told the little girl that he didn't know where she was and that he missed her. This was going to be a day that the case worker will never forget. The school buses started to pull up and the children started piling out and they all ran up the steps and out into the big dining room for their after school snack. The weather determined what snacks we would lay out for them said the lady in charge of the home Pat Ruth. On some real cold days we would have some nice warm chicken noodle soup ready for them and in the summer we might have fruit. It varied all the time, the most important thing we serve up here is love. No home should be without it.

Jenny being at home all day she could give Chris a lot of care and when Chris was sleeping Jenny was studying and taking courses on her computer. She loved it and just might be lucky enough to get a degree someday. She was willing to spend the time to do it. She couldn't make up her mind as to what she wanted to major in. She finally decided to pursue the Wall Street trading degree, she feels like she could succeed there. The income potential was very high and it was just what she was looking for. She definitely had the looks to be a great sales person. She proved that when she was an insurance agent. Good looks wouldn't hurt and these companies would know that a pretty face goes a long way on the stock exchange. If she is going to go back to work she would like to wait until Chris is at least eighteen or if she could get a position during her school hours.

Jenny wanted to take a computer class to perfect her computer skills, because she will have to have good computer skills to be successful in the stock and brokerage offices where she will probably end up. She hasn't giving up on working at home and thinks she will love it. Keeping herself busy will be good for her; it's not easy being alone. It's not easy being alone and without a man. Jenny hasn't had a man for around eight years now and is at the point that she is probably a virgin again having gone this long without a man. Her priority at this time is Chris and all the others come second.

She did join a health club and hired a trainer to put her back in shape and give her back her great looking body. The trainer worked with her two days a week and she felt this was what she needed. The question is what is she going to do with Chris and the answer is that she was going to take her to exercise class with her. The trainer thought it was a good idea and said if she didn't mind he didn't mind. When she was finished her class she would shower at home and not at the health club. It felt safer for her and whenever she didn't feel safe. She would either not go or she would carry her concealed weapon that she has a permit to carry. The gun classes that Jenny took trained her to use her weapon if her life is in danger. Little Chris slept through her classes and was a big hit at the health club.

Her trainer Bob was built pretty good but when Jenny looked closely at him she could tell that he wasn't a certified trainer and looked like he wasn't long at it no matter what he said. He rarely talked about himself probably because there wasn't anything to talk about. Jenny was happy with him and his workout program he had her on, she was interested in toning up and nothing else. She has had two babies and she wasn't looking for miracles. The only way anyone would see her would be with her clothes on and not see her small stretch marks from having two babies. This girl still could win any beauty contest if she should enter. She had this beauty and never strutted around like she was hot stuff, she just wasn't that way. She was one of the few beauties that didn't know how beautiful she was and therefore she was down to earth and easy to talk to.

Living by herself she needed to fire her gun at the range so she hired one of the girls from the clinic where she had the baby just for an hour that was long enough to drop Chris off fire her new weapon it was a 9 mm baby Glock that fires fifteen rounds and easy to conceal. It was easy to keep on target at 10 to 12 ft. She likes her 9 mm Glock 19 that holds 15 rounds that gives Jenny a better chance in a shootout. She couldn't imagine herself in a shootout but knew 15 rounds were better than 7 rounds. Either way she can carry the baby Glock in a small purse and the Glock 19 in a concealed belly pouch. Either way someone is in deep do do if they try to mess with her and do her some harm.

Jenny had made up her mind that she would not suffer the loss of this child or have someone stalk her and rape her thinking that she was helpless and not capable of defending herself. This girl is a train wreck waiting to derail some unsuspecting amateur if he should pick her out to do her some harm. The clinic idea worked out real well they are very responsible and she trust them and their employees who have a very extensive background check. The clinic had their employee's finger printed and looked at by the FBI. She only fired a hundred rounds from her baby Glock and practiced her three round rapid fires until she got it right. She was instructed to fire in three round spurts and at ten feet or less someone was going to die.

There wasn't a whole lot for Jenny to do every day raising an infant she got up early and went to bed early. She would give Chris her whole attention and while she slept she would do her school work on the computer a little each day one subject at a time. She wasn't in any hurry and had plenty of time to perfect her studies with a goal of getting a high passing grade. She knew what these Wall Street people would expect from her and she had to be ready to show her skills. Its funny how a dream or a goal can motivate you to heights that you thought were not attainable. Jenny has suffered a lot and had some good fortunes come across her path. The pain was greater than the good fortune and she would have to fight off any misfortune that might await her.

Sonny sat on the porch with the case worker and looked at all the lonely children who were truly happy to be at the home with Pat Ruth who she showed her love to every day all day. They were happy to be here at the home and grateful for that. Pat asked the case worked if she had the date of birth for Sonny and who his parents were and all that other stuff. Pat said she thought the lady where Sonny lived with last was Harris so we will call him Sonny Harris. She didn't know it was Brown As far as his date of birth is we will have to guess at 8/21/1980. Pat told the case worker she would make up a file for him that will give him a life after he leaves us later on. I am going to get him a birth certificate that he cannot be without. Ann Roberts the case worker was really taken back at what she has seen here at the home and wanted to come back and visit with Sonny at least once a month. Pat told her to come as often as she wishes.

Pat took Sonny out in the kitchen where there were three ladies with aprons on and rosy cheeks just having a good time preparing dinner for the children. She called out to the ladies that this is our new child and his name is Sonny. They all replied hello Sonny and Sonny waived to them. Pat told Sonny that it wouldn't hurt to stay on the good side of these ladies they will give you anything you want as long as you're a good boy. She looked at Sonny and said that not everyone here is a good person you might run across one or two that have evil in their hearts. We try to spot this and weed them out to the reform school where they belong.

It was time to enroll Sonny into another school and it was Pat's job to do it so she took his new folder with her and drove down to the new school where all the kids go from the home. It was a new school called Lincoln elementary. Pat knew where to go and sat Sonny outside the office while she spoke to the girl in charge of enrollment. The girl asked her what grade will he be in and Pat replied that he was home schooled for over two years and was in the second grade in Baltimore Elementary in Baltimore. The girl picked up the phone and called the school and they did confirm that he was in the second grade there and was only there a couple of weeks before he stopped coming to school. They have been looking for him and it's as if he dropped off the earth. The girl told her that he is here with her now and will be living at the Mores home out here in Prince Edward County.

The clerk at the school started looking through Sonny's folder and put it down and said to Pat that all of this is just filled in information. Pat told her that they didn't even know his name or his real mothers name or his date of birth or where he was born, or anything else. He is a displaced person and it's up to us to take care of him and turn him into a productive citizen that we can be proud of. She didn't have any alternative but to give him an identity or his life when he gets older will be a sham. Pat told her she thought he would be a good student; he has good manners and can add to the schools good reputation. Pat went out to tell Sonny that he was going to be in the second grade and that someone will take him to his room shortly. Sonny could see this girl coming up the hall way and walked up to Sonny and asked him if his name was Sonny Brown he said it was and he was to follow her to his new class. Just then Pat came out and told Sonny that he was to go to his new class and he was to catch the number 44 school bus back home. He said he would and walked down the hall way with the girl until she stopped in front of the room that said Rm. 37 Mrs. Johnson and opened up the door.

Sonny started to get a few butterflies as they walked in together; the children were doing an assignment and only the teacher Mrs. Johnson who was going to introduce herself to him. Sonny's escort left him and went to her desk. There was a desk vacant next to Sonny's escort. He heard the teacher call her Marie that was easy for him to remember. It was his lucky day he was assigned to the vacant seat next to Marie. Sonny didn't have any lunch so Marie shared hers with him. Sonny was never going to forget that and he thought she was cute. The last school bell rang and everyone ran outside they all were clamoring for their bus number and wouldn't you know it Sonny's bus was the last one in line. When he got on it was half full, he didn't know anybody so he picked a seat and sat near the window. Out of nowhere Marie stepped on to the bus and saw Sonny and walked towards him and sat with him for the ride home. She also was staying at the home and she liked Sonny as well.

Marie and Sonny were always together, that was ok because it made them comfortable. Tonight was going to be Sonny's first dinner; he just took a slice of meatloaf and a spoon of corn with some brown gravy and a slice of bread and a small bottle of milk. Marie was late coming to the dining room and she sat by herself so Sonny picked up his tray and went to her table. She was happy to see him and said that she had fallen asleep reviewing her homework and woke up to the birds singing outside her window. Sonny asked Marie if she could show him what he had to do for homework, she said she would and they met in the study room. He could see that he had this in his home study courses and whizzed right through it. Marie was impressed with that display.

Sonny was tired and was happy to have met Marie, Sonny's room had seven beds and his bed was against the wall and it seemed a little dark but never the less it was safe and clean. Wake up was at 6:30 and they were expected to be in the dining room by 7:00 Wake up consisted of an adult coming to the bed and asking the person to wake up. There were no showers in the morning, only at night because of the time restraints. The school busses came at 7:25 and left sharply at 7:30 with or without you. If you missed the bus there wasn't any way for you to get to school so you had to clean the house all day with only a break for lunch, most of the time you would be cleaning the bathrooms from head to toe. By the time the kids got home from school you would never miss a bus again.

Mrs. Johnson was a good teacher and loved her students; she could see that Sonny has had this work before and was hoping he could be as good with the subjects that come after what he has already had before. Every time he would look over at Marie she would be looking at him, he could see that they liked each other and everyone else could see it as well. Marie was told not to spend so much time with Sonny and her reply was that she was only showing him around the home and all they ever did was to have breakfast and dinner with each other. Never the less she was told to mix it up a little; he needs to meet some boys his own age.

The next morning when Marie came down to the dining room she sat at a table that was full after she joined them. There wasn't any room for Sonny at Marie's table so he was left with a table of boys that were trying to outdo each other. Sonny felt uncomfortable, but he knew he had to listen and learn and not get in trouble there could only be one stop and that was the Farris Reform School where there was a lock down every night and there were boys there who were criminally insane. No one in their right mind would trade the home for that. Sonny found a football and it needed air so he went to Pat and asked her if she could inflate it, she found an old bicycle pump and in no time she had it like new. Sonny found a couple boys his age and they had a catch out back behind the home until dinner. They had a lot of fun and made plans to do it as often as they can.

There was a flier floating around at school for tryouts for the midget football team the next evening. So he went to Pat and asked her if he could tryout and she asked where the tryouts were and Sonny told her that they would be at the school football field. She told him he would need a ride home.

Pat got a hold of the coach and told him that one of her boys wanted to try out and needed a ride home after practice. He told Pat let's see if he is good enough to make the team and we will go from there. The first tryout they asked Sonny what he would like to try out for and he said quarterback.

"Another quarterback."

"Are you the boy from the home and Sonny said yes?"

"Go over to that fellow in the orange shirt and tell him you are trying out for quarterback."

"Excuse me but the coach told me to tell you that I am trying out for quarterback."

"Ok son pick up a football and when I tell you to throw it you throw it over the head of that fellow standing down there in the white shirt."

OF course Sonny was the last to throw and he threw it a mile over the guy's head so the coach gave him another football and waved the fellow back five steps and told Sonny to throw the football. He did and it still went over the head of the receiver. They brought up five boys and asked them to throw their football over the head of the fellow waving at them. Not one of them could do it, so the coach asked the fellow to move back five more steps and Sonny threw five straight footballs in the guy's arms without moving one step. The coach walked down to the assistant in the white shirt and said did you ever see anything like that before; he has the arm of a ten year old. Do you have any idea what this kid could do in a football game; if we can test some receivers that can run like a deer we will be unbeatable. These other teams won't know what hit them.

So now it was time to work with him and polish him up to start at quarterback, they worked with him the whole practice until he was better than good he was great. The different coaches took turns getting him home before lights out at 9 pm. Marie would help him with his homework and Sonny was ready for his first game. Sonny didn't start the third quarter because the score was 42 to 0 so he was benched so as not to devour the other team. The coach was right, no one could come close to beating them and now the sports reporter was writing articles about him calling him the boy with the golden arm. The last game the entire school piled into six buses and went to the championship game. The cheering was loud and clear and everyone was excited that they had a kid from the school that was a star. Needless to say that the Prince Edwards hawks won the game 49 to 7 it made all the newspapers in Maryland and Sonny rode back to the home with his friends in the school buses that Pat had rented just for this occasion.

They celebrated back at the home and the coaches brought ice cream and cake for everyone. A lot of his team mates showed up with their parents, this turned out to be the biggest thing that has happened at the home in years. The newspaper reporters were all over Sonny taking pictures all the time of this little kid that throws a football accurate all the time. Marie tried to stay close to Sonny and Sonny wanted her to stay close. He whispered to her that if she could stay with him he would feel better; maybe they will take our picture together. The season is over now and Sonny didn't quite understand what was happening to him, the coaches did. They talked about how good will he be next year with one more year to play with the under eight year olds. None of the coaches bugged him; he would be too young to put pressure on. Right now he's just a little kid playing football.

With Marie and him studying together they were constantly improving their grades and after a while they would let other kids in their study group and they were improving. Pat could see that these two have found something that they could share with the rest of their friends and bring up their average one grade from C to B and that was nothing to sneeze at. They were no longer telling Marie to spend less time with Sonny they could see that the two of them had some good ideas. One day while Sonny was rifling through one of the closets he found a nice set of golf clubs and asked Pat if he could use them. She told him that that were to long for him but would look into getting him a few golf clubs that were cut down that he could practice with. She called one of the football coaches and asked him if he could get Sonny some cut down golf clubs for him to use; he wants to practice some golf. Her called Pat back the next day and said he found a golf pro that will give me some clubs for him to use.

All the kids at the home knew that Sonny could be found down in the field hitting golf balls all the time especially on the weekends. All he needed was some water, sometimes Marie would bring him a ham and cheese sandwich. Some time she would sit in the shade under a tree and watch him hit balls for hours until he would quit for dinner at 5 pm. picking them up was a trip he didn't have the ball picker up device that can pick up fifty golf balls in ten minutes. He had to bend over and pick them up. He was the only kid at the home that was interested in golf. He didn't know how prejudice a country club could be especially to a kid that lives in a home for homeless children. Sonny knew that some of his football coaches could get him on the putting greens for him to practice his putting.

There was one of the coaches that worked a deal with the pro at the local public golf club to let Sonny practice his putting late Friday and Saturday evenings for an hour or so. The football coach said he would pick him up and drop him off and if he couldn't make it he would find someone to do it. Sonny was so excited about this he could hardly sleep; he was going to be putting on a real golf green. He's been reading all about the sport and has taken a liking to Jack Nicklaus and wanted to swing like him. He showed him that he was a perfect gentleman and he admired that in him. Putting was a part of the game that required a special touch and an ability to see a line that the ball would take on its journey to the hole. Sonny never got tired of golf and had to rely on other people for some assistance in his practicing the sport. Not even eight years old was too young to know what independent meant but he would learn some day that it was a goal to achieve in his elevator ride to the top.

*S*onny has been at the home now about six or seven months and he is very happy that he isn't getting beat up and having roaches eating him all night, right now he thinks he's in heaven and other people outside the home either look down on the children or they feel sorry for them. Either way it's not nice of them to feel the way they do. What's the old saying, "There for the grace of god, go I?" When you think of the pain and mental torture that some of these children went through before they came to this home would break your heart just to think about it. They live amongst each other having had the same pain and are still able to get on their knees and pray to God for his guidance and never once questioning him as to why he doesn't help them see their parents. Most of the children in this home don't even have visitors. Imagine no parents, no visitors no birthday parties and so on. The old ladies are trying to recognize the children's birthdays even if it's just a cup cake with a candle on it. When they grow up they will looked down on by these people that were lucky enough to not of had this life.

Some of them went in the service and were killed on the battle field defending those very people's lives, the one that would look down on them and spit on them when they return home like they did the Viet Nam veteran. I could get sick just thinking about it. These poor orphans grew up not having known their parents joined the service when they became of age, not knowing how good America is and yet joining the service and killed on the battle field never have had a good day in America. You know what I say don't you. It is grossly unfair.

The ladies in the kitchen would have a newspaper delivered every day except Sunday by a young boy whom they called Babe. He was the only boy that would deliver the newspaper eight city blocks from his home. The paperboys that lived closer refused to deliver. So Babe would jump on his bike and ride it down to Mores Lane. The kids knew his schedule and would wait *for him to show up, sometimes there were ten or twelve of them waiting for him to ride up the drive way and as soon as he put his bike down they were all over him like a ton of rocks. They would wrestle with him and when he stood up they would hold on to his legs and the real little ones would call him daddy. There were two or three of them hanging on to his legs and he would drag them over to the high wooden steps and sit with them so he could catch his breath.*

They made Babe feel important and they were very lonely, they needed some out sider to hold them and play with them and Babe was the guy. Babe's mother made sure his brothers and sisters weren't put in a home because of their father she kept them together and out of the family court system. He loved being with the kids and would never miss a day to deliver the paper to the ladies in the kitchen. Babe would ask the children to let him take the newspaper to the ladies and he would come right back and play some more. He always kept his word and came back to where they were waiting for him. This went on for every single day there was a newspaper delivered there. As bad as Babe had it these children had it worse. He made them feel good and they made him feel good so they were helping each other. If he ever missed a day of delivery he would have to tell the children where he was and why he couldn't come, they would all have long faces while he explained where he was. When they would make a long face to him he would make one back and they could see how they looked to him and laugh for the longest time. Babe helped those children more then he knew he has, there were a lot of kids that would just sit around watching the little ones love him. They looked forward to loving him every day; it was therapeutic for them both. I know some day Babe would look back on those years and be glad he was part of their lives and not trade one second of it. How could anyone be so lucky to have experiences such a beautiful thing and if the truth were known he probably never told anyone about it?

Babe was almost like Santa Clause he would bring them something every day and got nothing in return but their love, which was the greatest thing that anyone could receive. Babe was about fifteen and even if he were caddying or playing golf he was at the home with the newspaper for the ladies in the kitchen.

Jenny didn't have any idea that all of this was going on and her son was a good little football player and was within fifty miles from her. How could she know this, she couldn't. But that didn't stop her from missing him every day since he was kidnapped. The new baby helped take her mind off of him. She became very guarded of Chris and didn't want any repeat performance.

Sonny was real popular at the home, because of football everyone knew him even the older kids. It seemed like the older the children got the less self esteem they had. Pat had posters around the different rooms like the dining room and the study room with motivational messages on them but it was hard when you're gloomy. Now take Sonny he was able to put a crack in that wall out there that prevented the children from the home from being recognized for anything. Now that he's done it they would start to see more cracks in the wall that they put there. How about the girl from the home winning the spelling bee? How about the boy who was accepted in the University of Notre Dame? The kids could see some openings for them to wiggle through and would work hard to do it.

Please don't think that things are so rosy at the home because they're not. You can't have that many children living without any parents to be enthusiastic about anything, no matter how hard Pat would try to be the missing link it wasn't enough. Look at the love they have for the paper boy Babe who could use some loving himself and got his fill at the home. That was therapeutic for him, that's why he loved going there so much, someone loved him and was willing to show it. It seemed like Sonny had Marie now and she loved him and didn't even know it, she thought he was awesome and didn't know what love is. His next football season she never missed a game. He played for a different team and they lost their opening game. The coaches knew where the weaknesses were and practiced to close them up. They had a nine game season and it was going to be a tough one.

Sonny was called aside one game and said that the opposition coach has filed a complaint about Sonny that he was older and wanted him investigated as to his DOB. They didn't want him to play until his age could be substantiated. They looked everywhere and there wasn't any record of his birth, his parents or anything that could identify him. Pat was fuming about all this and called in the county lawyer to get Sonny a birth certificate. It wasn't easy but he got one for Pat and now Sonny could relax about his age. The coach put Sonny in the last game and his team was playing the team that their coach was the one to complain about Sonny he just wanted to win no matter who he hurt. Needless to say the coach got his team fired up and they went on to win with Sonny in the whole game 72 to 0. When the two coaches met after the game at the center of the field the loosing coach told Sonny's coach that he didn't have to run up the score like he did. Sonny's coach told him that he was right but he wanted to get even for the low down move that he made on Sonny so he could win a football game. He asked him where did it get him; he just looked at him and started to turn away when Sonny's coach told him that he would regret trying to hurt a small kid for his own recognition someday. You will never be a head coach any higher then you are now because you're no good.

Sonny got a good write up in the sports page and was already getting offers from the new league that he would be playing in. His golf was coming on big time he would hit all his clubs without any problem and could putt like a pro, but was still awfully young so he was told to still practice and soon he will be allowed to play on the public golf course where he practices his putting. Sonny is eight now and going on nine and has really developed nicely always studying and hitting golf balls. Playing football got him motivated to do better and Marie tells him that he can do it as well. Sonny sat on the steps one day waiting for Babe to show up, the kids spotted him coming down the road and jumped to their feet waving and screaming out here comes Babe. Sonny was brought to tears and covered it up by rubbing his eyes; he thought how one person a boy himself could be so important to these little kids. The look on their little faces would bring anyone to tears.

Sonny stood away from the little kids and took it all in. Babe spotted Sonny and said I know you, you're that quarterback with that good arm. Babe walked up to him and shook his hand and told him he plays quarterback as well. There was a football sitting on the step and Babe picked it up and they had a catch it was fun and Babe said we could do it again. Sonny asked Babe if he plays golf and Babe told him he plays as much as he can. Babe asked him if he plays and sonny said that he still is practicing and will be able to play soon. With that Babe said good maybe we can play some day and Sonny's eyes lit up and said he would be ready soon. He just needs a little more time. Babe left for home after a very busy day, not knowing what was in store for him when he got there. Those little kids didn't know what was going on behind the scenes just what they saw and they saw Babe happy go lucky, that's all they knew.

Babe's mother was asked a lot of times if she wanted to move the children to public housing where there would be no mortgage payments. It was on a very bad side of town and she would have to give up everything she and the children worked hard for. She turned down the local do gooders and Babe could keep his paper route. Like I said earlier no one knew this but the Catholic Priest who wanted his troubled family out of his hair and his diocese. Babe knew that if his mother wanted to he would be living at the home.

The children were very well protected at the home; the police were always ready to respond for calls of help from the home. The fire departments were always ready to respond for calls of help also. They knew that the home was seventy five years old and made of all wood it would burn like a match. Marie was getting very attached to Sonny and Sonny didn't notice that she was, he just took it for granted that she would always be there. They were trusted by all the adults there and no one had any bad thoughts about them always being together. It was just two nine year olds trying to survive in the environment they were living in. Every now and then Sonny would have thoughts of leaving the home someday and being on his own somewhere. He would tell Marie about it and she said she didn't have anywhere to go. That was when Sonny told her she could go with him if she wanted to. She told him she didn't know how to say no to that, she had no one or nowhere to go.

Marie asked Sonny did he know what going steady meant.

"No I don't know that one."

"Well it means that you are only seen with one boy and only go out with one boy."

"What do you mean go out?"

"I mean go out and be seen together."

"You mean like we are now, we don't go anywhere without each other."

"I don't want to go out with anyone else, just you."

"You probably don't want me to go out with anyone else but you either. We aren't allowed to go anywhere but on the porch or the study room, or take a walk down the lane that leads to nowhere."

"Yes that is what they call going steady."

"What is in it for me?"

"Anything you want there to be in it for you."

"Why can't we just continue to do what we are doing now and not complicate things?"

"That's fine with me."

"Ok then let's keep it as it is, we don't have any problems. I like that."

Jenny has just about lost all thoughts of finding Rome, because of spending so much time raising Chris. She is so horney and doesn't even realize it. It's been almost ten years since she has had sex and that last one got her pregnant. Chris is turning into a beautiful little girl, which was not a shock seeing as how her mother was a knock out. Jenny liked not working and could live easily off of the interest her money was earning. Chris is only three years old and Jenny thought she would home school her to see how it goes.

She can get her involved with other children when it came time. Jenny was too independent and really didn't need anyone or anything from anyone. Hell she didn't even have to have sex to have her baby. She has kept a slow pace with her studies on the stock market and whatever goes with it. She will be able to graduate in ten years getting her degree on the computer. The timing couldn't be any better; she could go back to work when Chris would be able to spend all day at school. With a degree and her looks she should be very successful.

The neighbors are friendly but she notices the wives won't let the husbands help her if she would ever need help lifting something or digging something. She would call a company that would do the job in relation to the problem and not have a problem with any neighbor. They all admired her and her effort in raising Chris on her own. They were mystified how she didn't have to work and was never in need for anything. She was always invited to all the community parties but she never went, she was very uncomfortable around men that drank too much and wanted to show off to her so they could be noticed by her. She had one agenda and that was to raise Chris to be the best she could be. She would have all the benefits of a rich little girl. Jenny would take Chris to the grave of Mrs. Topkis and she would tell Mrs. Topkis how grateful she was for ever having met her. She would always tell her she loved her and walk away. She was hoping someday that Chris would go there on her own and visit Mrs. Topkis.

The visit to the grave yard was the tenth anniversary of meeting Mrs. Topkis and moving in with her. At first they were strangers but soon became good friends. Unlike her family who didn't want any parts of her. She knew if Rome was alive he would almost be ten years old. Rome was ten and was a good looking young man;

All you have to do is to see Marie who was starting to become attractive in her own rite. Thank God the two of them weren't overly attractive to each other it was much better the way it is, they were consumed by their interest and not have a lot of idle time on their hands to get in trouble with. Sonny was practicing his golf and was getting good at it. He went out for football, for the next league up and made first string quarterback. This league was a lot rougher where as in the midget league you weren't allowed to hit the quarterback. The line men lived to hurt the quarterback and would come after Sonny with a vengeance so the coach made up a lot of plays that had quick releases and they were very successful at it. Usually when he was hit it was roughing the quarterback because he had already thrown the ball much earlier.

They were undefeated going into their last game and there were a lot of people wanting to see Sonny's team win with a perfect season so it was standing room only and every kid from the home was there and every sports reporter from around was there. If Sonny could win this game big he will become well known around the state as a quarterback. Marie made sure she told Sonny how much she was rooting for him and all the kids from the home would be too. The coach practiced with Sonny all week on plays that were tricky and deceitful now you see it and now you don't. Sonny liked that new series and playing from the single tee with two of the fastest boys on the team as running backs the opponents were going to be in for a new kind of football and a Houdini style football game.

Sonny's team won the coin toss and they elected to receive, the opening play Sonny made a fake run to the right and gave the ball to the speed demon coming at him and handed it off once he made the turn he ran for seventy yards everyone else was chasing after Sonny who didn't have the ball. The next time they got the ball they did the same play only this time the runner flicked it back to Sonny and sonny threw it down field to one of his receivers who was wide open and scored. They had two plays and scored two touchdowns. By the time the first half ended the score was 49 to 0 the coach didn't want to run the score up so he played the backup quarterback and Sonny played as a receiver. Sonny scored two touchdowns and the coach pulled all the starters and only played the backups the final score was 63 to 13

Some people said that they saw it on national TV as a sport news clip. He was carried from the side lines around the field on his team mate's shoulders. It was a great day for Sonny and the home that was getting a lot of publicity. Some companies in the area wanted to paint the home and some wanted to put some large additions on and build a large dining room and furnish the kitchen with all the latest cooking devices and a large walk in refrigerator. They even wanted to put a couple dozen rockers on the porch. Things couldn't be any better for Sonny or the home. There were numerous numbers of requests to adopt Sonny and Sonny turned down every one. He did ask the people wanting him to pick some of the little ones they were still in the need for some parents. He was glad to see some of the little ones get adopted.

Now on the other hand some of the little one didn't want to leave Babe and cried their little hearts out. They were promised that if they would write

Babe a letter and mail it to the home they would see to it that Babe would get it. It was not a nice sight to see these little ones say good bye to Babe even Mr. hard as nails Babe was balling like a little baby and had to be seated on the porch in a rocking chair and consoled by Pat for the longest time. It wasn't easy but the ladies from the kitchen helped the little one with their new parents. One of the new parents wanted to know who this Babe was. One of the ladies from the kitchen told her he was just someone that took a genuine interest in them and they could feel it in their bones. Little children know when someone loves them and when someone doesn't and they knew how Babe felt. They were lucky enough to see Sonny play in the championship football game last month and those little kids were the ones cheering the loudest. We wish more people would know more about him and these kids, maybe someday they will. Babe isn't looking for any publicity that's how special he is. He is very special to us and we would never want anything to happen to him. You might say that he is a legend here at the home.

Marie didn't know what was wrong with her so she sat with Pat and had long talk about boys and Sonny in general she told Pat that she loved touching him and looking into his eyes and seeing him smile at her and she would love to find ways to be with him using an excuse to study and do their homework. When he spoke to her she could feel her legs get weak and her far head get damp. She wanted to be in his company whenever she could. Pat told her to make sure that she doesn't do anything that would turn him off or he will go against you and you will lose someone so dear to you that you will feel the pain for the rest of your life Pat reached for Marie's hand and told her that she loved Sonny with all of her heart and that she really has it bad. She went on to tell her that when girls feel this way they will do anything that their lover wants them to do. She told her that she would have to be in full control of herself and not let Sonny use her for anything. It won't be easy and you might get hurt so be careful, because what you just described to me was a girl very much in love with a boy. He's not a man yet and will be capable of loving you back or hurting you very deeply. Men are hard to figure out and it takes a very special young lady to keep her man under control.

Marie left Pat and went back to her bed and just laid there looking up at the ceiling and thinking of Sonny until the pain was unbearable not to see him now or the thought of not seeing him anymore. The most important thing to her was not to lose him to anyone else because of her stupidity. She felt that she could have a life with him and knew that she could never say anything like that to him. She might have been only ten but she felt like an adult.

Sonny had no idea about this sudden outburst of love coming from Marie and she had to hide it as best she could. How do you hide it when your legs are weak from seeing someone whom you love so much that you can't control yourself and cover up the hot flash you're getting when he comes into your presence with the damp fare head? This was a tall order for a young girl but she had to do it.

Marie was really helping Sonny with his school work and it started to come easy for him, thanks to Marie. He wanted to be able to walk on a golf course and shoot in the seventies. Marie knew what his goals were and would even try to help him practicing, she even knew what his swing should look like and started coaching him and he could see an improvement in hitting his balls. When he did as Marie told him to do the ball went perfectly straight and long. This gave her a chance to be with him for a longer time. Pat could see out the window and see them practicing hitting golf balls for hours together. It warmed her heart to see her being with the one she loved and get along so well together. Sonny respected Marie enough not to hurt her feelings or hurt her personally.

Soon it would be time to play his first round of golf, he saw Babe and told him he was ready for his first round. He told Babe that Pat would drive him and pick him up and Babe told him to meet him at the Rock at 9 am Tuesday and he would be there. The clubs that he practiced with were a fine set of clubs but he didn't have any balls so Babe gave him a half dozen golf balls and told him if he should lose one of them he wouldn't break eighty and if he should lose two of them he wouldn't break ninety. Sonny was nervous driving with Pat to the Rock and she gave him some change to call her when he's finished and get himself a hot dog and a soda. This was definitely beyond the call of duty but Pat was that close to these kids she was doing things that a mother would do for her children, the hand book said to keep a distance from them and not to get close. There wasn't a cloud in the sky and the air was clean you could smell the grass being cut and the flowers that were planted all around the clubhouse.

abe was on the putting green when he saw Sonny walking towards him, Babe shook his hand and told him they could tee off anytime they felt like it. Luther the caretaker came out to meet Sonny and told him that he read all about him in the newspaper and if he can play golf like he can throw a football then he was going to be one hell of a golfer. Luther told Sonny that Babe was a good athlete also; he just didn't get the notoriety that you got. Babe can throw a football and hit whatever he was aiming at. He tries real hard at golf and some day he will get it right. We waived your fee for today and we want you to have a great day, Luther gave him a sleeve of balls and told him to have a great day. Sonny practiced his putting and told Babe he was ready to play. Sonny thanked Luther and they walked to the starter whom Babe called Grumpy but his real name was Mr. Bush. He was not a happy camper.

Babe introduced Sonny to Grumpy and as expected grumpy told Babe if he heard anything going on out there he was coming out to get them and don't hold anyone up, let them play through. Babe showed Sonny where the hole was and how far away it was and everything he had to know to successfully play the hole including the out of bounds to the right. He told Sonny to hit first and while he was teeing up his ball for his drive he thought of Marie and how she practiced with him all those days for him to be good at this sport too. He took his stance and hit this thunderous drive down the middle right side of the fairway that would shorten the hole by one club length. It was Babes turn and Babe did the same and their balls were lying together. They walked together down the first fairway; Sonny knew this was going to be his sport, There wasn't anyone wanting to tear his head off and take him out of the play. They both pared the first hole and they played head to head but Babe couldn't par every hole

Babe thought being four and a half years older than Sonny he would probably score better than him. Well it wasn't going to happen, Sonny might not know what he was doing but he sure could hit different shots and make the ball go where he wanted it to go. He could hit the ball solid every time and Babe couldn't. They had a run in with one of the bums that hung out at the golf course and Babe told the bum that he was going to turn him into Mr. Bush and he would be barred from coming here from now on. The bum told Babe he didn't see his ball come in the woods, he would rather keep the ball and sell it, then to get a quarter for finding It and giving it back. The bum found it under some leaves and Babe picked it up and walked away, he got nothing.

They walked off the ninth green Babe shot a 41 and Sonny shot a 36 two over par. Babe told Sonny that was a great score for someone his age and being his first round of golf. The tenth tee was open so they teed up right away and hit big drives. Sonny was quiet and taking in all there was to see at the rock. Sonny was having a great back nine and managed to birdie the long par five along the RR track, Babe has yet to get his first birdie. He was impressed with Sonny's first round. He parred the eighteenth and finished with a 36 again, so his first round of golf was a four over par 72. That was a great round of golf; Babe shot a 42 on the back nine for an 83 for eighteen holes.

They both were starving for something to eat so they stopped by the snack bar for their famous hot dog with plenty of onions and an ice cold soda. Babe chose a nice spot down by the putting green and they both polished off their hot dogs and sat back on their chairs. Babe told Sonny it doesn't get much better than this. Sonny wanted to do this every day and knew it could never happen. Sonny asked Babe where the phone was so he could call Pat at the home and tell her he was finished. She didn't come for him for almost an hour; he appreciated the extra time with Babe and practiced his putting. Babe and he would play and see who was the best on every hole putting and it was very close. Pat walked to the putting green where Babe and Sonny were and asked Sonny how he did. Babe told her that Sonny was really good and had a very good round today. If he keeps practicing he will be a champion. Pat said that she can see a good life for Sonny some day in sports.

Pat was telling Babe that Sonny is probably the best quarterback in his age bracket in the state and the high school that he will go to will have a great football season. He has a while to go yet and once a high school can see that he will be attending there school, the students that want to play with him will be trying to enroll in that school so they can play on Sonny's team and maybe get sucked along in the vacuum that will surely be there. Pat had made up her mind to help Sonny where ever she can, the most he will ever need is some clothes and a ride every now and then. The ride back to the home went fast and Marie was sitting on the porch waiting for Sonny to come back. Pat left him off at the porch steps and Sonny carried his clubs up the steps and laid them down on the porch floor where Marie was sitting in her new rocker.

Sonny skin color was starting to look nice and tan from his four hour round of golf. Marie couldn't stop looking at him and when he spoke to her about his round of golf at the Rock she would hope that he would take all day. This girl was suffering from being a little more mature then Sonny and didn't have any way to relieve her anxieties. She could see that Sonny wasn't suffering from anything at least it wasn't showing. Sonny looked sleepy and kept dozing a little until he heard Marie ask him if he wanted to have some dinner. He told her he was starving and asked her if she was ready. They both walked into the dining room together and the old ladies behind the serving line were all happy to see Sonny and asked him how his golf game went today. He said it went well and was happy with his score. These old ladies felt as if these children were there's and took a deep interest in them and when they were not feeling good they didn't feel good.

They picked a table by the window and they could see out the window at where Sonny practices hitting golf balls. Sonny told Marie that he missed her not being with him today, it was something that she thought she would never hear from him. There were some tears that ran down her face and she quickly wiped them away. Sonny apologized if he said something wrong and she told him that it touched her heart to hear him say that. She placed her hand on his and gave his hand a gentle squeeze with that he could finally see how she felt about him. He went on to tell her how he missed her swing analysis and her little bits of confidence she would give him. She reminded him that he was only four over par on his first round; you flatter me when you think I could have improved on that score. He knows that if she was there with him he would have played better. Here comes the tears again and with that Sonny asked to be excused and left the table, which made it worse for Marie. She knows that he doesn't understand girls.

Sonny went to bed early and was awaken by a dream of this beautiful woman who was walking with him down a street holding his hand. He didn't know what to think of that dream; it didn't make any sense to him. The woman was beautiful and spoke very kindly to him. He didn't recognize anything in the dream but never the less he loved seeing that beautiful woman in the dream. He wondered who she could be and why was he with her, holding her hand. It didn't take long for him to come to the conclusion that she must be his mother. Who else could she be, that was the first time he ever had this dream. He was awake because he was scared to let it continue and learn something else. He thought that if he should let it continue the next time he will learn more.

The next morning Sonny sat with Marie for breakfast and told her what happened, she was amazed to hear him describe the woman in his dreams. She was anxious to hear who Sonny thought she was. Finally he told her that he thought she could have been his mother. Marie told Sonny that he could have the opportunity to hear her call his name and find out if Sonny is your real name or not. He told Marie that sometimes you can't recall things said in your dreams. She told him that he was right and if he makes a point to try and remember this, he just might be lucky enough to hear her call him by his name and remember it after he wakes up.

Jenny was doing well being a mother to young Chris who is four years old now and with Jenny's help she is turning her into a real lady. One Saturday she found Chris watching golf and really taking an interest in the game, she asked her if she liked golf and Chris told her it was her favorite. While Chris was in school she bought her a putter and a dozen balls and a putting green hole and told her to practice all day if she wants too on the short hair rug that would be slow compared to a golf green. She still can develop a good putting stroke. Jenny would watch her without Chris seeing her and would be very impressed with this little girls putting on the rug. It was Chris's idea and not Jenny's so all the pressure to practice was on Chris because Jenny would leave it all up to her.

Jenny knew she could work with Chris if she should pursue this sport. Her looks at four showed Jenny that she would probably be a cheerleader for football and an athlete in other sports. The home schooling was going good; Jenny had made arrangements to have a Micro Chip placed in Chris's meaty part of her shoulder so that if she needs to find her the Micro Chip will locate her anywhere in the world. Once burnt twice shy would be the only way Jenny could handle having a child growing up in this world today. She feels that if her son Rome had a chip they would have found him fast, before he was absorbed in the community and easily not traceable. The only way she could recognize him is that he has a heart shaped red birth mark behind his right ear. Jenny has no hope of ever seeing him again, it seems like the police have all but given up in this case.

There are no leads to work on, there was a report that someone saw a woman with little boy being drug on board a bus one day around the time that the police were raiding that run downed house and found nothing. No one followed up on that lead and it died in the steel case cabinet draw. Maybe somebody someday will take an interest and see that it was a good lead to follow up on. If Jenny knew what was in her folder, she would have screamed the building down. Because of the time that has lapsed even if they knew the bus stop where Betty got off the bus that's all they would know. Betty never took Sonny out of the house to be seen by anyone the house was eventually bulldozed and there wasn't anyone around that knew anything about the woman that lived there. The neighborhood was slowly being bulldozed and would take a while before they could have enough land to build some townhouses. It's going to take someone extremely interested in that case to track down Rome and find him. It is possible; there is still a trail to follow.

The home has taken on a drastic change with all the notoriety and all the changes that are being made. Sonny is twelve now and looking good. Football season is coming on fast, and Sonny had a good summer practicing his golf and playing a few times with Babe. He sees Babe almost every day bringing the paper and sitting with the children on the steps or up on the porch telling them stories that were a little scary. He made sure before he left that they weren't scared, he would never leave them like that. Babe saw Sonny and told him that he might be giving up the paper route soon, but found it very hard to do because of the children's attachment to him. He is not looking forward to that day when he delivers his last paper. Sonny asked him to make sure he stays in touch with him.

There were a lot of people that wanted to adopt Sonny but Sonny refused because of all the love that was bestowed on him at the home. Even though he didn't have all the material things that other children had Sonny felt happy to be at the home. Both Sonny and Marie were taking on changes in their bodies at first were a shock but soon adapted to it. Marie had it the worst because Pat had to help her through her first menstrual period this was something a mother had to do. Sonny noticed some changes in Marie and she was getting prettier, and with a little tan she got over the summer she was really attractive. Pat had her hands full with all the girls that were there but if she needed help she would ask for it.

With football season starting up Sonny was playing quarter back in the 12 to 14 year old class. He was still heads over the other players because of his ability to throw a football and place it where he wanted it. He caught the

84

flu and had to stay in bed for a week and get better so he missed two games in which they lost one and won one. Marie would visit and sit with him for hours and talk about her future and what she wanted to do. She didn't realize it but she was giving Sonny the impression that he wouldn't be in her life after the home. Sonny never said anything or asked her any questions. Marie didn't know that she was giving Sonny the wrong impression. So for the first time he started to stay away from Marie and would purposely avoid her in the dining room or in study hall and even on the bus. It wasn't long before Marie came to Sonny's room and asked him what he was doing avoiding her for these last two weeks.

He told her that when she was talking about leaving the home at eighteen years of age, it seemed like he was not included in any of her plans. You were always in my plans, how could I have a life after being with you all of these years. We have been together for almost six years now where would I go without you? Sonny just sat and looked at her and never said a word. She sat on the bed and motioned him to come to her and he said he was ok sitting where he was. She told him that he didn't like her anymore and stood up to leave. Sonny didn't know how she got that impression and stood up to walk her to the door when Marie turned and stopped and Sonny had to stop. That's when she kissed Sonny for the first time on the lips and she almost collapsed on the floor. She never realized that kissing a boy could be so great; in this case she loved Sonny and still has never told him.

Sonny was back at practice and the team needed to make the playoffs or the season was going to be over soon. The coach was making new plays that would keep the other teams trying to figure out what was going to be next after each play. Needless to say they won the rest of their games and had worked themselves in the championship game that was getting a lot of notoriety from the local press. Sonny's team practiced very hard to come on the field with a set of plays that the pros don't have and they have Sonny to pull it off. Half time Sonny's team was down 10 points and the coach at half time told them that Mr. Hughes the assistant coach that died a few weeks ago is watching them and is probably not feeling to good seeing them give this game away. If that is all the respect you have for him then go ahead and go out there and lose the game and disgrace his name. The coach left the locker room and Sonny stood up and said that he would quit right now if this is the best we can play, do you know how many people that are counting on us to win this game. I don't know about you but there are a lot of little children from my home innocent children routing for us to win and I am not going to let them down.

They were late coming on to the field and the coach could see a change in them and told Sonny he noticed it. They were going to receive the ball on the kick off; the young boy that caught the ball on the 25 yard line ran his ass off and scored a touchdown to start the second half. This team was fired up and nothing could stop them either on offence or defense. The second half was not like the first half every time they scored a touchdown that would always go for the two pointers. The other side was trying to keep up but didn't have the momentum and lost 32 to 48 in one of the most hotly contested championships games ever played in that league. Needless to say the newspapers had a field day on how Sonny motivated his team to go out and win that game for Coach Hughes.

There was a big party at the home and all the old ladies brought their husbands and children and a good time was had by all. There was school the next day and Sonny needed some minor medical attention so Marie told Sonny that she would bring her medical kit to his room in five minutes. Sonny made sure he said goodbye to Babe who had to come to the party at the home and congratulate Sonny on a great game. Sonny was starting to get sore and told Marie that he had to take a hot shower and would return in five minutes. He returned with his pajamas on and sat in the chair by his bed while Marie walked up to him and asked Sonny what he wanted her to fix first. He told her anywhere because he ached all over she sat next to him and would press her body against his and clean some of his cuts and Sonny could feel like he wasn't supposed to feel her. She told him that it was ok because she had to work close so she could better clean his cuts up.

Sonny was too scared to do anything because he honestly didn't know what to do, or even know if he was supposed to do anything. He just let her rub herself all over his arms until he noticed her starting to breathe a little heavy. That's when he told her she was out of condition and she should run the track a little to build up her stamina. She stormed out of his room and left some of his cuts unclean so he stood in front of the mirror and did it himself. He doesn't know what gets in to her sometimes with this crying for nothing and now mad because he told her she was out of shape and needed to run the track, what next. They met for breakfast and Sonny was so sore he could hardly walk; he could barely carry his tray to the table.

Marie came in the dining room late and Sonny asked her where she was and she told him that she was running up and down Mores lane to get in shape seeing as how she is out of breath all the time. Sonny told her he was proud of her for exercising and someday soon it would pay off. She told him that she hopes so because she can't be out of breath all the time. Sonny could hardly stand up when he was finished eating and he had to carry his tray to the drop off area and carry his books to the bus stop out front. Marie asked him if she could help him and he said no he had to help himself or it would take longer to work out his soreness. It was hard to believe how sore he was until he had to go down the steep steps out front to the bus stop. It felt worse doing that then getting hit in a football game.

There were banners everywhere in the hall ways praising Sonny for his win in the championship game, there were a lot of kids that would come up to him and congratulate him on winning the game after being down by 10 points. Once they got to school he only saw Marie in one class and that was in their math class. Sometimes they would meet for lunch; it was hard because they didn't have the same lunch either. There were a lot of girls that wanted to go out with Sonny but he didn't want any part of it, he was comfortable with Marie and didn't feel comfortable being around girls his age. He didn't know why and didn't care. His teachers loved him and they always looked forward to having him in class. He had been schooled on manners because he was very respectful to the teachers and any person with authority.

When the girls had grouped together in the hall way between classes and Sonny would walk by they would all say at once Hi Sonny and he would smile at them, one of the girls would say, "what a hunk he is." Marie knew the pressure he was under and never interfered with him meeting other girls, he just didn't want to. Marie thought how lucky she was to have met him in school first when she escorted him to his first class from the principal's office. Now she has to hang on to him and see where he is going with his life. Sonny didn't know where he was going and he would have to see what strikes his interest. Marie could see that someone was going to scoop him up and paint this great picture of how life would be with them and she would hope he would see if he was being used or not. Marie was going to do her best and hope that Sonny would choose to spend the rest of his life with her; she knows they would be good together. They were so young and there were a lot of obstacles to overcome if Marie's dream were to come true.

Sonny was only getting a high B average and Marie wanted him to do a little better than that because of his success in sports he would be expected to do better than B's. and get in to a good college. She figured on him getting a scholarship to just about any college he wanted to go to for free as far as money goes but would be under their jurisdiction to as to his time away from the sport that got him there. Sonny wasn't going to be led around by the nose and they would soon find that out. Anyway that is in the future and Marie wanted to stick to their lives now at the home and what high school they would go to.

Behind the scene there were lots of request for Sonny to go to the different high schools around the Home and Pat would tell them that Sonny would pick the high school he wanted to go to and not her. Sonny was sitting out on the porch with Marie when Babe came with the newspaper, the small children were all over him and Babe looked very sad and Marie asked him what was wrong.

"Today is my last day to deliver the paper"

"O no."

"This isn't going to be easy to tell the children."

"Marie started to cry and left the porch for fear of upsetting the little children."

"Sonny asked Babe what was he going to do in place of his paper route."

"The guy that is my boss wanted to belittle me in front of his assistant and I quit on the spot and it would take more than missing the little ones for me to keep this paper route under those circumstances."

"What are you going to do?"

"I am going to join the Rock and play golf every day and join the Air Force in the fall and take it from there."

"You know these little ones are going to miss you."

"I know they will but I want you to help me out and step in and be the one they love in place of me."

"No one could take your place Babe."

"I am counting on you to do it. Please it is very important to me that you try real hard."

Marie came back to the porch with all the ladies from the Kitchen and Pat and they were hugging Babe and said they would miss him. Babe assured them he would come back from time to time and see how things are going. Now all the little children started to gather on the porch and Babe had to tell them good bye. He tried to do it but failed miserably he could hardly talk; it was a site that I wouldn't want to wish on anyone. To see a teen age boy crying like a baby is not a good thing to wittiness and the little children hanging on to him like it was the end of time. To the children it was just another let down in the many they had experienced. Babe left the porch and never looked back because he couldn't bear to see their sad faces. Babe was wrecked when he got home and didn't want to deal with the route manager trying to talk him into reconsidering and taking back his route. No matter how much he apologized Babe told him he had made up his mind and wouldn't come back under any circumstances. The next time he wanted to flex his mussels on some young person he better think it over. They couldn't find anyone to deliver Babe's route so the mean manager had to do it. He would take hours to do a forty five minute job. When they found someone to take over the route the manager was fired.

10

Sonny would follow the sports section in the newspaper showing the state junior championship and who shot what. That year they played at the Rock and Babe had an opening round of 83. Sonny was pulling for him to score better the next day. Babe shot an 81 and with the two day total babe was 13th in the field and Sonny knew that Babe would try too hard and not get the round he wanted. Babe had football energy in a cool calm and collective tournament. It wasn't long after that that they found out at the home that Babe had joined the Air Force and was sent away to Savannah Ga. as a military policeman (AP). Sonny was enrolled in the high school closest to the home and the only one that he could legally attend. They had a ho hum football team and a coach that drank a lot. Marie went their also and went out for cheerleaders and the golf team. Sonny went out for football and the golf team as well. There weren't too many players that wanted to play on the golf team and the girl's team only had three golfers.

This would be a hectic year watching the coach trying to talk other kids in to going out for the team. He would sell them on they had the best quarter back in the state and they could go undefeated for the first time in the history of the school. The first day of practice Sonny was showing the coaches how the players could do things that would get them in shape; this was what he could remember from the other teams he played on. Sonny was the quarter back and would play defense as well. The press was calling Sonny the all American kid. He was the only player in high school football that was playing both offence and defense. The coach asked Sonny if he could give him some of the plays that won some of his titles. Sonny was happy to do so because he didn't want to lose all of their games.

He showed the coaches the single tee and all the plays they could run off of it and they agreed to use that formation with no huddles. This would wreck any team trying to defend against that sort of play. They had practiced

8 to 12 plays off the single tee that wrecked the other team they were being penalized every time the ball changed hands by the time the fourth quarter came around Sonny was getting tired but was having the time of their lives they had racked up a score of 48 to 27 and won their season opener that no one predicted they could do. They just ran plays that no one has ever seen and with no huddle the other players couldn't make the proper changes from offense to defense and take the five yard penalty. The newspapers had a field day with this opener and made Sonny into a school hero.

Marie was the home coming queen and was expected to be at the home coming dance. Pat had to take them and pick them up. Marie wanted Sonny to be her date and he told her he didn't know how to dance. Marie told him that she would show him what to do and if he could play football he could slow dance with her. The home paid for their clothes and Pat took the best looking couple at that dance that night. There were banners hanging in the gym saying the name of the school Warner high the fighting orioles. The dance was only for the ninth graders but some senior classmen wanted to meet Sonny so they came in the locker room door without a problem. They thought he would be playing varsity next year with them

There was quite a crown starting to build up around Sonny and Marie wanted some of Sonny's time. Sonny slow danced with Marie and told her if this was the best she could handle herself in a situation like this then she won't be invited to accompany him anymore. He told her that she was jealous of his popularity and the no interest she was getting. Sonny walked her to a chair and asked her to be seated he would be back to get her. The next thing Sonny saw was Marie dancing with some guy who thought he was a jock on the football team. When the dance was over and she returned to her seat Sonny came over to her and said that he wanted to leave and that Pat was on her way for them.

"You're mad because I danced with your friend."

"He's not my friend and the only reason you danced with him was to get back at me. Well it worked you really have me pissed off, so now you are out of my life and you can date him from now on."

"Sonny your acting jealous of him."

"I am not jealous of him when I can get any girl I want anytime I want her."

"I knew what you were doing when you were rubbing yourself against me the night you were cleaning my cuts and I told you to take up track to build up your stamina. I guess you thought I was brain dead, I was just trying to

keep you safe. So now that you have tried to hurt me I no longer wish to let you be in the elite group and have unlimited access to me."

"Don't you think that you are carrying this childish act a little too far?"

"I didn't deserve this kind of treatment and I don't want to have a relationship with you anymore."

"You acted in a harsh manner when I needed you to do as I told you to do you tried to make me jealous of you. Sorry I wasn't and you will be jealous of me because I am going to meet someone I can trust to do as I ask them to do. By the way I didn't want you around those guys because they were starting to curse and I didn't want them to do that in front of you. Thank you for your kind appreciation of my thoughtfulness. I hope you know how to get up with that guy and I hope he will show you the respect that I did. I suspect you will be putting out to him to get his attention."

"Now sonny this is not like you to be so angry about a little thing like this."

"Your right Marie if you look at it through 20/20 hindsight vision, where you went wrong was when you tried to hurt me or make me jealous. Suppose a fight broke out or something like that, would you have been happier about that."

"No I wouldn't have, I just wanted your attention when I thought I was losing it. I guess it was a girlie thing."

"I don't know about girlie things, but I do know how a guy will react to a girl that has no reason to be jealous of anything and wants the spot light on her. We can still speak to each other but we can't be friends, because I can't trust you anymore. Please don't walk around the home being the martyr because if you do I will tell everyone what you tried to do to me. Who do you think they will believe?"

Just then Pat drove up and the two got in the car and were very quiet all the way back to the home. Sonny thanked Pat for all of her help this evening and said, "He was going to bed." He wanted to lock his door but was too tired to get back up, he could hear his door open quietly and there was Marie with a very thin white sleeping gown on so when she walked to his bed the moonlight lit up her white gown that left no guessing as to whether she was a girl or not. She knelt on the floor and put her head on Sonny's chest and said, "That she couldn't let this night go by without making it up to him." She slipped off her robe and stood in front of him so he could see her well-developed body and hope that Sonny would reconsider after seeing what he has just given up.

Marie didn't leave Sonny's room until after 3: am she was happy that Sonny had taken her cherry and she had taken his. With that behind them Marie knew that she better never mess up like that again. Marie laid on her bed and felt tingle all over and wanted Sonny all the more, now that she knows what it feels like to have him inside her. Sonny on the other hand didn't think he would ever forgive her but boy he did big time. He definitely wanted more of her but didn't know where he could have her and not get caught. There wasn't any school so they met for breakfast and were all starry eyed and without saying it they wanted more. Marie told Sonny it was the best experience she ever had and wants more and where can they do it safely and he had to wear a condom to be safe. Sonny didn't like it but he agreed. She told him there would be times when he could penetrate her but had to pull out before he came. He said he could do it and she trusted him that he would.

They hit golf balls for most of the day and she was all over him like melted cheese, she was really pushing him for some more sex and he didn't want to do it anywhere because it was too good to waste doing it in some bushes. She agreed and said she will find a place but will have to look around, there had to be some place safe to do it. Sonny was keeping his focus on school and football there were a lot of people relying on him and he didn't want to let them down. He was marked as the man to hit in a football game; he needed all the protection he could get. The coach knew that if they lose him to injuries that they will in all likely hood lose the game. Not only was he good he was the team leader.

The coach was relying on Sonny to help him out with the single tee because if they could run the football game using the single tee, they could cause havoc with all the different ways they can run the ball, hand off the ball and pass the ball and don't use a huddle can win most all of their games. The next game they were well practiced and put the single tee into effect and ran rough herd over their opponents. The newspapers had a field day on this one and were painting Sonny as the up and coming quarterback to watch out for. This made the opponents want to hurt him all the more. He had to have a lot of protection and not hold the ball for a max of 2 to 2 ½ seconds or be slaughtered. The coach had them practice stripping the ball if the game was not going good for them and it worked because it gave Sonny another chance to score a touchdown.

He was getting hit a lot and after every game he could hardly shower, the coach knew this would have to stop or Sonny's playing days might be over soon. The next week of practice concentrated on blocking for Sonny I mean really blocking because as the coach told them Sonny might not last the season, he is taking to many hits. He is doing his part and he needs you all to do yours. One paper was saying that if he should continue to be hit savagely like he is then he should either quit or play another position. The answer lies in the blocking, the coach knows it and the reporters know it and Sonny knows it.

The next game was a world of difference Sonny got all the blocking he needed and was hardly touched and the few times he was the ref's called unnecessary roughness on the defense. They played a picture book game and won by three touchdowns. Sonny continued to get all the publicly any one could ever need Pat would take him and Marie back to the home after the game, where Sonny wanted to get some dinner that was left there in the kitchen for Sonny and Marie to eat. She noticed the more Marie got some sun tan the more beautiful she looked. He looked at her eating dinner and she definitely wanted him and asked him if he felt like taking a walk. He told her he just finished a football game and felt like doing something but not taking a walk. She told him that her roommate is away for the weekend with the girl scouts and her bedroom was going to waste.

It was still daylight and Sonny asked her to sit on the porch with him and just rock and talk a little. He told Marie that if he should win a scholar ship the only way he would accept it is if she had a scholarship as well at the same school with him. Isn't that asking too much and he said he didn't know what the limits were, he definitely knew what he would want to play for some college that would make a lot of money on him playing sports. Marie told him that she never looked at it that way. Do you think you can pull that off? He told her if they want me to play football for them they will have to agree with what I want. It was starting to get dark and Marie told Sonny that she was going back to her room and shower and gave him this beautiful smile that made him want to come to her later on.

Sonny went back to his room and laid down for a few minutes and the next thing he knew, it was 1 am and had fallen asleep and missed out on what Marie had to offer. They say things happen for the best, what was so good about falling asleep and a young woman waiting for you and take care of all your desires that you could have with her. He will still have to work this out in his mind. Sonny got up early and went down to breakfast and found Marie sitting all alone. She saw Sonny walk into the dining room and was hoping he would come and sit with her. That football game yesterday made him hungry for a big breakfast, so the women made him a big gut buster. He was too active to gain any weight playing football so a breakfast like the gut buster was nothing.

Marie asked Sonny if he fell asleep or did he chicken out, her looked at her and said he fell asleep and didn't wake up until the middle of the night. Marie told him she fell asleep also she woke up in the middle of the night with a chill for not having any clothes on. So she had to look for her pajamas and get back under the blankets before she froze to death. She told Sonny that she was really looking forward to being with him and was disappointed that they both fell asleep. Sonny said there will be other moments, the desire is still there and is growing greater every day. He told her as seeing as how it was the weekend maybe they can hit some balls, because she will have to be good when she goes to college and she will have to get high grades to try and win a scholarship. In other words she will have to be marketable to the school when Sonny tells them that he comes as a package. If you want me then you will have to want her, it's that simple and Sonny wanted to keep it simple.

Marie knew exactly what Sonny was up to and he would leave it up to the college that wanted him the most. They must have hit balls for three hours and were bushed; they hit the dining room for lunch that was a bowl of soup and a grill cheese sandwich with ham and tomato. Sonny loved that lunch and felt comfortable after he finished that he didn't feel bloated. They both wanted to study in Sonny's room and break for dinner. Marie liked that and went to her room for her books. Marie was a good helper in some of Sonny's weaker studies and was determined to bring up his grades to a higher average. Now is as good time as any to start and make him very marketable. She had three years to get it done and that would be plenty of time for her.

Sonny had come to the time now that he had lost all of his concentration and wanted Marie to take her clothes off. She stood up and went over to the door and locked it and then took off her clothes for Sonny to have his way with her. She was so giving until it was 2 am in the morning and had to walk to her room knowing she just had the best four hours any woman could ever dream of. Sonny didn't want her to leave but she had to because they pull a bed check unannounced and God help you if you weren't in bed. The next day at breakfast Pat strolled in and sat with the two of them and asked Marie in front of Sonny where she was at the midnight bed check. She never flinched and said she was in Sonny's room helping him improve his grades for college down the road. She could show her all the notes and test papers and Pat said it wasn't necessary, but never the less the rules were broken and you

Marie have to be written up for not making the bed check at midnight and you Sonny for having a girl in your room after 9 am. What does writing us up mean and Pat said that for someone who breaks the rules and doesn't care it doesn't mean anything. Now on the other hand if someone cares then they won't want to do that again. We don't play favorites here the same rules apply to everyone.

The last game was coming up Friday and Sonny's coaches were practicing an extra hour every night. They would have to win this upcoming game and their opponents would have to loose for Sonny's team to get into a championship game. They were practicing like that was exactly what was going to happen. Marie was looking for some extra attention from Sonny and Sonny told her to back off. Sonny wanted to win this game and he had his team mates feeling the same way. It would be a Friday night game and the fighting oriole would be ready. A lot of kids from the home would be there, thanks to Pat and her getting some cars to get the kids there. Sonny spent some time with Marie and they smooched a little he stopped because he didn't want to spoil what they could have over the weekend.

The orioles got to the stadium early and put on a fake practice session to mislead their opponents on how they would play their game. They had their spies everywhere and the Orioles had them by the short hairs. The Orioles won the toss and said they would receive. It was a great game and the other side was absolutely out played in every aspect and Sonny was taken out of the game in the third quarter when there was no fear of losing. The sports reporters were asking for interviews before the game was over, the coach told them to stay away and we will see how things go after the game. The game finally ended and the Orioles won by four touchdowns. There was chaos on the field and the police were assigned to get Sonny off the field and into the locker room. They got out of there and took their showers back at their school.

Pat and Marie were busy getting the kids back to the home and one of the coaches took Sonny back to the home and left him off safely at the front door. Everyone was waiting for him and Pat had ice cream and strawberries to spread around for everyone to enjoy. Marie ran to Sonny and hugged him with everyone watching, Pat knew it was going to be impossible to keep them separated but it was her duty to do it or she would have a problem with the powers to be. Sonny was well protected in that game and the coaches were thrilled about that. The celebration broke out and they were partying with root beer floats and pizza, these kids were never going to forget this night.

Everything quieted down and Pat told everyone to go to their rooms and get a good night sleep.

Marie was so frustrated she could hardly talk, Sonny told her that there isn't anything wrong with sitting around and talking they will have plenty of time to get closer. Marie knew that she will probably not see him next week at all because they would be practicing till nine every night and with the players not having a chance to have supper the coaches had to find ways to feed them. With the coach doing a lot of calling around to the parents at 5 pm the ladies had a food table ready for the players to get something to eat and still not be so bloated that they can't practice. That was a hard task, but there were a lot of fruits and veggies and some sliced turkey and chicken with mashed potatoes and gravy. Come Thursday they had practiced their plan and were in good shape to pull off a championship. Sonny wanted this win real bad and his team mates knew it.

The Orioles were going to show up ready to play a tough game and they planned on being tough themselves. They were going to work that single tee and do it with no huddle which would be even harder. The orioles lost the toss and their opponents scored on their first three downs. Sonny was in shock because they were playing a game like they planned to play theirs. The orioles took the kickoff and ran it back forty yards and with the no huddle single tee they scored just as fast as their opponents did. This went back and forth the whole first half and the coach had them change a few things and go heavily into stripping the ball and be ready to pick up the fumble.

The Oriole's received the opening kickoff for the second half and showed their opponents some football that has never been seen before. Sonny mixed it up with fake runs on his part and then some short passes and had taken a ten point lead. With two minutes to go in the fourth quarter the other team was on the move. Mixing up the plays until one of the Oriole's line men charged the line and sacked their quarterback and on forth and short yardage and the Oriole's ran out the clock and won the game by three points. Three points or not it was a great game. They were calling Sonny an all American and a future Hizeman trophy winner. With their win they were the States high school champions and Pat and the coaches wanted to have pizza delivered to the home and cases of their favorite sodas and really have a great time. Those kids at the home really liked all the celebration that Sonny was responsible for. The celebration didn't break up until way after eight o'clock. His coach made sure that none of the news reporters got near him asking their stupid questions. Sonny was too young for that.

Sonny told Marie that they had to concentrate on improving their golf game this summer and he had to find out if he would be allowed to get his driver's license. Pat had to go before the county review board and ask them if Sonny who was a very active athlete to get his license and be able to get around on his own to his golf matches and football games. If the county supplied a car it could only be used for his athletic use and not running out for pizza. Pat reminded them that it was Sonny's football fame that got the home all of it new alterations and additions and furniture plus the new kitchen. They thought that it was wonderful and did approve Sonny to get his driver's license and use the county car that was at the home for football practice and his golf practice. Sonny was excited to hear the good news and told Pat that he would do what they expected him to do and not run around the city that he didn't have any knowledge of in the first place.

The weekend was going to be long if he and Marie didn't find something to do. His coach asked Sonny and Marie if they wanted to play golf this afternoon at 1 pm and they said they would and were ready standing at the steps for their ride. They both had on some very proper golf clothes and the coach told them it was all covered and when they went into the pro shop the pro Mr. Douglas recognized Sonny and shook his hand. His coach told him outside that recognition was nothing compared to the national recognition he will be getting some day. You won't be able to pay for anything and if you're a decent guy they will love you all the more. They were just a threesome and the starter put a forth with them. He introduced himself as Jake Warner he was the Physical director at Sonny's school. Sonny said he knew of him and he told Sonny that he knew all about him as well. He went on to say that if he can play golf like he can play football he could go to any school in the country. Sonny told Mr. Warner that Marie goes where he goes or he don't go. He told him not to sweat it they will do anything you want.

Sonny played great and shot a one over par 35 and Mr. Warner said he would like to see him shoot par for the back nine or below. Marie shot a 39 and the two men thought that was great. It was turning out to be a great day and they were hoping that Sonny and Marie were enjoying themselves. He was standing on the seventeenth tee and wanted to position his drive for a good spot in the fairway to hit the green in two. Marie could hit a long ball and could almost stay even with Sonny off the ladies tee. They both birdied the seventeenth and put Sonny in a good position to shoot par for his round. Sonny's second shot on eighteen went into a trap and stopped in some ones unraked foot print. He would need a miracle to get his trap shot close to the hole, and he would need to sink his forth shot in order to shoot par for the round. His trap shot was horrible and he had a twenty footer to get his par four. He missed it and had to settle for a one over bogey or a one over par 71 for his round. The two adults couldn't believe what they just saw because Marie shot a one over par on the back nine 36 and finished the day with a 75 their probably not five women in the state her age that could come close to that. It was hard to conceive that these were two kids that didn't have parents and lived in a home for children that was run by the county. We are talking about something that proves that you can live under these circumstances and still excel.

They had to stop for their popular hot dog and soda and chat a little about school and what they wanted to do when they got out of college. They both weren't sure and felt they had plenty of time to plan their future. There wasn't any reason to pursue that conversation so it was left alone and not spoil a perfect day.

11

Sonny received a letter from Babe and he has joined the Air Force and was assigned to the Air Police. He told Sonny that he was first stationed in Savannah Ga. and has now signed up for a three year tour in Oxford England. He wanted to know how he was doing with his golf and football and how was everything going at the home. He said to say hello to everyone and Marie. Sonny was happy to get the letter it was the first letter he had ever received, he made sure that he said hello to everyone for him and let Marie read it. Sonny thought about Babe being a policeman and had a smile come to his face, he knew that Babe would be good at anything he wanted to do. He thought about Babe playing golf in England and how lucky he was to be there. Babe almost felt that way, he was still away from home and even though it wasn't much of a home he missed his mother who was working hard at the luncheonette and she missed him helping out at night.

Sonny wanted to improve on his golfing and so did Marie she wanted to do the same so between that and him studying for his driver's license test he was going to have a busy summer. He couldn't take his test until he took drivers Ed in the fall school semester. Sonny signed up for drivers Ed before school let out for the summer. Three months was going to feel like an eternity. Marie thought that Sonny getting his license to drive was exciting. Sonny explained to her how it worked and she said that it was perfect for them to get to the golf course and back and probably run errands for the ladies there. Now he has a way home from football practice from now on. He has to come from the football field straight to the home with no breaks in between or lose his right to drive the county cars. Sonny knew he wouldn't do anything wrong to lose that right.

With all that Sonny did for the home with all of the publicity they were getting, the county opened up two junior memberships for Marie and Sonny that they wanted to use every day. They didn't have a ride so Pat paid *someone to pick them up at the home every morning at 9: am and drive them to the golf course and bring them back by 3: pm weather permitting. They had a wonderful time playing and made a lot of friends with other junior members. The word must have been out about where they live because no one ever invited them anywhere in fact they felt an animosity towards them. It took a while for these junior members to realize who Sonny was; he was the guy that was in the newspapers all the time during football season. Now that was different and now he could fit in but by then Marie and Sonny didn't want to fit in so they would turn down all invites and only play as a twosome and not allow anyone to join them. Now they put the shoe on their foot and they didn't like it. Sonny found out who was the one trying to stir up some trouble and dragged him before the pro Mr. Douglas and told him what this kid was doing to their names and reputation here at the club and the pro asked the boy if that was true and he said yes. He told the boy he could revoke his membership but was going to let him stay on under a probation period and he better never talk about these to fine people again.*

Mr. Douglas asked the boy to leave and commended Sonny and Marie for bringing the boy to him and let him settle this. Because if it turned out that he got into a fight with them he would have lost his membership as well. All of the sudden life got better at the Rock and they were having a wonderful time. Mr. Douglas knew where Sonny and Marie were living and he could see that they would make very good citizens and they were proud to have them as members at the Rock and not allow anyone to try and make them be second class citizens. Sonny and Marie were going to enter the State junior championship being held at the Rock this year and Marie and Sonny were very familiar with the layout. They really practiced very hard and were in the sunlight every day all day and had a great tan. Sonny couldn't see how Marie could lose the women's title while Sonny was going to have some tough competition.

The first two days were metal play, in other words it was the score they shot added up for two days and then broken down into pairs and the ones playing for the title were in the top eight and they were paired by the draw. So it started out with eight golfers the second day four and on Friday the fifth day the remaining two would play for the champion ship. Sonny breezed through his first elimination round and so did Marie and the second round they both won again. Now on the third and championship round Sonny was going to be playing the defending champion and two years older than Sonny. Now Marie was also playing in the championship round her opponent called in sick and Marie was automatically declared the winner and the ladies state champion.

She wanted to walk with Sonny and help him if he needed her help. The match was all even after nine and someone had put the word out that Sonny was playing for the state Junior golf Championship and the reporters were showing up in droves. Luther and some of the county people working at the Rock pitched in to keep the reporters away from the two golfers. The match had everything that the pros have and then some. This kid from a county home was playing for the states junior championship and his friend had already won the lady's title. The match was going back and forth and it was coming down to the eighteenth hole where Sonny was in the fairway and his opponent was in the edge of the woods. He knew he would need a good shot if he was going to beat Sonny. He reached down to move a leaf and his ball moved, he had to take a one stroke penalty and walked out on the fairway and waived Sonny over and told him what happened and walked back to his ball and halfheartedly hit his ball out into the fairway and looked over at Sonny. Sonny was nervous but not as nervous as him needing two yards for a first down in one of his football games. In golf this is what was expected of the golfer to call a penalty even though no one saw it.

Sonny went on to knock it stiff and his opponent finished with a two over par six, while Sonny dropped his birdie putt and was now the new Junior state champion. The reporters were everywhere with their human interest story of the poor boy that made it good and the new ladies state champion was from the same home. Luther could see that the crowd was too much for these inexperienced kids so he had the reporters give them room or he would call the police in and have them removed from the golf course for disrupting the play on the course. They had some TV coverage one from Wilm. De and one from Phil. Pa. Luther thought that these two kids were going to get plenty or notoriety after this tournament.

Luther called Pat with the news and said he would like to get these two out of here before some of these reporters get out of hand and try to pull a fast one and start misquoting them just to get a story. Pat was there in twenty minutes and could hardly move between people and finally get to Marie and Sonny she gave them both a hug and someone called out that must be the mother. She ignored that and asked them if they wanted to leave they said they were ready while Luther had their clubs they walked towards Pats car and left slowly because no one would get out of the way. The flash bulbs were everywhere. Pat was out of her mind with praise for them and was going to have a celebration for them when they get back. She has ordered ten large pizzas and ten 32 ounce bottles of mixed sodas. Everyone at the home was waiting and the ladies in the kitchen were ready to celebrate. When Pat pulled up to the steps the whole place went crazy and Marie and Sonny could hardly walk up the steps to the porch. It wasn't but a few minutes when the van pulled up with the pizzas and sodas. This party went on till 9 pm and Sonny's coach Jake Warner came a little later and he was all over Marie and Sonny congratulating them for a great duel win.

Sonny's coach was happy that some of these reporters didn't follow them back to the home that would have been bad. Mr. Warner said it would have been bad for them not us. Both Marie and Sonny had golfers tan and when they took off their hats their far heads were white. They never stayed around for their trophies and Mr. Warner said he would find out where they were and get them. Come to find out that they wanted the two of them to come back to the Rock and partake in the award ceremony the next day at 1 pm. Pat drove them back to the Rock for a big sports ceremony even the Governor was there, now that's impressive. They both were given a $1,000.00 bond and a beautiful silver plate with the tournament name engraved on it and the year it was won. There were a lot of questions from the reporters and finally things quieted down enough to enjoy the moment. One reporter asked Sonny doesn't he think that being a member gave him the edge. He thanked him for the question and said his opponent was the reining state champion and I won because he called a penalty stroke on himself and asked the reporter back what advantage did he have in that. The reporter didn't reply he just held his head down in shame. Another reporter asked Marie how she felt about wining without playing anyone. Just then the Governor took the microphone and blasted that reporter for asking a young woman a question like that. He went on to tell him that these are children being asked mean questions from mean reporters.

The question session broke up and the reporters wanted to kill those two reporters that wanted to treat the two state champions mean and unfair. Marie and Sonny posed for some pictures and the Pro Mr. Douglas sent the reporters away and finally congratulated them and told them both he was very proud of them. He told them that they bring honor to the Rock and they will make up two awards that will hang on the walls of our clubhouse for as long as there is a Rock. Luther was very proud of Marie and Sonny as well and this day will live on in his memory for the rest of his life. Finally Pat got them back to the home for them to relax and have a nice cold soda on the *back porch where the two of them could talk about each other's match. Marie said she didn't have a match so there wasn't anything for her to talk about. Sonny told her he almost died when his opponent waved him over and said he was going to call a one shot penalty on himself for causing the ball to move. It must have torn the heart out of him because he never hit the ball good after that.*

Marie told Sonny that she was watching him throughout the match and how she wanted him so bad and had to control herself and not let you see her with that look on her face. She wasn't going to mess him up and loose the match. Sonny asked her how she felt now alone with him and she said she would like his hand down her shorts but it was too risky. Pat seems to have eyes in the back of her head anymore and was determined to keep them apart. Sonny said now that we know she's making bed checks we can't use our rooms anymore. Marie thought this is so frustrating sitting here and can't do anything about it.

They didn't play golf for a week just to let the fanfare pass but were eager to get back with a month to go before school starts up and Sonny takes his Drivers Ed class and gets his license. There wasn't much to do at the home because there wasn't anyone there to do it with. Sonny could have gotten out of the home years ago there were a lot of people that wanted him to come and live with them but He wanted to stay at the home with Marie and the children whom he loved and loved to be with. That afternoon everything was right for them two to meet in Marie's room with Pat going into town and Marie's roommate gone for the rest of the day. They met in Marie's room and she was ready for him and made no bones about it. She let him see her naked again and that was all he needed because Oliver was doing everything but the twist. Marie couldn't tell Sonny enough how much she loved him, it was that great. They met back on the porch afterwards and had a cold ice tea. Marie just sat there with her glass of ice tea and kept smiling at him.

Meanwhile Jenny and Chris were having a great time together; Chris was the only thing in her life right now besides her computer classes in the stock market. She is thirty four now and still looks like a twenty year old. Chris has turned out to be a beautiful young lady with light hair and a deep interest in golf and always liked to watch it on TV. Jenny decided to take Chris out to the club for an evaluation before joining. They met in the pro shop and he picked up some balls and said to follow him. They walked to the driving range and the pro asked Chris to take a few practice swings. She did real good and said it was great, so now he wanted Chris to hit some golf balls and was amazed how good she was without any lessons. He asked Jenny how her putting was and Jenny said wait till you see. He dropped three balls on the putting green and told her to putt to number three pin. She made one out of three the other two were rims. He told her to putt to number eight she made two out of three. Finally he had her putt across the green about twenty feet and she made one. He asked them to come into the pro shop and talk. He told Chris to putt some more and that her mother would be right inside the window looking at her.

He put the clubs away and looked up at Jenny and said that if her daughter would practice and follow his instructions she could be great. Not because of him but because of her ability to strike the ball solid and of course the love of the game is very apparent. Jenny asked him if she could join as a social member or should join as a golf membership and get it over with. He told her to take the golf membership and that he would sponsor them, they wouldn't have any problems. He would spend around three days a week with her and then you can either play nine holes with her or you could just walk with her. Jenny told Mark the golf pro that she will require some lessons as well and probably be better if he did her on school days while Chris is at school.

Chris's first lesion, Mark had her hitting the ball longer in the air then before her lesson and it was going further as well. Chris has had half dozen lessons before Jenny was ready. She was approved right away without any waiting period. She had to get some wardrobe from head to toe for them both. At first being a member of a country club is not easy, but if everyone tries to be friendly then it becomes easier. Jenny didn't have any plans on getting into a click. She just wanted to advance Chris's chances on being a good golfer. Mark the pro was going to be a big help, Chris couldn't play a round of golf until after 3: pm and had to be with an adult the whole time. So they were playing in the worst time of the day when the sun was the hottest. After a while people were starting to see Chris and her mother together all the time. They would use the dining room as long as they had a food requirement each month. They had to eat four hundred dollars' worth of food in twelve months between the two of them, or forfeit it. Chris was over nine now and could shoot a 42 for nine holes, not bad for a young girl.

Chris and Jenny kept up their lessons and could only improve so by the end of the summer they were very good and trying to break forty. But the weather was changing fast and Mark asked Jenny and Chris if they wanted to practice hitting balls at his indoor screen and come out next year ready to shoot low scores. He wanted Chris to practice her putting whenever she had a chance to because that was the secret of shooting par. That meant the Jenny had to bring her to the putting green and she might as well practice with her and have some putting contest to make it interesting. The only time they weren't putting was when it was raining or snowing, the rest of the time they were hitting balls and putting. By the time that spring came along they both had a 14 handicap and it was posted on the handicap board for all the ladies to see.

Jenny was getting request to join the beginners, the nine hollers' and the eighteen hollers. She was very diplomatic about turning them down and always made sure that they accepted her reason that she was devoting her time with Chris and when she is on her feet she will join them when she can. She was going to be a friend to everyone which made her very popular at the club. Everyone wanted to be seen with her and knew she was a single parent. Both Chris and her broke out and were shooting good scores, thanks to Mark who really took an interest in them both and so did marks wife Lisa who also took a liking to them both. Mark was only charging Jenny four hundred dollars a month for unlimited golf lessons for Chris and lessons for Jenny three times a week, which sounds high but was a bargain. This attention was going to put them over the top of their game. Mark was happy that they were good students which made it easier for him to teach them. His prize student was Chris and some day he was going to release her on the golf scene and raise a few eyebrows.

With the high visibility of Jenny at the club the men were very reluctant to do anymore then say hello for fear of someone making more out of it than just a simple hello. Some of the women felt uneasy and how she could attract attention just walking through the parking lot. Jenny only wanted what was best for her daughter and she took a second seat to that. If Jenny was bored at home she has her hands full with Golf and raising Chris. This country club life style was nice and it sheltered them from another part of life that Chris was not seeing. This made Jenny very happy and thought the investment was worth it. Spring golf was a little tougher because the ground was soft and the air was moist and the grass was struggling to be nice but would need a little more time to show it's better face. Soon the grass would have to cut twice a week with the hot weather.

One day the pro asked Jenny if this young man can join them for a round of golf. His name was Brad Casey and his father was the president of the largest bank in Wilmington. Jenny thought it would be good for Chris to have some outside competition to see how Chris will react. He was ten and one year older then Chris but not as good a golfer as Chris. I am sure after today's round he will be practicing to beat her because he probably thought he couldn't lose to a girl. They said goodbye on the eighteenth green and Brad walked away in shock. I am sure that Mark will be hearing about the round today. Now when Jenny and Chris go into the dining room everyone says hello and they also said hello to Chris as they are being escorted to their table. This fabulously dressed man came over to their table and introduced himself as Brad's Father Timothy Casey and thanked them for playing with his son today. Jenny told him that his son was a perfect gentleman and they were happy to have him join us.

He went back to his table where he had this woman that was dressed as good as he was. Jenny recognized his sport coat as a Hickey Freeman one of the best out there. This is exactly what she wanted Chris to be exposed to and develop friendships that will not only be lasting but beneficial in her social life. She didn't see a wedding ring on his finger and didn't give it another thought. Chris was secretly hoping that Brad would want to play some more someday. But in the mean time she was practicing her putting with a vengeance, she felt that if she can get on the green she would have to make the putt to win. Mark could see that Chris was going to be the best student he ever had and that Brad might never beat her in match play or metal play. Jenny wasn't any slouch either she was breaking eighty regularly now and the other ladies members wanted her on their golf teams as well.

Jenny wasn't going to lose sight of her goal and to give Chris the best life she can. To her it seemed like the country club was a good thing. It would be up to Chris to tidy up the loose ends and make some lasting friendships. With her grades and golf ability she should be able to get a scholar ship anywhere. Jenny knows that when Chris starts dating and going away too school she better have something to fill the void or she is going to be very lonely. Right now Jenny is in the prime of her life and the fruit is ripe on the vine for some young wealthy man to come along and eat the forbidden fruit.

12

Sonny was going to try out for the varsity football team, as a sophomore it would be tough but he had the talent to do it. The training was brutal; he could hardly walk to his car. This one day after practice he was cornered by his car by four seniors on the team and was told to go away or they were going to kick his ass. So he decided to quit the team and stay away like they said. The coach was frantic looking for Sonny and found him eating his lunch in the cafeteria. He asked Sonny was he sick or hurt?

"No I just decided to quit the team before some of the seniors were going to make him quit."

"I don't understand what you're telling me."

"I don't want to play on a team where the players don't want me to play on."

"What players? What the hell are you talking about?"

"Sonny told him to find out for himself, I am sick of this shit. I thought winning the game was what this was all about and having some fun doing it."

"It looks like you're not going to tell me anything so I'll have to find out for myself."

The coach got up from the table, knocked over a chair and everyone in the cafeteria saw it and stormed out. Three days later Sonny was asked to show up at the gym after school for a meeting. When he got there the whole football team was seated in the bleachers. Sonny took a seat with them and a few minutes later coach Warner came into the gym and told the players that he had to kick four players off the team last evening because they tried to strong arm one of our players to quit the team or have his ass kicked. He told them that we don't condone that kind of vigilantes on our football team. Everyone trying out has a fair chance to make the first team or even make the team. We will resume practice tomorrow and would expect to see everyone that wants to *play football for the Fighting Oriels to show up. Coach Warner left the gym and everyone was looking for answers as to what he was talking about and nobody knew anything*

Practice the next day Sonny showed up to see what was happening and there was a couple of guys that wanted to play quarterback as well. Sonny was the youngest and the other two were very good but never played the single tee or could they throw with either hand. The composition was heavy and the coach knew the best man would win the position. Sonny was so good at hiding the football and playing without a huddle that eventually he won out the position and from now on it was going to be some tough football. They practiced a lot of quick releases that would prevent the defense from hitting him too often, because that's how most quarterbacks get injured by getting hit too much. The first game was going to be how the season might go so everyone was on pins and needles but Sonny. He had a lot of experience in this format and felt comfortable running it. The no huddle let the offence run more plays and keep the defense on the field for a longer time tiring them out.

Marie was a wreck and kissed Sonny goodbye before he left for the game. Sonny found it hard to leave her because she didn't make it easy pressing against him like she would to get his attention. Coach Warner had them leave early so to sharpen up on a few things and allow the other team to see them doing things that they won't be doing at game time. They won the toss and scored in three plays, their opponents never saw anything like it. The game wasn't over it was just beginning and by half time the Oriels were up by ten points. The talk in the locker room was to play a little different than they did the first half and confuse them all the more. They went to a direct center and switched all throughout the game and won easily by twenty four points. It was the worst their opponents were ever defeated in the history of their school.

Sonny was given another good write up in the newspaper and Coach Warner was thrilled how easy Sonny made it look. That's what experience can do for someone. This was going to be another great year for Sonny as long as he doesn't get hurt. There were more people gunning for him then there were hunters at the opening of deer season. Every game they would want to do him in and he knew it. The first win was the sweetest because of all the uncertainty they all had. Sonny gave Marie a ride back to the home and they parked and smooched for a short while and headed to the home and not get in trouble. Thank God they stopped or she would of had all her clothes off. She didn't have that much on to begin with seeing as how she only had on those skimpy cheerleader uniforms. It was way past bed time and everyone was in their rooms at 10 pm so Marie took Sonny down to the tool shed not for a beating but for some way overdue loving. She stripped for him to see her fine body and that was all he needed to see, they must have went at it for thirty minutes before they finished. They walked back to the home hand in hand in the moonlight.

They both were starving to death and went immediately to the kitchen for something to eat. Here the ladies left them some dinner and thought how lucky they were to have such thoughtful people looking after them. Marie told Sonny that she didn't want to get pregnant so please pull out early enough so she won't. He promised her he would. Now that they have a car they can stop on their way to where ever they are going and buy some rubbers and stash them somewhere safe so Pat won't find them probably the shed would be the best place seeing as how they are always in there for their golf balls and ball retriever. Varsity practice is very tough and can wear out the best of them.

After the fourth game they were undefeated and they were going to play the other undefeated team next Friday. What a hell of a game that was going to be. All week there were banners everywhere and on Friday afternoon there was a big pep rally in the gym and the cheer leaders were kicking those legs extra high and the degenerates up front loved it. Those girls got the crown all worked up for the game this evening, there should be quite a turn out to see two undefeated schools go at it and break each other's streak. There were police cars everywhere to make sure the parking went easy and no gang fighting like at some other games that had to be stopped on account of the fighting, before they were over.

The practice went well and when they huddled just before the game started Coach Warner told them that they had to hit harder, run harder go for the sacks and look for a good opportunity to intercept and hand off when you are sure it will work. They won the kickoff and when their receiver caught the ball he ran across the field and did a hand off that was professional and stopped the opponents in their tracks, they didn't know who had the ball. They scored a touchdown on a 65 yard kick off to start the game and demoralized the other team right off the bat. They weren't undefeated for nothing they came right back and scored on a long pass to a receiver that out ran the defensive back by three steps. Coach Warner was livid and told the defensive back he had to make that up somehow. On the next set of downs that the other side had the ball the defensive back we talked about was watching the quarterback enough when he knew who he was going to throw *the ball to and was right there for a clear interception and scored easily. It was half time and the fighting Orioles were only up by seven points.*

Coach Warner told them that if they keep playing the way they are they should win but they had to be up for another tension filled second half. The coach told Sonny to run when he has a good chance to get some long yardage out of one of his fakes don't give it to the second runner either keep it and run like hell. The Orioles had to kick off and the defensive team caused a fumble and the orioles had the ball on the twenty yard line. Sonny called a fake double hand off and kept it and scored easily but was hit crossing the line and had the wind knocked out of him. What a scare that was, Marie was crying on the side lines and stopped when she saw Sonny walking off the field. She couldn't run to him like she wanted to because it was strictly forbidden and she would have been kicked off the cheerleader squad for having any contact with a player during the game.

Sonny was ok by the kickoff and was ready to go when they got the ball. Thank God that it was only the wind knocked out of him, his team needed him so bad it wouldn't be funny if he couldn't play, it would be a disaster. Coach Warner had the backup's practicing to take Sonny's place if he should ever get hurt but they still couldn't master what Sonny could do on the field. Throwing a pass with either hand, he was the best anyone could see doing it. The football scouts were everywhere and wouldn't take their eyes off of him. There was two minutes to go in the forth quarter and the Orioles were up by seven points. They were on the twenty yard line when the orioles stripped the ball and fell on it with forty seconds left on the clock and Sonny took two knees and the game was over and so was the undefeated season of the opponents.

Sonny played a great game and it was highlighted on a lot of the news networks throughout the city. Sonny lived such a quiet life back at the home most people his age were out drinking, smoking, partying and staying out till the early hours of the morning. Instead Sonny was at the home basically an orphan with no parents and probably the most recognized young man in the city and with all of his publicly he didn't have two cents to rub together. This was really sad; it was going to make him a better man because he doesn't feel out of place or less than his peers. He doesn't feel like an orphan, he has had plenty of successes just the way they were. Sonny and Marie rode back to the home after Sonny showered at the school and turned in his uniform. Marie told Sonny how good he smelt and he told her how good she smelt. They were real close to the home so they decided to go there and see if there was anything to eat. There was so they warmed it up and sat out on the porch and had a beautiful meal, thanks to the ladies in the kitchen who always took care of Sonny and Marie.

Saturday was a good day to play golf at the Rock so Marie and Sonny headed for the course around 11 am and as they were to tee off, the starter asked them if they would mind if this couple could join them. They said they didn't mind and they introduced themselves as Dr. and Mrs. Smith from Newark De. He was a plastic surgeon and was in town on a convention. Sonny asked him and his wife to hit first and they hit two beautiful drives right down the middle of the fairway. So now it was Sonny and Marie's turn and both of their balls went by them in the air, as the doctor went to his bag the starter told him that Sonny and Marie were the reigning Junior State Champions. The doctor had a cart and Sonny and Marie had to carry their own bag. It wasn't a problem for them because they didn't know any better. Even though they were a twelve handicap they couldn't keep up with Sonny and Marie.

It was a long four hours and the Doctor and his wife were very impressed with the way they played golf and their manners for a couple of young kids. He never saw two young kids be so nice to each other and polite to them. The Doctor was walking off the eighteen green and asked Sonny and Marie if they would like to be there guest for dinner at the Hotel Baltimore this evening. Sonny told him that they couldn't.

"You can't."

"No we live in an orphan's home and we have to get back in a reasonable time, or we will lose our driving privileges. We can't let that happen."

"Now son let me try and clear something up. You live in an orphanage and you have access to a golf club and can use a car to get to and from and I found out from the starter that you two are the reigning junior state champions."

"Yes that's true."

"This is an unbelievable story, how you two have made so many achievements under those hardships."

"It's not just us two, there are fifty three of us at the home, and we don't miss anything because we never had anything, so you might say we don't know what we're missing."

"Very well put Sonny, you don't have anything clogging your thinking. Do you?"

"No we try not to complicate things."

"It certainly was a pleasure meeting you both and we will remember you always."

The doctor and his wife walked away to their car while Sonny and Marie putted a little and decided to get back before it was late. Dinner was just starting to finish when they walked in the dining room and grabbed their dish and loaded up on some chicken and mashed potatoes and some warm apple pie. What do you do at an orphanage on a Saturday night? Not a whole lot but get in trouble. Marie lost her roommate through an adoption and was hoping that they wouldn't put anyone with her. She had plans on using the room when she could and with no roommate she can get Sonny in and out of there without getting caught with no problem. Marie liked it best in her room. Sonny wasn't that easy to lure back to her room with Pat snooping around he was too nervous to really enjoy it. Marie knew it but couldn't do any better than no roommate and to know when Pat was going to be away and for how long and between what times. She knew that was safe and couldn't get any safer.

Marie wanted it all the time, that was great for Sonny but he should have been the one wanting it all the time and not her. It was all new to them and they had to get use to each other. They were too young to be rational about it. Sonny had a lot of things to take care of like college, he wasn't going to attend any college without Marie, and can they defend their state golf titles next year. His football season was coming to an end with the playing of the school championship next week. This was going to be a first for the coach and with a state championship under his belt he might move on to the higher rated schools out west, or down south and land a much higher paying job. He knows that thanks to Sonny for teaching him about the single wing and how he can play it. Right now coach Warner was concentrating on the game and how best Sonny can play it.

They practiced every night till 8: 30 and Sonny was dragging ass when he got back to the home. Marie was busy with homework and Sonny didn't have that much but enough to keep him up until 11 o'clock most every night. Friday was a big day at school. They planned a pep rally and dress for the game afterwards and go out to their practice field and practice ten plays without a huddle until they got it right. The defense was put through a grueling practice and was ready to go to the ball park in just enough time to start the game. You talking about being ready, these guys were ready like a fine tuned clock. This game was definitely going to prove who the state high school champions were.

The oriole players were playing the game for Sonny and Sonny was speechless for them wanting to do that for him. The orioles won the toss and took a great kickoff return down to the thirty two yard line. Now it is Sonny's turn to shine and boy did he ever he took two plays of faking handoffs and he scored the first touchdown. The place went berserk and the orioles knew that the other team was going to give them the game of their lives. They took their kickoff and scored and now it was crunch time. They scored because of missed tackles and Coach Warner asked the defense if this is how they plan on winning this game for Sonny. Their heads were low but they weren't going to make these mistakes again.

Sonny called for two straight short passes and the third would be a fake pass and a run around left end and hand it to the runner coming from the opposite direction. He went about thirty five yards before they tackled him from behind. Sonny reminded his right end that they are expecting another short pass so he told him and only him, to start off very slow and take off like a rabbit with his tail on fire and he better be in the clear. The play went well and his receiver was wide open and Sonny hit him on the run and he scored easy. They are up by seven and they need a turn over before the half. They got one on a blitz and their quarterback fumbled and the orioles had the ball on the twelve yard line with a minute and forty seconds to go in the half. That was plenty of time for Sonny to score he did some fake hands offs and when they were stumped he ran around right end and scored his second touchdown. The half has ended and it was off to the locker room for some ass chewing.

Coach Warner was in good spirits and reminded the boys that their opponents weren't going to sit around and allow us to ride rough herd over them. They were going to come out a blazing; he went on to tell them if we can keep them from scoring the third quarter we will take the wind out of their sails. He told Sonny to make sure that his backs know what the play is. Finally he told them to expect them to start stripping the ball Remember the rule due un to others applies in this game. The knights were getting the kickoff for the second half and you can expect the orioles to hit very hard and strip on every play. They wanted to increase their lead to twenty one points.

Sonny was short passing them to death and just as they thought he was going to pass he kept the ball and ran twenty five yards for a touchdown. Now that's three td's in as little more than a half. The knights took the kickoff and kept the ball for nine minutes and only scored a field goal and now they are down by eighteen points. They need touchdowns not field goals. Sonny called about five plays on the side lines before they took the field. The Orioles went back in and their first play the center hiked it directly to the right running back and with a fake hand off that sonny made to the left running back as if he had the ball the running back took off for the goal line and scored a beautiful Td The defense didn't expect them to pull any trick plays. Now they are up twenty five points, with fifteen minutes to play. The Knights were in serious trouble, they did score after five minutes. The coach told Sonny to run the clock down, so they ran one run play after another now they are down to the twelve yard line the play was to fake a hand off and throw a short pass behind the lines. Sonny did that and ran into the end zone unguarded and the running back hit Sonny in the end zone for his fourth touchdown of the game. The game was over but not the celebrating, everyone met in the center of the field and the Knights coach gave Sonny a hug and told him he was going far if he wanted to.

Sonny was glad he had shoulder pads on because everyone was hitting him on the shoulders for good luck and praise. He really felt good about the game, there had to be at least seventy reporters wanting him to say something. He thought for a few minutes and told them if they wanted to show their appreciation make sure that some of the children at the home have cars and a few wardrobe changes twice a year. He went on to say that there must be a few people out there that can help some of my friends out. They also need an allowance to buy their own little things instead of waiting for the county to bring it to them. We are all going to leave the home someday and we need to make it on our own and be good citizens like we all want to be.

Well it made national news, it was everywhere on TV and on every talk show and in every newspaper and some overseas. Marie was waiting back at the school for a huge pep rally out back in the bleachers on the football field. There was all kind of praises but none more than the one Sonny got, he received the most valuable player trophy. Someone lit the huge bonfire and the kid's sang for hours. Sonny told Marie that they should leave now and get back to the home. Marie didn't want to leave so Sonny told her to get a ride. She grabbed Sonny and told him she didn't want to leave because she was having too much fun, but she was ready to leave now or any time he wanted, after all Sonny this is your night. You did all that scoring on the field and now it's time to see if you can score off the field. He burst out laughing and grabbed Marie and left for the car. With everyone at the pep rally Sonny took Marie to the back seat and gave her the shot she wanted from him. She slept all the way back to the home.

It was a little after 11 o'clock when they got back, there were only a few dim lights on around the home and Sonny and Marie didn't know what to do. Marie ran into the kitchen and found some hamburgers and French fries and heated everything up and put everything on them she could find and brought the ketchup with her. They had a great time just having their snack together on the porch watching the moon go by overhead. Marie got a little chilly from the night air so Sonny put his arm around her to keep her warm. Sonny told Marie that they better go to bed and find something to do on Saturday.

Saturday morning was hectic there were calls from all over the world wanting to help the children at the home. There were numerous TV stations wanting an interview with Sonny and the county told them he was very young to be giving an interview one on one. The county finally relented and said that he can do an interview at the home with some people present from the county to assist Sonny if he should need their help. The county rep. told the head of the reporters that if there is one question asked that is considered to be in bad taste the interview will stop and you all will be escorted from the property. Sonny was informed how much money was coming in so far and it was a little over $3 mil. Sonny told the gentleman from the county that the money was for the children at the home and some home improvements and not anything else. The county rep. told Sonny they know where and how to spend the money. Sonny went on to tell the gent not to forget the children's allowance either.

Come time for the interview with Sonny only half of the reporters showed up and only one TV station. The county people didn't think it was going to be that long of an interview. Sonny was seated at the center of the table along with some county people and a couple of their lawyers. The first question came from a Delaware reporter.

"Sonny how long have you be at the home?"

"Sonny quickly answered the reporter and said somewhere around eight or nine years."

"Do you like it here?"

"Yes, I don't know about anything else just the home."

"What do you like to play the most football or Golf?"

"Football is rough sports the defensive players want to inflict pain on me, being the quarterback every chance they get. Now Golf is a little different, it's a gentleman's game and you can't beat that. We play with different balls."

"Is it true that you showed your coach how to play the single tee?"

"No I merely showed him how we played it in the minor league and he improved it. Coach Warner knows his football and knows how to win his games"

"When will you leave the home?"

"I will probably leave the home when I go off to college."

"Will you come back to live."

"Do you mean after college?"

"Yes will you ever come back to the home to live?"

"No once I leave here I will not come back to live, but I would love to visit whenever I can."

"Are you looking to get a scholarship for college?"

"That would be nice because I don't have any money to pay my way through."

"Have you picked a college that you would like to attend?"

"To be honest with you I haven't."

"I understand that you are furnished a car to get around in and get to school and your practices. Isn't that nice?"

"On the surface it's nice, but I have nothing, no assets, no one tucking me in at night. I don't have any money in my pocket or in the bank. I have to be given money when I play golf so I can get a hot dog and a drink when I am finished. The membership is paid for by the county, in short I don't have access to a single Lincoln penny. I am what is known as busted."

"It is truly remarkable how you continue to play the sports as good as you do after the picture you have just painted for us."

"If I were to sit around crying about how bad I am doing in some people's eyes, I would never get anything accomplished."

The meeting ended and Sonny thanked the reporters for being kind and said goodbye. Marie ran up to Sonny and hugged him and told him she loved him and that he was the only one that could hear her say that. They decided to play nine holes at the Rock and practice their putting. They told the starter that they wanted to play alone and he said he understood. It was a beautiful afternoon and they had packed a couple of ham sandwiches and could top off the day while down on the putting green.

13

*S*onny was somewhat alarmed about his reoccurring dream of him and this pretty woman that would hold his hand and take him to the park. He wanted to talk to Pat about this dream and if someone could help him figure it out. Maybe it's nothing and maybe it's something he should know about. He stopped by her office and asked to see her, she asked him to wait a few minutes and she could see him. He sat on the only chair that was available to sit in and before he could get settled she came and got him. She knew this was important or he would have never come to her. Sonny has never needed her help or anyone else's help at the home. He was as nervous as anyone could get under these circumstances.

She looked him straight in the eye and he could tell that she wanted to help him no matter what his problem might be. So he started off gently about his reoccurring dream and this beautiful woman holding his hand. She asked him, if she ever spoke to him and without hesitation he answered no. She told Sonny of some reoccurring dreams she had that didn't amount to anything and have never came back to her for years now. He told her that was her choice or decision not to look into them, but in his case this was a woman who was showing him some love or affection and she was something to him, but what. She asked him if he wanted to see a doctor about it or does he want it to run its course and see if it still continues.

He asked her what would be the point in waiting and she said, "That maybe more might start to come from his dreams. She might even call you by name or their might be some conversation that we might be able to look into." He chose to wait a little while longer and hope something can come from it. Pat said that was a good decision and to inform her as to any changes in his dreams. Sonny doesn't know all what Pat went through to get him a birth certificate and the investigation that went into determining his date of birth and the last name of the woman that he was last with Judy Cole *who was almost untraceable except that she was in prison and no history of having a son. So where did Sonny come from? It would take an unbelievable investigation that no one could afford to find the answers to those questions, so maybe if sonny can give the doctor under hypnotism more then what he can recall about his dream might be a big advance in finding out who this woman is.*

Most of the view he gets of the woman is below her shoulders and no voice. Good luck to anyone that can get something out of that. Marie met him out on the porch and asked him how it went and he told her that they have decided to wait a little and see if anything develops from the dream. Marie is interested in knowing who this woman is and will help Sonny out anyway she can to get this resolved. They both worked on their school studies to improve their grade average that will help them come scholarship time. No one is spending more time with each other than Sonny and Marie, They are very close and Marie has told Sonny that she loved him probably from the first time she saw him. Sonny loved her too but wasn't as open about it like Marie. She loved him totally and wanted sex with him any time he would want her, it was the ultimate in loving someone.

Jenny on the other hand was spending a lot of time with Chris who she wanted to have all she could give her especially the country club that had a lot to offer anyone that wanted a little more than just playing golf. Chris was a big hit with all of the golfers out there and there wasn't a single boy that didn't want to play eighteen holes with her. Her stock market class was going good and she was right on schedule to complete her studies in four more years. That was what she wanted was to complete her class and get her degree around the same time Chris was close to graduating from high school. She knew that Chris would be away at school leaving Jenny by herself. Chris was only 11 yrs old and still had a way to go before she would go to college. She was working real hard on her game to be the state champion; Jenny was a big inspiration on that goal.

Chris was real popular at school and she was getting a lot of request to go to the movies and parties taking her away from mom that was overseeing everything that Chris did and didn't want Chris to fall prey to some fast talking dude who would promise her everything but give her nothing. Jenny knew it wasn't too early to start supervising those activities. Being 11 she was determined to supervise at best she could. Jenny still wasn't dating anyone and was perfectly happy with that, with the bad experience she had with men you might say that she was once burnt. Chris keeps her busy and not much time to think about men. She just loved golf and all the challenges that were there. Chris knew if she could go 18 holes with the guys she could do anything. They were rude to her and didn't show much respect, not all of um but most of um. They didn't act that way in front of Jenny or there would have been hell to pay.

Now when Chris played with some of the ladies including her mother she was very good, because no one was giving her a bad time. Farting in the back swing was about the hardest to get use too. She was able to get over anything or walk off the course, which was not what she wanted to do. Boys were going to be boys no matter what and take advantage whenever they could. Her chances for her to win a club championship looked good for one of these years; she had a reputation of being a strong player thanks to the boys. Going into the sixth grade was different, her body was starting to change, and it made her feel uncomfortable at times. Jenny had to start buying her some different underwear and bra's and things like that. Once the girls started developing some breast the boys would stare. The girls had to get use too it or wear baggy clothes. The baggier the clothes that some of the girls would wear the more talking by the boys about what they must be hiding.

Chris wasn't in on all this boy business she stayed focused on her grades and her golf and was much better off with that thinking. Let's face it she is too young to be playing those games she is still a little girl growing up quickly in a great environment. Chris loves her home that Mrs. Topkis left them and how her mom has fixed it up with all the latest appliances and furniture and a great computer for her school work, there's not a month that goes by that they don't visit the grave of Mrs. Topkis and thank her for what she has done for them. Jenny always makes sure that she changes the flowers on the grave. They never rush off they pay their respects and gratitude that she deserves. Chris knows how important Mrs. Topkis is to her mother.

Jenny told her how her first child Rome was kid napped from the park when Mrs. Topkis fell asleep sitting on the park bench. Someone saw her sleeping and took him away, never to be seen again. She told Chris how she looked and stayed on top of the police to find him but the trail got cold fast and there weren't any more Leeds to follow. Chris felt sad to hear that she had an older brother that was taken away and she will never see him. They didn't dwell on it because it hurt too much. You would think that time would make it a lot easier to talk about it but it hasn't for Jenny and Chris. Without asking, Chris knew that Rome was born out of wed lock and the father didn't step up and take any responsibility. She never asked her mother anything about Rome's father.

Sonny is in his senior year and his reoccurring dream has not come back to him about the pretty woman holding his hand. The only pretty woman holding his hand is Marie and she won't let go, she loves Sonny so much and wants to be a part of his life and knew it would have to be football and golf the two very things that Sonny is taking a deep interest in. For a young man he has gotten a lot of publicity from Football. Now that this was going to be his senior year there were request for interviews and request for him to go to their college on a full scholarship. He wants to concentrate on the upcoming football season after he and Marie have won the state junior golf championship. The two kids from the home have won another title and are getting huge coverage from the press along with plenty of photos. They are in big demand from at least twelve colleges and Sonny knew he was going to select the one that was going to offer him the most as far as education goes and everything that his needs to get through a typical day. He was going to be tough to negotiate with because he doesn't have anyone running interference for him, so he won't trust anyone that will represent any college.

Football tryouts were in a week and Sonny knew that there were a few guys that wanted his position real bad but they didn't have his experience and would probably have to settle for back up. The first day of try outs the weather was hot, up in the low eighties, thank God there was plenty of cold water to drink and towels to wipe off with. Coach Warner was excited to coach Sonny in his final year and wanted to win the state title for him and the school. Sonny never looked better and was hitting his receiver's right in the numbers. With sonny being able to throw either hand coach Warner wanted to use that against his opponents and make it too hard to defend against. He also knew that the scouts were going around like flies and was hoping that they wouldn't distract Sonny from what he had to do. Too much attention for Sonny might turn off the rest of the team; this was a delicate matter that Coach Warner had to keep an eye on. Sonny wasn't looking for anything special he just wanted to play the game and win.

Coach Warner wanted to come on the field for the first game and score a touchdown in the first three downs. That was asking a lot even though they have done it before they weren't trying to score a touchdown in the first three plays. The bad thing about this goal is if they don't score in the first three downs they will be crushed. The night before the home coming game, Marie hadn't seen Sonny for weeks and wanted to give him an evening with *her and something for him to remember. She was able to lure him in to the back seat of the car they used to get around in and let Sonny score on his first play. Marie wanted so much to be with Sonny and not have to sneak around all the time in fear of getting caught. With the big pep rally in the gym the pressure was mounting for the kick off later on that evening. Their first game was Friday night under the lights.*

Marie was the Capt. of the cheerleaders and also the best one, she was also the homecoming queen and she had a very high exposure this week at the school and was handling it very good. As the team rode the bus to the field Sonny was thinking of Marie and their future and he wanted her in his life and so did she want him in her life. They weren't going to let some scholarship get in their way. With all the noise on the bus he soon got into the swing of singing and cheering and was ready for their opening game and what it meant to the coaches and the students for the team to win this one. The stadium was packed full with 4000 fans screaming their heads off; this was Sonny's senior year and they were all there to support him.

The team entrance to the locker room was crowded with people standing around to get a glimpse of the players, some of them were friendly and some were unfriendly. The friendly ones were cheering and saying nice things and the unfriendly ones were yelling obscenities at the players and wishing that they would lose badly. When they were settled down in the locker room Coach Warner reminded them of how important the game was to their opponents and how bad they were going to come at us. When they took the field for practice they made sure they gave the wrong signals. He had the receivers run slow after their passes and Sonny worked off the tee, which was a complete surprise for the other coaches to see.

With a short time before kick off the team met in the locker room for the final time and that was where Coach Warner told the team of some of the players parents that were deceased were watching tonight so let's not let them down and this one was for Sonny who gives his all for us, let's not let him down either. The chant outside in the stands was Sonny, Sonny, Sonny, Sonny until the entire stadium was chanting Sonny it was really exciting to be at the stadium and be a part of this special moment, the team wanted to get the game underway and were lucky enough to win the toss and elected to receive. This was it, there wasn't any changing the plans now everything was in place. The plays were pre called and they were going to play off the single wing.

When they went out on the field they weren't the same team that was in practice, they were deceitful so to lure them into the wrong defense and be able to run and pass as they choose. The receivers were told to start off slow and then take off like a rabbit and get a couple of steps on the defense. The kick off was something to see the Oriels ran the ball back forty yards and started their play on the thirty eight yard line. Sonny ran on to the field and the team knew what was coming next, for the next five or six plays without a huddle. The first play was a fake pass and a flip hand off to one of the backs who picked up twelve yards. The fans are howling for more and the chant Sonny is picking up again and getting louder and louder. The second play was meant to be a score play where Sonny fakes a handoff and tosses it to the receiver coming across the center of the field. It worked down to the four yard line, so now it's first and four and Sonny called for a double fake handoff and he would keep it and go in for the score. It worked and they scored in three plays so now the other side in shambles.

By half time the score was 21 to 0 and the other team was walking off the field with their heads down, the oriels locker room was quiet, they knew there was still more to do. Coach Warner asked Sonny if he minded if they put his backup in to see how he can do and Sonny said he didn't mind at all. They let the backup quarterback play for a quarter and the other team only scored seven points. Sonny was going back in for the fourth quarter and the other side was going to see some crazy ball handling. He was playing left handed and he put on a clinic on passing that the fans won't forget for a long time. The scouts for the colleges were there and they were writing up some strong reports about Sonny that will open a lot of doors.

The game ended 42 to 7 with Sonny having four touchdowns, the coaching staff was elated for the win and the other coach never came out on the field to congratulate Coach Warner. The reporters picked up on that and will tear him up for not having the sportsmanship to come out at mid field and congratulating Coach Warner. He would eventually be let go by the school for not showing good leadership and setting a bad example to his players under these hard circumstances. Marie was waiting outside the school gym parking lot for Sonny, it was almost an hour before he came out and she wanted to express to Sonny how much she loved him. Sonny was a very lucky guy that night because she expressed her love for him in many ways and for the longest time. Sonny thought that life with her was going to be good and knew some day they would get married and share a life together. They were overdue getting back to the home and they sat out on the porch with cheeseburgers and fries that the ladies in the kitchen left for them. The *newspapers were really giving Sonny a huge write up that led the colleges to come after him in droves.*

He asked Coach Warner to sit in on the recruiting seeing as how he hadn't any experience in that field before. He was happy to do so and they would meet at the home where Sonny grew up and give them a flavor of who they are dealing with. These recruiters would have mixed feelings after seeing Sonny at the home being a poor orphan and all that. The school that wanted him the most would have to be the school that would have to give up the most. It looked like it was a tossup between Penn State and Florida State, Sonny wanted to play on the golf team as well so he would end up choosing Florida State. There was a hurdle that FL State was having trouble with and that was that they had to give a full scholarship to Marie or he would go somewhere else. Coach Warner came back to Sonny and said they wouldn't do it and Sonny stood up and looked them in the eye and told them when he leaves this room he will never play for them, ever. They were looking at their notes and Sonny walked out of the room with Coach Warner and heard the door close and reopen quickly the recruiters ask Sonny to come back and Sonny told them that it was too late for them that they made their decision and they were pre warned what was going to happen.

They asked the coach to intervene and help them out and he told them that they should have picked up on his vibes and could clearly see that Sonny and Marie were deeply in love and they were not going to be separated. The coach told them that they have just lost the best quarterback in the country and an excellent golfer with three state titles. Now if that is not enough, you just lost a woman's state golf champion and both of them have their grades up to better then a 4 point average. He wanted to know where their thinking was, they said it must have not been there because they have just made the biggest mistake in their careers if they still have a career. They asked the coach to bring Sonny back to hear all that the school was going to do for both of them. He told them he would try but Sonny is a very head strong person and when he makes up his mind that's it, over and done, end of the situation. It took the coach almost an hour to get Sonny back in that room to allow the recruiters to restate their position once and for all. Sonny was not a happy person to go back in their but only did it for the coach whom he trusted a lot.

Sonny went back in and took the same seat and it was all business from this moment on. They thanked him for coming back and wanted to make him and Marie an offer that was never offered to anyone before. Sonny just nodded with that approval like tell me more. Coach Warner was thinking how could they have this offer and not offer it to Sonny before he walked out and now that he proved that he would leave they changed their minds and make the offer that was approved to offer Sonny.

"Ok Sonny here goes and we will put it in writing Coach. We will give you and Marie a full scholarship with no strings attached, no pay backs, no grades attachments for you and Marie single quarters with no roommates in separate buildings, fully furnished with a computer and TV and DVD player. You will be required to work an hour on the weekends and we will in turn we will deposit a check for each one of you for $200.00 a week for expenses for your new Ford Mustang that will be provided for you to use the whole time you're at FL State, you and Marie. There's more, you and Marie will have your own food pass for three meals a day and we usually only offer two meals. We will also pay your on line computer hook up and any school expense such as books or any passes you might need to go to the basketball games or any other games. If you are able to make the golf teams we will clothe you and supply you with all the new golf balls you might need for the entire stay here at FL State. I assume you have your own golf clubs and if you would like to change set we will take care of that too."

Sonny looked at the coach and he asked them if they could be alone for a few minutes and they said yes because they knew that was the best package ever given to anyone or in this case two students in the history of recruiting. They were together now and the coach told Sonny they must want you bad to make you such an offer. It has to be the best offer ever given to anyone. That business of working for an hour on the weekend is a giveaway. It is the only legal way they can give you money. The car is not yours it's only a vehicle for you to use, once again it's legal and that is what they need. He asked Sonny what he thought and he was speechless, but finally said all of this and they never met Marie. The coach told Sonny that they don't have to meet her they know all about her, any girl that can golf like her they know all about her and will take her and you in a package deal if need be. She is the icing in the cake and all good cakes have icing. Sonny asked Coach Warner how will they make money out of all this and his reply was they will fill the stands sell more hot dogs and anything else plus sell the TV rights to some local or national TV station to broadcast all the home games. He told Sonny they will make hundreds and hundreds of millions of dollars over the next four years, yours is a pitons to all that.

The recruiters told Sonny that they will need some papers filled out and signed by him and Marie and they will contact him for the signatures when the time comes. They also would want the coach present as well; he would be a witness on behalf of Sonny and Marie. Sonny asked the coach what guarantees do they have that Fl. State can't back out of this before the required signatures. Mr. Warner told Sonny that he would get a letter of intent signed before they left. Promising Sonny and Marie all the things that were promised to them could not be reversed. They will be guaranteed in writing all the conditions discussed earlier. Sonny and Mr. Warner left the room and were very happy about the contract and Sonny couldn't wait to tell Marie who was waiting back at the home for him to return with the news. Sonny sat with her on the porch and was happy that they will be together for the rest of their lives.

With the final game of the season coming up and the pressure is on, there are so many people wanting to be at the final game that they were sold out now for two months. Sonny has already gotten his scholarship and could sit this one out. He would never do that and the fans would not understand that decision. Sonny was ready and has spent a lot of time with his coaches to win his final game that he will play for his high school. Marie will be on the field as well as a cheerleader, she has grown into a real beauty and the two of them make a great couple.

Pat wanted to meet with both of them a week after the game for a long talk about their future at the home. This was going to be a very important meeting and they will probably be set free from all ties from the state and the home and they will be definitely on their own. Sonny didn't expect that this might happen to them; they have never given this any thought, but will soon be given what is inevitable and they know they can trust Pat.

14

*T*he last game was so big that the city of Baltimore has never seen a high school game like this one before. Sonny played the whole game and scored four touchdowns, he was carried off the field by his team mate's right to the waiting arms of his favorite fan. Marie, Marie was all over him and didn't care who saw her she loved him and couldn't help showing it. She wanted to be with Sonny but they didn't have anywhere to go or any money to go there. Sonny knew that was going to change as soon as they check in to their new home in Florida in the fall. There was some time to go before that. It was time to meet with Pat and see what she wanted to discuss with Sonny and Marie. Pat's secretary told Pat they were here and Pat came out to get them.

They walked into Pat's office and were a little apprehensive but Pat put them right at ease. They really liked her and trusted her and her decisions that she has made on their behalf over the years were real good for them.

"Soon it was going to be time to move on and not only were you going to graduate from high school you both were going to graduate from the home and no longer will you two have that stigma over your heads. You both will be going out to the real world where you have made your way without any help from anyone and you did it with your skills. You didn't sit around without any goals and hope someone was going to help you out. I am very proud of you two and I know that you will be very successful. You have worked out a beautiful scholarship and should have anything you need."

Now I want to discuss with you two what the responsibility of the state is once you leave here for your new school. Once you leave here the state no longer has any responsibility for you two. Because of you Sonny this home has millions in the bank from donations that were made from all over the world when they read about you and you living without any parents here at the home and still able to play sports good and get good grades. I am going to put in the bank for you two to share equally $28,000. for you two to *live on at your new residence in Florida. If you are thrifty you should not have any problems. You will be having an income of $400.00 a week. That should cover your expenses. When you leave here in July the money will be transferred to an account that you choose for easy access for the both of you."*

"They are giving us $200.00 a week to live on so we won't need that $28,000 that you're going to give us"

"You know Sonny only you can be that honest to refuse our $28,000 gift because you're each getting $200.00 a week from the school. You are about the most honest person that I have ever met. All the money that has been spent at the home because of you Sonny is staggering."

"I just played a game and kept myself busy."

"I know that, but you did it in such a way that a lot of what was brought into the home came from you just playing a game as you say. You can be proud of it and we are proud of you for doing it. This home is the only home you can remember that you ever had and Marie that goes for you as well. You will always think back about this place and all the memories you'll have that will last you a long time."

Pat handed them each a 3x5 card with all the info they would need to contact her or where their money is and things like that. There was about six months to go before they would leave for college they would still have plenty of time left at the home. It was somewhat boring waiting to embark on a new life far away from here. There wouldn't be anything in Florida that would closely resemble Baltimore, even the insects were different. Marie was more excited than Sonny was because this would be the first time she could be alone with him and they would both need each other more than ever. Whereas the home was their shelter now it will be the college but not in a family way, it would be more like business.

Right after they graduated from High School a letter came to Sonny and Marie giving them a schedule and a time to report and a time for Sonny to report for football tryouts. Marie's reporting date was different from Sonny's so they decided to use some of the money and get a room at the hotel down town until their dorms were ready to move into. Sonny did call and request his car to be parked in front of the hotel where they would be staying temporary until they could move in on campus. They did a little shopping for clothes before they left and Pat had set up a Farwell party for the two of them that she wanted everyone to attend, including his old coach Mr. Warner. There wasn't any booze just soda's and juice but everyone was happy and sad to see them leave, still the room was electrifying.

Sonny was looking at Mr. Warner when he saw Babe walk into the room he didn't believe that he would ever see him again. They ran to each other and gave each other a big bear hug Marie ran over as well, it was quite an occasion. Sonny asked Babe what he was doing and he said he was making engineering models.

"You mean like toys."

"No not toys, they use them to build their factories hoping I would find the problems in the model instead of on the real thing."

"How interesting that must be."

"I look forward coming to work every morning."

"How was your tour of duty in the Air Force?"

"It wasn't like being at home but it was good for me."

"What did you do in the service?"

"I was in the Air Police."

"You were a policeman that must have been awfully exciting."

"It was and four years was exciting enough."

"Now what are you up to?"

"Marie and I have scholarships at Fl. State and will be leaving in two days; I have to report for football try outs and all that stuff."

"That is a different kind of football in college; they play a little more intensely. Stay in shape and stay healthy."

Babe said he had to go and wished them both good luck and walked out of the room and never looking back, Mr. Warner gave Sonny his card and said to call the number on the card if he should need help, that he would come to his aid as fast as he could. They hugged each other and he walked away wiping his eye when he had his back turned away from Sonny. Now Pat was making her way towards Sonny who was crying a little and was hugging Marie and she told Sonny she could still remember seeing them for the first time and how sorry she felt for them and now she can see that their stay at the home was a good thing and hoped they felt the same way.

They told her they did appreciate the State looking after them and made sure they would never let them down. We both didn't realize that there was a stigma that came from living at the home, not on their part but by the people living outside the home. We were able to overcome all that stuff and stay focused on what was important to us and the home. He went on to tell Pat that it wasn't there choice to be placed in the home, at the time it was the best thing that could be done for them and it turns out that it was the right thing to do.

Sonny and Marie left very early in the morning so as not to cause any commotion between them and the younger children. They were on their own now and the meaning of it hasn't hit them yet. They were too busy loving the feeling they had for each other that could easily overcome any little problem that could creep up. The car rental company gave them the rental for three times the normal price because they were only eighteen. He knew Sonny and he knew he was reporting to his new school in Fl. and got permission from all the way up. They stopped for lunch and held hands the whole time they sat there, they had been through so much together and now it was their time to enjoy the moment. They decided to stop and get a nice room around 5 o'clock. There were plenty of places to choose from so they picked the holiday inn; they even had a small restaurant so they wouldn't have to leave for anything once they check in

They were both tired from their drive but after their shower they got a second wind. Sonny could see that Marie had a sculptured body that could only make Sonny a very happy man. She was all his and for all his needs to be fulfilled. Being together like this was going to be good for their relationship; Marie wasn't inhibited and walked around sometimes naked and sometimes in a robe. They both wanted to stop at some outlets and each get a wardrobe so they wouldn't look like where they came from. They had the money and needed the clothes. They never bought clothes for themselves so it was going to be an experience.

The next morning they came across some outlets in Savannah and decided to pull in and have a look see. Every store they went in they bought something, it was fun and Marie remarked to Sonny she could get use to this. Sonny was smart enough to make sure not to draw any attention to themselves; they put the clothes in the trunk of the rented car and went on their way. The college was in Gainesville Fl. so they kept an eye out for the signs that would tell them how far away they were seeing as how they never did this before they were extra cautious not to miss any signs. They knew they were getting close to Gainesville because there were plenty of billboards reminding everyone where they were and who the FL Gators were.

They decided to stay in a motel outside of the campus this evening because it was Sunday and no use in trying to find something open on campus on the weekend. They carried in their new clothes and were very conscience of being alone out in the world on their own for the first time and they didn't want any trouble or get robbed of any of the money they were carrying until they could get to a local bank on Monday. They decided on a joint checking and savings account after all the money belonged to both of them.

They were doing real good being on there own for the first time. They didn't go to any bars or bring some liquor back to their room and drink and raise hell. They weren't that kind of people and didn't want that kind of lifestyle. Marie would hold Sonny in her arms all night just to have Sonny as close to her as was humanly possible. She knew that holding Sonny so close to her was going to go to a higher level and he would want more than just holding her. She was hoping that he would roll her over and give her a good pounding that would put them both to sleep for the evening Marie was taking the pill so she wouldn't get pregnant It was too soon to have his babies and knew there would be plenty of time to raise a family. Sonny was in full agreement.

The next morning they decided to drive on campus and check in with administrations and see what was in store for them. When they walked in all the heads in the place looked up at the same time, they were expecting them and one of them wanted to be the one to sign them in. Sonny gave this young woman their names, Anna was hers and she immediately looked in the file and found them together. She pulled out their folders and took a minute to review it. When she finished she looked up and said welcome to the Uni. of Fl.

Sonny said they were glad to be here after a couple days drive. Anna asked them where they drove from and Sonny told her Baltimore. Md. She said that she has a brother there working at the airport (BWI) He told her he knew where it was and how nice of an airport it is. Sonny couldn't wait for her to say something about the mustang, so he brought it up and she told him she would get to that in due time. She wanted to get to the crux of their scholarship and move on to other things. She gave them their food passes and she told them it was strictly theirs and nobody else's everything that you do here will be scrutinized. Your scholarship package is very expensive; in fact I've never seen one like it. Everybody that is somebody on campus knows who you two are, you won't know it but they will.

The dorms are for the assigned students and not to be used as a place to meet and have sex and shack up with their friends. There are plenty of places off campus to get a room. Now let's talk about your job here at the college where you and Marie earn $200.00 a week. You will be expected to show up here every Thursday and dust down the offices for one hour and you money will be deposited in to the account you give us every Friday. This will end on

June 1st and start back up on Sept 1st. Now about your mustang that you will be using as long as you are a student here at the school, you will be expected to keep it in showroom condition. We have plenty of ins. on it with a $250 ded coll. and $100 ded comp. We don't want you to loan your car to anyone under no circumstances. You can lose your use of this car one by getting a DUI or using the car in a convicted felony. Anna had them sign a lot of papers and told them to take the tour that goes twice a day and meets at the cafeteria at 10 am sharp and 2 pm sharp.

Anna reminded Sonny that he was to report at the football gym at 7: am tomorrow morning for what was to be his try outs for the football team. Sonny knew that no one expected him to get the starting position but they did expect him to be heads above all the others. He and Marie turned their rental car in and started using their mustang. They stayed in their motel off campus for the last evening and really made a night of it; Sonny knew he would need all the energy he could muster up to get through his first day. Marie was always with him in his heart and could easily call on her in spirit to give him the energy he needed to go forward.

Sonny sat on the bench in the locker room suiting up when he heard someone ask him was he Sonny Harris? He turned to see who was asking him who he was and saw this very distinguished man with a nice looking shirt that said Coach Shaw. He reached for Sonny's hand and said, "He was the head football coach."

"I am very pleased to meet you Coach Shaw I must confess I haven't heard of you."

"That's ok son you will before you graduate from this wonderful school. I've been looking over your rather thick book that somebody has made up on you and it has taken me a long time to finish it. You grew up in a home that was sponsored by the state. No parents to speak of, but a whole lot of talent on the football field and an equal amount on the golf course as well. You're not even the starting quarter back and have a scholarship better than our starting QB Jeff Pabst. He's good and you will have a hard time taking over that spot."

"I plan on giving you my best every day and we shall see what the outcome is."

"That's what I like, spunk and a desire to lead and win. Who is Marie? How did she get such a good scholarship?"

"Marie is my child hood sweetheart and goes where I go. She's part of the deal or there is no deal."

"*Try to understand me Sonny your deal has already been made and I don't have any plans towards it.*"

"*Good because that is the one thing that is not going to be changed. We will never be separated.*"

"*Can she interfere with your football goals?*"

"*Only if anyone here that would like to flex their mussel to me in an unfair manner. I think it would be fair to say that if someone were out to get me or Marie it would be a career move, I promise you.*"

"*I'm sorry we have taken up this conversation, so let's forget it and move on. You have won most of your games since you were eight years old. You've won every championship you ever played in. You can throw the football with either hand and with the same accuracy. You are definitely going to give our starting QB a run for his money. He knows it and will be extra sharp like you will be. I'll see you on the field.*"

When Sonny walked on the field everything stopped and one of the coaches walked over to him and told him to take three laps for starters, he was probably a touch late and when the coach saw him running and asked the coach why was Sonny running the track they said he was one minute late. Coach Shaw told them that they were talking in the locker room and we both were late. He wanted to know whose decision was it to flex their muscles on this new player, the asst. coach put his hand up and Coach Shaw told him to give him 16 laps or resign now. You are too anxious to hurt someone that you couldn't even shine his shoes. Let this be a lesion to you be careful who you pick on because you might be opening up something that could hurt this school for a long time.

When Sonny finished his three laps the Coach called him over and apologized to him for that strict enforcement of the late rule that wasn't Sonny's fault for being late. They were talking in the locker room and that is what caused that. Plus you had no idea of a late rule. I had the overzealous coach give me a few laps to calm him down to our level. Everyone was gathering on the field for calisthenics that would take forty five minutes and then they would take a twenty minute break and drink plenty of water.

There were different places around the field that had signs that told what position they were trying out for. The QB had about six to eight players standing around looking pretty and waiting for someone to tell them what to do. Coach Shaw lined them up and told them he wanted to see how fast they could run. Sonny came in second and Jeff came in first. Coach Shaw asked Jeff if he could do some long passes, he threw about twelve very long and very *accurate ones. He went through the whole bunch and finally called on Sonny to do the same, he threw twelve very beautiful passed right on the money. The rest of the spots on the field were very busy with the centers to linemen and so on. By the end of the first day everyone was bushed. The coach that ran the twelve laps apologized to Sonny and Sonny told him it was ok.*

The shower really felt good and Sonny was hoping that Marie would be outside to take him to his dorm or go for dinner. As luck would have it she was waiting and they kissed and Sonny asked Marie if she would like to eat now, she was hungry and they headed for the cafeteria. She reminded Sonny that classes don't start for a few weeks yet. Try outs for the cheerleaders starts in a week and she wants to see if she can make it. Marie took Sonny to her room to show him how good it looks, like the contract says she will be living alone and so was Sonny. They know they will be cautious at first and they both know that one of these days they will lock the doors and get it on.

Sonny told Marie that he had to be on the field by 8: am sharp or do three laps. She laughed and got the hint that Sonny wanted to go to bed and rest for a big day tomorrow. They smooch a little back in Sonny's room and Sonny had his hands all over her, that she wanted but he wanted to rest. Marie experienced all of this before this was not her first football try out. Sonny slept real good and met Marie in the cafeteria at 7: am for breakfast and it was really enjoyable for them both to be together for a short time. Sonny wanted Marie to take him to the gym thirty minutes early so he could be suited up and ready to go five minutes before he was supposed to.

When he ran onto the field he spotted the overzealous coach and said, "Let's take a couple of laps to warm up." The coach thought that was nice and said lets go. Sonny was forming a friendship with him that would last for years. His name was Eddie Kautz and Eddie had never met a nicer guy. The calisthenics were rough and again they all looked forward to their twenty minute break with plenty of liquids. The QB's were called to a secluded part of the field where Coach Shaw wanted to see more of Sonny so he called over one of the receivers and asked Sonny to throw him six passes at different parts of the field. They were all good and then asked Sonny to do the same pass routes and throw left handed. Somehow the other players stopped to watch this exhibition, it was something they never saw a QB throwing the football with such accuracy from either hand.

Coach Shaw didn't want his starting QB to be demoralized so he had him throw some passes and hopefully that defused the whole moment. Soon the offence and defense lines would be formed and they could start scrimmaging and working on the plays that had to be learned by whoever is going to start the opening game. Jeff had the experience while Sonny had the edge on ability. There were two offensive lines and sonny practiced with the backup offensive linemen. Sonny looked so good with those back up linemen the coaches caught themselves watching when they should have been looking somewhere else. Sonny had a way of hiding the football that made it very hard for the defensive linemen to follow. Coach Shaw was going to keep three QB's hoping that was all he would need.

Coach Shaw asked Sonny to study and know all the plays by heart incase Jeff would get hurt.

"Does that mean that Jeff is going to be the starting QB?"

Coach Shaw said, "Yes he probably would start and if he is not up to snuff you're going in to relieve him of his responsibility."

"Believe me Coach I'm not complaining after all he has the experience and that counts too."

"That's the right way to feel Sonny, your head is clear, we don't get to see anyone as unselfish as you are."

The practice went well and Marie was waiting for Sonny in the parking lot, she was very quiet and never said a word all the way to the cafeteria. That didn't last long because she broke down crying at the table and Sonny held her hand and asked her what was wrong?

"I'm bored and I don't have anything to do."

"Why don't you go to the library or find the golf course that lets the golf team players play on and play and meet some girls."

"I want to play golf with you."

"Well that's out of the question right now, I have to honor my scholarship I did sign a contract just like you did. We have the best scholarship ever given by any school legally. After we finish our dinner I want to take you back to your dorm and make love to you for a long time."

"You think that is going to make me feel better."

"Well if it doesn't then we are wasting our time with each other. If I can't cheer you up then nothing can."

"Stop talking like that, can't a girl want her man and think that she is bored when she is having anxieties. We have never been alone like this before and I want all I can get from it."

"That's fine for you to think that way but I have to be strong enough to please you, the school, the coaches and myself and never have a letdown."

"Sonny that's why I love you so much, you are strong and I can count on you to be there for me and give me the right answers for my self-induced problem."

"Marie you will have to promise me that you are going to toughen up and help me get through these hard times for me as well."

"When you find something to do please keep me in mind now that you have set a president in picking me up after practice and things like that, please don't leave me stranded and tell me that this is what happens when you told me to find something to do. Please don't do that to me, because I will react in such a way that will not make you a very happy camper."

"I would never do anything like that Sonny, I love you too much."

"Good because I love you as well and would be very hurt if that should happen. Now do you want me to take you back to your dorm or do you want to drop me off at mine."

"Don't be silly Sonny I want you, why do you think I'm in such a state wanting you so much. A woman can only be so aggressive."

Needless to say the evening went great and Marie was back to her old self again. Sonny stayed until 9 o'clock and crashed when he got back to his room, he just knew that tomorrow was going to be tough. Sonny had all the plays memorized and felt he could call a game. He might just have to tomorrow.

They arrived on the field and Coach Shaw had Jeff take the team down the field and score anyway he could. He kept it up for almost an hour when he called them off the field and called for Sonny to come on with his 2ⁿᵈ team and told Sonny to do the same as Jeff did. He was to score as much as he could. Well it was something to see, the ball handling was professional the passing was great even the left hand passing left the defense standing there with their jocks hanging off. The assistant coaches were amazed at this kid ball handling not to mention his scrambling when he had to.

It was time to break for lunch and Sonny was very hungry he didn't get enough to eat last night. The coaches sat by themselves and the players sat with the players they were practicing with which left the three QB's sitting at the same table. Jeff respected Sonny a lot and it showed when they talked, he knew that Sonny was a perfect gentleman capable of tearing you to bits on the football field and yet off the field he was very humble and even quiet. He was hoping to get a degree in marketing that is what turned him on the most.

The afternoon was hot and they worked on no huddle plays for the rest of the day this was going to throw off the defenses of the other teams and not allow the right defensive guys on the field. Once you get it working right it would be hard to win a game when the oposing QB doesn't call the plays in the huddle. Both QB's were being watched intently to see who could do it the best and it turns out that they were both good at it. Sonny was very comfortable playing QB and no matter how hard they would rush him he could still throw the ball with either hand. When the fans see this for the first time the place is going to go crazy.

Marie met Sonny as usual and said that she thinks that she has made the cheerleading team, but won't know for a few more days. Sonny was happy for her and said he was having almost the same problem. He knows that he's made the team he just doesn't know if he will be the starting QB. He feels with the experience that Jeff has that he should probably be the starter and Sonny can learn a lot watching and maybe getting in for a short time in some of games. No one has made any announcements who was playing what and who was going to be the starting QB. Usually by this time in the tryouts there would be some announcements.

This time when Sonny met Marie for dinner she was so excited and couldn't wait to tell Sonny that she had made the team and gets her uniforms tomorrow for a private fitting in the girl's locker room. She was told that the cheerleaders couldn't be seen talking to any of the players during the game. She told the cheerleading coach that her boyfriend and her have joint scholarships and some of the wording might trump what she is saying. She told Marie that she would look into it and get back to her, but in the meantime follow the rules. Marie told her that just because I have a boyfriend on the team doesn't mean that we would be talking during the game.

It was only a few days later that they announced who were the starting players in all the positions and Sonny was to be the backup QB. That was fine with him he knew he could take over in a very short notice and feel comfortable leading the team. The pressure building up to the first game were almost unbearable, their opening game was at home and with the Citadel. It was a night game and one game they had to win. Marie modeled her cheerleading outfits for Sonny and he couldn't take much of that so he caught her in between changes and made an evening of it. Marie was always happy to know that she could still turn her man on. They have been together for ten years and no one was going to separate them. The powers to be at the school knew it and other people were starting to get the picture. Leave them alone, they have a different scholarship from the others.

Let's face it the coaches couldn't replace Jeff as the starting GB he would have to play below the standards of Sonny and then they could pull him out of the game and replace him with Sonny. What a clever way of changing starters, there could be no bitching because Jeff would have done it, not the coaches. There were giant reminders all around for everyone to come to the opening pep rally and give their team the recognition they deserve to win this opener. Sonny was very nervous with all the hype that was going on about this game and that it is a must win and it was a night game being televised on national television. It's hard to believe how Sonny was not that well known on the college circuit. The fact that he was such a good QB was not that known and passing with either hand with the same accuracy was definitely unheard of, if he should get in that opening game he will be on every television in the country including the eleven o'clock news. Sonny didn't know that he was going to be so popular, but under certain circumstance he was going to be.

The night before the game Sonny went over the entire play book just in case he would be put in. There were too many people counting on him to take over in a game as the new leader and lead the players to victory. It was hard not being with Marie this evening but he explain it to her how important it was for him to be ready, he told her that this was the first time that he ever played back up to anyone. He felt comfortable with it because he was going to learn how important it was to be #2 before he could be good at #1.

15

Jenny never looked better turning thirty then most women looked turning twenty working out was good for her two days a week can't hurt. She loved to walk every morning and always carried her gun in her specially made belly bag, just in case. She felt like she owed it to Chris not to have another tragedy that could be avoided. She was happy working on the computer for a degree in investment management; short for "stock market broker" she wanted to finish her course when Christine graduated from high school. Jenny was a very good looking woman and wouldn't have any trouble closing a sale especially if it was taking place in person. She had planned to have her picture on her business card. Jenny paid extra to have a guidance counselor help her with her courses and steer her in the right direction to break in to a very lucrative occupation. Her counselor's name was Jean Wood and they got along real good probably because Jean was a single mother as well.

Christine was 11 now and full of energy and wanted to play golf all she could. She would show up at the golf course and hit a bucket of balls and putt until she found someone that wanted to play with her. There were times that her mother would go out with her. The boys at the club were from good stock but were never the less boys. Let's just say they were everything including Rude and disrespectful. It definitely was a good test for Chris to find someone that wasn't so disrespectful. One day at the range Brad came by and asked Chris is she going to play today and Chris said she was and asked him, was he? He said he was and did she want to join up and play. He told her he would be at the putting green when she was ready. Brad knew that playing with Chris would help him in his shyness around girls. Four hours with Chris would have to help. It was only when one boy was with another the rudeness and ignorance and all that surfaced, it was almost like who could be the most ignorant. You might think that the better looking the girl the less ignorance they would be. No they were just as bad even if they were playing with miss ugly USA.

There were a lot of boys that didn't want to play golf with any girls; they made sure they didn't get caught in a situation that would have them paired up with girls. Any girl that could survive playing golf with these ignorant boys for a summer could play in any environment and be very successful. Some of these boys were fifteen and would whip out their Johnson and piss behind a bush that didn't leave much to anyone's imagination. There was no use in Chris complaining to anyone because it would only get worse and no one would have anything to do with her after that. Chris was hesitant to telling her mother as well about all the ignorant things the boys were doing and saying to her. She knows her mother would loose her cool and confront these guys about their attitudes.

The pro didn't know that this was going on among the juniors at his club and if he did there would be hell to pay. He was making sure that anyone that played 18 holes had to post their score for a valid handicap. Like the sign says in both locker rooms, all rounds have to be posted, anyone caught not posting their score within 24 hours after they shot it would be stripped of their handicap and have to play scratch meaning they wouldn't get any help in playing the better golfers. It's not strict it's the only way it can be kept fair and honest. Chris knew that all the tournaments at the club are handicap tournaments.

Jenny's golf game was improving and her and Chris were becoming the partners to beat and they would enter all the tournaments at the club. Jenny was a 12 handicapper and Chris was a 14. They both were improving almost every round and were the talk of the club. They looked like sisters and not mother and daughter. They dressed very stylish and had no trouble keeping up with the rest of the members in fact the members had to keep up to them. Mark the pro and his wife Cathy were very good to them and very good to all the juniors. Mark would give Chris a lesson almost every day and had her putting at least thirty minutes a day as well.

Jenny was still turning down the single men for dates; she couldn't handle a boyfriend and a very active daughter at this point in her life. Her school work on the computer was very interesting and she loved the math side of it. She could see that she has picked the career that she would love a lot. Jenny wants to take Chris to the gun range and improve their shooting so that they feel comfortable handling their pistol and knowing how to load the clips. The instructor at the gun range told them that most shootings take place within

8 ft. so he had them practice at the 8 ft. distance and do three rounds rapid fire until they felt comfortable doing it. He had them practicing rapid reloads dropping the clip and reloading as fast as they can. He introduced them to a shoulder holster and a belly bag that is made to carry a concealed weapon that looks like those belly bags that people use to carry their money or things like that in. He wants them to feel comfortable in drawing their weapons and using it without any second thoughts. He would tell them to practice the need to pull the weapon and when that need arises they will be able to do it like they practiced.

Jenny has her Concealed Deadly Weapon permit and wants Chris to get hers when she is old enough. Jenny loved going to the gun range and so did Chris, to them it's a necessary evil and being a woman, having a gun is an equalizer for them. God help any man who approaches them who doesn't have good intentions. Jenny was looking to buy another Glock 9 mm they were easy to take care of and easy to fire seeing as how it was almost totally plastic it was light for a woman to carry and if necessary she could put it in her handbag or even put it in her jeans pocket. The cost of the ammo was very cheap and affordable. Jenny likes the little kick that comes from the 9 mm baby Glock that allows her to recover for a second shot quickly, that's important for a person firing a pistol when their life is in danger.

Jenny made sure that the home Mrs. Topkis left her has all the latest kitchen additions and bathroom updates as well as all the latest appliances. The house was an easy one to keep clean. Jenny asked Chris if she would like to go to Arizona for ten days. Chris said she would love it. Jenny let the travel agent set it up and she got the set up in Phoenix Arizona staying at the camel back inn. They both were excited and were counting the days before they left.

The morning of the flight, they were at the Phil airport at 7: am in the morning for their 9 o'clock departure. With a small layover they arrived at the phoenix airport at 1:10 pm their time. It was different with all the Indian artwork. They caught the hotel shuttle and were standing at the hotel check in desk in one hour. Jenny knew this was a four star hotel and they had a room on the edge of the desert and a golf cart to bring them back to the pool and dining rooms instead of walking in that heat. The clerk drove them to their hotel room that was a two bedroom Spanish style building at the end of the desert with cactus everywhere. When they saw the inside they both gulped when they saw how nice it is. They even had a fire place for those chilly nights to take the chill off the inside. Their beds were high and they needed a step stool just to climb in. They both had their own shower and bath rooms.

The decorator really did a beautiful job and Jenny could see that no cost was spared.

They wanted to go back to the hotel and have dinner in the dining room just off the pool and desert. Jenny drove they felt good driving their golf cart through the desert air after their shower. They were seated by a big window and were asked if they wanted something to drink, they ordered two ice teas with extra ice. The dinner took hours and they could hardly move after finishing up with their desert of apple pie and vanilla ice cream. Chris couldn't be any happier; they talked about what they wanted to do. They wanted to visit an old western town, play golf at the camel back c.c. They wanted to take some dune buggy rides in the desert with their own experienced drivers. They wanted to have supper in a chuck wagon experience high in the mountains with real cowboys and a Hollywood shoot out. They wanted a helicopter rental for a two hour tour of the Grand Canyon and visit an Indian reservation. Spend a few days at the pool and play a second round of golf at the local PGA golf course. This was a large order and one that Jenny knew they could afford with no problem.

They stopped at the travel desk to get this started. They wanted to rent a car for a few days, the days they didn't have anything planned. It took a while but the agent set up everything for them. The next morning she had them set up for the desert dune buggy rides with professional drivers all day and their lunches were in the coolers on the back of the buggy. The next morning couldn't come soon enough for them; they had their breakfast alongside of the pool out on the pool deck and wanted to wait out front for their van to pick them up. They both had sun block on, hats and a wind breaker when the van pulled into the starting point the outside thermometer read 102 degrees Jenny told Chris she was glad they are prepared for this hot day.

They stepped from the van and were immediately greeted by what looked like the two drivers that were clean and had on safari clothing that really made them look the part. They shook hands and were led into this building where they would receive so instructions on what to expect and what not to expect. Joe told them that they will be going as fast as they could safely go and that they would sometimes be ten feet in the air. He went on to tell them that at the speeds they will be going they could turn over but the buggy's were designed to take the roll and no one would get hurt as long as their arms were inside the buggy holding on to the hand grips. Joe showed them where they would be going on the map; they had to Ronda view with their fuel station that was no more than a little four foot box where their refuel would be.

He showed them where they would break for lunch near one of the famous monuments; Jenny had her camera and was going to take a lot of pictures. He told them they might be scared at first but that would change fast when they saw that everything was safe. Chris liked her driver; he called himself Shank and wanted her to feel free to call him Shank. The two girls were really excited and were ready, Joe asked the girls if they had to go to the last toilet in the next sixty miles. They both ran real quick and when they returned and strapped themselves in and took off like the buggy was on fire. Thank god they were given goggles to protect their eyes because they would need it. There was plenty of sand in the air the drivers made sure not to get behind each other and no closer than a hundred yards because of the sand that their buggies would throw up in the air.

Jenny didn't have time to look for Chris she was too busy hanging on for dear life. Their buggy's would sail over the dunes and be air born for a few seconds that would give the girls butterflies in their stomachs. They rode through shallow creeks and the water was everywhere and their buggies were right in the middle of it. The drivers would give out their cat yells that added to the flavor of the ride. This was far more then what Jenny expected from this ride and was overwhelmed with excitement. When they got on to the real hard compacted roads their drivers would take the curves on two wheels. Jenny would let out some screams to really get in to it and Chris could hear her and it was contageous and scream as well.

This by far was the best time they ever had together and never wanted it to end. Their helmets had speakers in them and the drivers would talk to them throughout their journey. The two girls could talk to each other as well; they would point out all the movies that were filmed where they were. The two drivers would talk to each other and were planning where to stop for lunch. The time there was radio silence the girls knew that something big was going to happen. Joe picked his favorite spot under a very high cliff. Their view was breath taking and Jenny couldn't help but see that their drivers were carrying guns and when Jenny asked why, they said it was to protect them from the rattle snakes. She told them she hopes they were good shots and Joe's reply was let's hope they don't meet up with any rattlers.

Their lunch was fantastic; it was the combination of the food and the view. Jenny knew that this was going to be just a taste of what was in store for them this vacation and this would be hard to beat. Food has never tasted better to either of them. The chicken and barbecued pork and beef ribs were never better. The cold ice tea was never colder and sweeter. They just sat there *after lunch just sucking in the view and the drivers had themselves a good smoke. Joe thought it was time to start the second leg of this buggy ride out in the desert where no one was. Chas told Joe that he would take the lead with Chris and he took off like lightning; he was out of sight in seconds. They kept contact on their microphones so all was good. It almost seemed like to Jenny that they wanted to turn over their buggies. They wanted to come close to flipping them but never did.*

They finally reached the refueling site and Chas was already there and refueled. He had walked away from the full containers of fuel to have a smoke while Joe refueled his buggy for their two hour ride back to the compound. Jenny knew if there was going to be some excitement it had to come somewhere on the way back. This time Joe took off and was out of sight in a matter of seconds. Chas wasn't concerned because he knew all the different routes that Joe knew back to the compound. They would ride the top of the sand ridges and scrape their bottoms that slowed them down and when the time was right they would swing a hard 90 degrees and turn down the steepest slope they could find. It was awesome for the girls to experience into what looked like a sure death plunge. It wasn't and everyone survived. There wasn't any more they could do because they had did it all and no one was hurt and arrived safely back at the compound all in one piece.

They went into the starters shack and the girl asked Jenny how she wanted to pay. Jenny said she had an Amex card. "How much was it again?"

"It was $250.00 each."

"I want to tip each driver $50.00 each so write me up for $600.00."

The cashier thanked her and there van would be ready to take them back to the hotel. They walked outside and saw the two drivers and Jenny thanked them for the ride of their life time. She told them that she left a tip with the cashier for both of them. They thanked her and said to tell a friend about us. The ride back to the hotel was boring they were used to something more exciting than this. Their golf cart was sitting where they left it and were on their way back to their hacienda for a shower and dress casual for a great dinner.

They didn't get to the dining room until after 7:30. They were starved and let the waiter know how hungry they were. He told them he has plenty of experience like this and left them for a second and came back with a sampler of food that would quiet them down for a while. They also wanted plenty of cold ice tea and would look over the menu for a meal that would top off the day. They both ordered filet mignon and just sat there looking out the big window at the desert. They weren't finished their meals until after 9 o'clock. Needless to say when they got back to the room they crashed and slept right through the evening until 7:30 the next morning.

They took their time getting ready for breakfast and arrived at the dining room just before breakfast was over. They talked about taking the rented car to the old western town and see how they lived over a hundred years ago. It was all laid out on their motor map and they were told to follow the map and you'll go right to the entrance. Jenny told Chris that they wanted to be back at the hotel showered up and ready to meet the hay ride up to the mountain top for a western cook out and gun fight by 6:30. In the mean time they walked into this old town and saw plenty of Indians sitting in chairs that were propped against the wall, just sitting there saying hello when someone said hello first.

The beer garden had swinging doors and sure enough there was Bell Star standing outside greeting everyone and inviting them in for lunch. Jenny had big plans for their dinner and told Chris that they should snack and save themselves for the big cook out tonight. They did everything that day from panning for gold to riding the old train around the outside of town along the desert where the Indian would put on a robbery and shoot um up. The sheriff was soon on their tail and chased them away at the end of the ride. The girls were having a great time and were never happier. They even shop a six shooter at a target and had their picture taken riding a bucking bronco that turned out great.

They were back at the hotel and showered off and out front of the hotel waiting for their ride up the mountain for their western cook out. Jenny could see off in a distance the wagons coming; they had so much hay in them it was spilling out over the top. Each wagon took eight people to the top wear there were some cowboys riding alongside the wagons all the way up they even stopped a few Indians trying to kidnap some people in the last wagon. Jenny and Chris were in the next to the last wagon and could see it all. Jenny was taking as many pictures as she could and still enjoy the ride. The ride was about thirty five minutes and the closer they got to the top they could start to smell the food. The food was sold as a big part of the outing and no one knowing about the big gun fight that went on during dinner.

The wagons finally got to the top and there were plenty of people to help everyone out and find them a great seat in front of this huge coral and barn and blacksmith shop. Every table had a great seat. The pace had picked up a little and the drinks were already on the table that was water, ice tea and soda. There was no liquor allowed for anyone to drink. Your waitress would ask everyone at the table who were also on the hay wagon how they wanted their steak cooked and if they wanted white potatoes or sweet potatoes and corn on the cob. There was plenty of butter and salt on each table. The crock of soup was a chopped steak soup with small potatoes and tomatoes and beans and corn. That was the best that Jenny had ever had. Chris was really taken back with all the authenticity being put into this meal.

It seemed like a fight had broken out at one of the tables down the end and you could hear someone call the other one out trying to take someone's food when they weren't looking. When the cowboy standing started to draw on the person sitting at the table someone else sitting at the table pulled his gun and shot him. Needless to say holy hell broke out and now the fight was on. Chris couldn't take her eyes off of the cowboys looking for a place to hide behind. When the sheriff rode in as he got off his horse he shot the person standing in the doorway over the barn doors and he fell forward and landed in the hay wagon that was going in the barn. Chris and Jenny sat there and watched this shoot out that was going to last a while. Jenny still managed to eat her corn on the cob regardless. It was clear this was the shootout that they were told that would happen. Jenny patted Chris on the leg and told her that it was ok.

What an experience this turned out to be, those six shooters had smoke and a big kick every time they would shoot them. Finally at the end and when they were serving desert and tea or coffee did they introduce all the cowboys that work for some of the movie studios in Hollywood they were told that it took hours to practice all the shootings and dress the applause was deafening in fact everyone stood to show their approval. Some of the cowboys would come around to the tables and shake hands with as many people they could and it was a big delight for Chris to meet a cowboy and shake his hand. He gave Chris an empty cartridge as a souvenir. She held it tight in her hand while Jenny gave her a big hug.

Everyone was told to go back to the wagon they came up in. That took a little time but when it was all said and done they were back at the hotel by 9:45. They were never going to forget this evening, Chris said, "Just think mom we had dinner in the middle of a shootout high on a mountain top."

Jenny reminded Chris not to lose her bullet casing that the cowboy gave her. They both were beat and went right to bed and crashed again. Every day was an adventure that they would have never experienced except out in the Arizona desert. They both awoke at the same time and Jenny reminded Chris *that they had a 10: am tee time at the Camel Back C.C. They had a small breakfast and took off for the golf course. Needless to say they were waiting for them and were told to tee off right away if they wish, so they decided to put off their shopping spree in the pro shop and go to the first tee and start. The course was in great shape and they finished in just a little over three hours just in time for lunch overlooking the putting green. They both bought a nice golf shirt with their logo on it and went back to their villa for a nice afternoon nap.*

Jenny set up a helicopter ride to fly over the Grand Canyon and see all the important sights to and from. Jenny was speechless the pilot was banking practically the whole flight. There was always something to see and more pictures to take. The pilot took them down into the canyons and close to the raging water and shot straight up over a thousand feet that made the girls stomachs feel like they were on a roller coaster ride.

The next day's Indian reservation visit was very disappointing, they had junk thrown all around the outside of their houses and never tried to keep their places tidy. The gift stores were very overpriced and some of the quality just wasn't there. Their blankets were of poor quality thread that looked like rope so Jenny pulled Chris's hand to go and they left. That was one fantasy that Jenny had that was destroyed very quickly. There doesn't seem to be any help for them when they don't have any incentive to accomplish anything. With only a couple of days left they did have a reserved tee time over at the PGA course and didn't want to miss that one.

As it turns out the golf was great, at first they didn't want Chris to play because of her age. Twelve year olds can't usually play until 4 o'clock but because they were so far from home and when the pro saw Chris hitting some balls on the driving range he told Jenny that there was no problem. It was going to be impossible for him to refuse them a round of golf as pretty as Jenny looked. The two of them presented themselves as a good looking twosome that would be hard to refuse anything to. The pro met them on the eighteen green and watched them both par the hole that he applauded them for doing. He invited them for lunch and told them that he went to the Uni of De for one year and still can remember the Newark Country Club where the golf team played their matches. Everything went great and they said their goodbyes and headed back to the hotel.

They didn't have anything planned for their last day but to pack and layout and just relax around the pool. Chris was a good swimmer because Jenny wanted her to have swimming lessons and swim on the club swimming team. She was able to swim against the other golf clubs swim teams and meet a lot of people. They couldn't ask for a better flight home and arrived in Philly at 5: pm the worst time to have to drive to Delaware. The shuttle driver that picked them up was used to it and to him it was just a job.

Jenny wanted Chris to play on the golf team, the same thing held true for swimming on the swim team were true for being on the golf team. If she was good enough she could really make a name for herself. She would have to be good because if there wasn't a girl to play against at the club they had their match with, then she had to play a boy. No boy wanted to lose to a girl so the matches would be ass kicking at best. The pressure that was on the girls was even worse for the boy that would lose his match to a girl. Both Chris and Jenny were happy that Chris only had one match against some boy that wasn't that good and the team used him as a match they could afford to lose rather than Chris beat one of their good golfers and too loose in the point total when they expected to win. The boy she played, anyone could beat, so he was the sacrificial lamb. They expected to lose that match. The boy she played couldn't win no matter what but she was good enough too.

Jenny loved the fact that her home didn't have any mortgage that gave them a lot of security knowing no matter what, they would have a home to come home too. She was proud of how much she fixed it up and looked brand new inside or out. She could see Chris living there some day if it came to that.

Jenny had a tough job telling Chris about the boys in general and how these beautiful boys only wanted one thing. She had to do this without destroying it for the really decent ones; it was hard to recognize the two so she would have to be leery of them all. Chris was having a hard time wondering why were the boys so obsessed with this one thing, as long as they got their way it was good for them. This was a tough thing that Jenny had to explain to Chris she suggested the one thing that Chris could use as a rule to go by, if the pressure was so great by the boy and if he's good enough to go to bed with then they are already engaged to be married. That would be her only safe decision that she could make not to get hurt. Chris was not that long into having her first periods and now this pep rally. She was a little scared, so Jenny told her not to be scared she has a plan to go with. The boys have their plan and she has hers. Somehow Chris knew that even she didn't completely understand what her mother was saying she would take her words as a precaution.

Chris was getting some request to go to the movies and Jenny was scared of the hand holding and the innocent arm going around them and so on. Jenny would tell Chris that if she was invited to the movies then go and watch the movie. There weren't that many movies that were suitable for a girl her age to really enjoy. Jenny knew that after the first date Chris would be on the circuit and things like was she a good kisser, did you put your tongue in her mouth and did she let you touch her she would get lined up for the next guy to use and follow up on. So if there wasn't anything in it for the cock smith's then there wouldn't be anything out there on the circuit for anyone to learn from. All they could say was that she was a nice girl and to remain a nice girl was all Jenny wanted. This going to the movies was nothing compared to dating in high school, this is where the partying starts.

Jenny knew that keeping Chris's nose in golf was going to be a good thing. As crude as the boys are playing golf with Chris she wasn't going to get turned on by those slobs they were shooting themselves in the foot. She was able to see firsthand that they could be Dr Jackal and Mr. Hide when around girls. They were afraid of girls so they reverted back to the Stone Age that gave them comfort and there excuse for being so rude and ignorant. These same nice looking guys that sat with their parents in the club dining room all dressed up, were treating the girl golfers like shit out on the golf course. When Jenny and Chris would walk by some of the tables while being escorted to their table you would bet all the money you had that those young men weren't like that. Chris knew they were because she was experiencing it firsthand. You could imagine any of those guys asking Chris for a date and what she would tell them. That's what I meant when I said they were shooting themselves in the foot. There's not a young lady who experienced their raft could ever want to go out with them. They have already showed their hand, there's nothing more to see.

Jenny was happy with Chris's grades in school and knew if they should change for the worst there would be something wrong. Chris was level headed and had someone to watch the good examples that she was setting for her daughter. Jenny wanted to give Chris an allowance for doing things around the house that would help Jenny out. She would give Chris $20.00 a week to spend or save, hoping that Chris would do the right thing. It was a good test, as far as the dating goes there wasn't anything out there for the boys to go on, only that she was a nice girl and nice girls aren't any fun.

16

finally it was time for Sonny to put down the play book and get a good night sleep. Thank God they didn't have to meet until one o'clock because the kick off wasn't until seven o'clock. Sonny thought that was a long time to wait. Sonny met Marie for breakfast they went off campus where they could be alone and not be looked at like they were breaking some rules. Marie was really in love with Sonny, he was so nice to her and considerate and she would always be in on any decision that would affect their lives. He would tell her how beautiful she is and how good she looked in her cheerleading outfit showing all her stuff for all to see. She reminded him that he got to touch her stuff and the only one that has ever touched her stuff. She asked him how did that make him feel and he said you'll see after the game just how I feel about it.

They took a little ride and would soon have to get back for Sonny's to report on time on the field for some warm up and some classroom talk of what they had coming at them from the Citadel this evening. It was the general conscientious that it was going to be a tough game it would be a bigger win for them then it would be for us. They were told that a big start with a couple of touchdowns would demoralize them for the rest of the evening. Sonny looked over a Jeff and he looked bored but Sonny knew he wasn't, he was going over every play in his head. God help the team that was going to try and stop him only they didn't know it. They did a lot of their practicing in the gym and wasn't about to give them a clue what to expect after the opening kickoff. There wasn't any doubt about it the gators were planning to win big time and not to give it away before the kickoff.

Coach Shaw had the men suit up an hour before the game and sat with Jeff and Sonny and asked them if they had any questions Sonny kept quiet and let Jeff do all the talking. It was sonny's place and Sonny knew his. They both walked out with the coach and the press finally saw the QB walking with another player and when they looked up his # it wasn't even on the list of players. They started scrambling to find out who he was and finally had to leave it to the runners to go down to the coach for# 5 name and position. By the time they got back it was time for the coin toss and #5 had to be put on the back burner until it was appropriate to bring it up.

The gators won the toss and elected to receive; the Citadel players wanted blood and would soon get their chance to get some. The return came back to the 33 yard line and Now Jeff was going to fire the first shot on them. He handed the ball off to the running back and only got three yards. The next play was designed to mix them up thinking they were going to run it again. This time Jeff kept the ball and started around the right side and was hit real hard and the lineman fell on him and Jeff screamed out in pain and just lay there moaning of course they stopped the game and Coach Shaw ran on to the field along with all the doctors and it was immediately concluded that he would have to be carried off the field on a gurney and a motorized vehicle.

Coach Shaw while still on one knee looked over his shoulder and could see Sonny throwing the ball to one of the ends he was ready to go in and take over where Jeff had them. Coach Shaw didn't know what to say to Sonny so he didn't say anything. Sonny ran on to the field and told everyone in the huddle that this one is for Jeff. The television announcers were dumb founded as to who this guy was. They even apologized to the audience that they didn't know anything about him but remarked that they would before the game was over.

Sonny called a right back hand off and said on one. The ball was hiked to Sonny and he had everyone believing that he was going to run it around the right side when all of a sudden he backed passed it to a running back blindly not looking where he was when he back handed it and the running back who caught it there wasn't anyone covering the ends because Sonny put on a great fake run that put two receivers in the clear heading for the end zone the running back hit the end longest down the field and scored without any problem. The defense has never seen a play like it, every student was on their feet screaming, they didn't expect to see a play like that one and neither did the coach. When Sonny went to the side lines the coach asked Sonny where that played come from. Sonny told him that they have been practicing it now for two weeks. He asked Sonny if they had any more plays like that one and Sonny said he did.

Sonny was asking Coach Shaw how Jeff was doing and he told Sonny that all he knew was that it was a serious injury and they were developing the seriousness of it. The citadel received the ball and the runner was hit so hard he fumbled on the 15 yard line and now it was time for Sonny to take over again and wreck this team. He would call the signals in such a way that the defense thought he was saying hike and they went off sides three times and the Gators scored a touchdown on penalties. The TV announcers were calling Sonny's play calling with only the short time he was on the field the best they have seen in years. Coach Shaw asked Sonny where have you been and Sonny said he was right under his nose, you were standing to close to see. I wouldn't want to be you when they question you about your decision to start Jeff. He looked at Sonny for an answer and he didn't have one for him.

The best the Citadel could do the first half was to get within a yard of getting a first down. It was really pitiful what the gators were doing to them; let's say Sonny was doing to them. At the end of the first half the score was 24 to 0. Sonny refused all request for interviews and ran off the field with the rest of his team mates as a show of unity. The locker room was hectic and it was Coach Shaw's job to get them quieted down. He wanted to tell them the extent of Jeff's injuries and told the men that he would be out for the season. He has a broken shoulder and two broken ribs. That hit that Jeff received from that lineman was excessive, that was all the defense wanted to hear. It looks like they were going to do some excessive hitting of their own. They knew the number of the lineman that hit Jeff and he was going to get the same.

The teams came back on the field and the Gators kicked off and put the guy that hurt Jeff out of the game with some tough injuries. The Citadel Coach was protesting the hit on his player and the referee told the Coach that the gators didn't complain about their QB being carried off the field and out for the season. He turned his back on the coach and walked away. Sonny came on the field and would short passing them to death and finally when they thought he would throw another short pass he would throw a long bomb to his receiver standing in the end zone all alone.

The coach took Sonny out of the game at the beginning of the 4th quarter the score was 48 to 0 when Sonny left the field. Sonny sat on the bench wiping his face clean and sipping on some gator aid not even watching the game. Sonny's QB scored two more touch downs that brought the score to 62 to 0 the worst beating in the history of college football. There were all kind of reporters wanting to talk to Sonny and they were all turned down because they weren't going to be friendly to Sonny because of the beating they gave the Citadel on national television. Sonny found out the Citadel coach wouldn't even shake coach's Shaw's hand he just walked by and said how much of a poor excuse he was for a coach.

Sonny quickly showered and snuck out of the locker room where there was a lot of celebration gone on. He had made plans to meet Marie in their usual parking spot outside the gym and left the campus to be alone with her. She was sitting there with the motor running waiting for her man. She was still in her cheerleader outfit but had a change of clothes in a bag in the back seat. Sonny drove while she changed and they drove out of town at least fifty miles away from campus where no one would know them. They stopped and got some groceries to make sandwiches in the room and some snacks and just be together without anyone snooping around. They checked into a very famous hotel that had great rooms and checked in before 11 o'clock Marie was all over Sonny she made him feel great and she kept reliving the game for Sonny from a spectators view and it was great. They finally fell asleep after making some good sandwiches and good conversation and some good sex and with nothing more to do it was near 3: am and they turned out the light and crashed.

They didn't wake early and used the excuse of going to bed late for sleeping in. They renewed the room for another night and decided to drive over to Naples and spend the day hanging around the board walk and finding a good place for lunch. Sonny picked up a newspaper and looked for the sports page and there it was the entire page was about the game last night and Sonny who wrecked the Citadel season opening and sent them home wagging their tails behind them. The question that the sports reporters wanted answers to was, who was Sonny Brown? He is a total unknown, except he played high school football for the ravens in Baltimore. The article went on to say that he went into the game as the backup QB and score twice the first two times he had possession in the first quarter.

The article went on to say that there wasn't anyone available for questions after the game including the coach we want to know why Sonny Brown wasn't the starting quarterback. Sonny Brown has disappeared after the game and hasn't been heard from up to when this article was sent to press. Sonny was getting favorable press it was the coach that was getting unfavorable questions about how he arrived at who started and who didn't. Sonny knows that the coach can avoid the press but knows that coach Shaw was going to have to answer to the sports committee at the school in the end. Another article called the worst whooping they have ever seen and now it came out that is this is the penalty for putting the star QB out circulation for the season because everything points to it. Sonny told Marie that if he is asked that question for print he will tell them that he is playing offence and takes his orders from the Coach. His job is to execute the play given to him and try to score a touchdown. Marie told Sonny that this was his first game and he has plenty more to play in so let it go and get ready for the next game, don't let these liberals reporters tie you up. Sonny told Marie that he doesn't want to speak to the press and they won't be able to misquote him.

Marie and Sonny were having a great time together and they knew they wouldn't have a moment's peace if they were back on campus. They still had enough food back in the room and they both wanted another command performance this evening. Sonny doesn't want to be dragged in to any squabbling that might be going on between the press, the school and Coach Shaw. They had to check out by 11: am and had no problem with it. They wanted to have lunch at the revolving restaurant overlooking the gulf; these two kids never experienced anything like this and were going to hold on as long as they could. The lunch took about two hours and was worth every penny. The restaurant made a little more than one rotation, it was awesome.

They headed back to school, it was going to be a couple hours' drive and still more time together that they needed. Sonny mentioned to Marie that the school has a life insurance policy on them for a million dollars so why don't they have one on each other for a million dollars. Marie said it was worth looking into. They pulled in on campus and they went to the cafeteria and picked a secluded spot to have their dinner. It didn't take long for people to start showing up and sitting with Marie and him there was one college news reporter mixed in and started to dominate the questioning until Sonny told him that we don't do interviews so why doesn't take a hike and let us students have a good dinner together. Well he was pissed off and said if he can't ask any questions then he will have to try and get the answer somewhere else. Sonny stopped him as he walked by and told him not to print any lies about him or Marie or he would come looking for him. The reporter told him not to threaten him and he will print what he wants to. Sonny reminded him that he heard what he said. The little elf walked away with nowhere to sit and no one to pester.

Sonny and Marie went back to their rooms and did a full review of their notes for tomorrow's classes. Every class that Sonny attended the students surrounded him and congratulated him on the game Friday night. Sonny had to meet in the gym this afternoon at 2:30 for some light practice and get filled in on Jeff's medical condition. Sonny walked in the gym and a lot of the players called out to him, the coach was waving him into his office and Sonny was asked to sit down while the door closed. Coach Shaw congratulated Sonny on the great game he played. He asked Sonny if he's had a chance to see any of the articles in the paper about them. Sonny said that he did

"Well Sonny they were nice to you and not that nice to me."

"They were picking on you today and will be picking on someone else tomorrow."

"That's probably true but in the mean time they keep on as to how I picked Jeff to be the starter."

"Did you ever wonder Sonny how I did that."

"To be honest with you Coach I really wasn't that interested in how you arrived at your choice. I couldn't put out anymore then I was. It was your decision and no one else's"

I'm sure when they get around to it Sonny they will be asking you that question as well."

Coach in case you don't know it, I don't give interviews under no circumstances. I have already told the school reporter not to print any lies about me or my girlfriend Marie. He told me in so many words that he would do as he wants and I told him that I would do what I want about any lie you print.

"Sonny don't you think that is a little tough what you did to that reporter?"

"What, making this guy aware that if he prints a lie about me or my girlfriend that I would be looking him up, now Coach are you having a problem with that?"

"No I just don't want you to get in trouble."

"As long that he doesn't print a lie about me or my girlfriend or give another reporter something that is slanderous and a blatant lie about him, then I will be ok.

"He has already gone to the school head professor about this and told them you threatened him."

"He knows that I didn't and is using this to get even with me for having the controlling hand. Now I just told you that I wasn't going to stand for any lies and he is lying, so now here is my response to this lie, either he is kicked off of the school paper or Marie and I will be leaving here tomorrow morning and you can stick this scholarship up his ass."

"Now Sonny this is not reasonable."

"He has brought a complaint about me that was a lie and wants to use the system and you to defend him. He still has to answer to me for telling this lie about me, so if I were you he is going to need security until I leave here tomorrow afternoon because I am going to make him pay for that lie. You have my notice now that I hereby resign from this spineless school."

Sonny stood up and left the Coaches office and walked out of the gym to his car and found Marie to tell her what happened. She never flinched she told Sonny that she was with him all the way no matter what. They went off campus for dinner and some privacy and didn't return until 8: o'clock. Marie stopped off at Sonny's room and in ten minutes the room was full of everybody that was somebody at the school were in his room telling him what happened to the school reporter that filed a false complaint about him. They went on to tell Sonny that they spoke to some of the people that were at your table and they confirmed your story and what the reporter had to say to you. The young man was asked to leave because he was serving an internship for a newspaper in Miami and was only signed up for this semester. He was just looking for a story no matter what or who he hurt. He never realized what going up against you could bring him.

"Now Sonny can we put all this behind us and start fresh and a new day tomorrow."

"I can as long as I don't see this bum on campus anywhere; I hope you told him that coming on campus is trespassing. In short you need to keep him away from me."

"Sonny we got the picture and we will see to it that he will be kept away from you and Marie."

They all filed out of the room and Marie told Sonny you must have some power around here. They weren't going to let the sun go down on this problem. We will have to keep an eye out for him in case he may want to try and get even with us. Marie was so happy that they didn't have to leave she really liked it here. Sonny told Marie that when you say something like I did you have to be ready to back it up or what you say will be worthless. She asked him if he was really going to leave tomorrow like he said he would. He told her there wasn't any doubt about it. Sonny walked Marie back to her room and kissed her good night and Sonny ran back to his dorm just for the exercise. He lost some time today not staying for practice and he would have to make it up tomorrow. He got there early and was ready to play some football.

The coach asked Sonny how he was able to draw that defective line off sides three times in a row. It was all in the cadence these linemen think that *any change in the calling of the signals means that the ball was going to be hiked. The biggest thing that had to be overcome was that our linemen couldn't even blink an eye. That has never been done before and made national news. I didn't see you practicing that back flip pass that flipped everyone on the field out of their jocks. He told the Coach that it had to be practiced until it was right and now that they have seen it we may not to be able to use it for a long time, unless we can make another play from the same line up. I'am sure we can do it with a lot of practice.*

17

It was Friday night all ready and Marie and Sonny barely saw each other they made plans for another sneak away somewhere close but not that close. They had another night game the kick off was at 6: o'clock and the overnight bags were in the car safely locked away. The game tomorrow was with NE Louisiana and if they could beat the Gators that would make national news. In order for that to happen they would need a QB better then Sonny and that wasn't gone to happen all the pressure was on Sonny to give a performance like he did last week. They were pre warned that there would be TV and newspapers reporters wanting to sit around the side lines and take some pictures that would lift them up to the who's who at their newspaper.

When the team met in the gym at 1: pm they stayed inside again and sonny showed the coach how he planned to open up the game like he did last week but he planned to alter it a little faking them out again and hopefully scoring a touchdown. When it was time to take the field the flashes were coming from everywhere. That Sonny was so cool he would throw the ball around no giving any hints of what was gone to happen. The coin toss went fast, the gators lost the toss and Louisiana elected to receive they ran the ball back to the thirty two yard line and the runner fumbled after being hit from the side and the ball spun out on the field where the gators recovered the fumble and Sonny and his team mates took the field. He told his team mates to listen up and called a fake back flip with a hand off and fake run, on one.

Sonny called signals and took the ball and started to go towards the left side line where as he went to the right last week, he did the fake flip and handed it to the runner passing in front of him while still running with no ball and looking like he very much had the ball and was looking to throw a sideline pass in the meantime the running back that Sonny handed the ball to was well on his way for a touchdown they were thinking that Sonny still had the ball. Once again Sonny scored a touchdown on the opening play. They *would kick to Louisiana again only this time they didn't fumble and their runner took the ball all the way down to their twenty yard line. Three plays later they scored and the game was all tied up.*

When they got the ball the next time when Sonny needed short yardage for a first down he would call the signals in such a way that an anxious defense would be jumpy and they would go off sides for a 5 yard penalty. They scored two more times by the half and the Gators defense stopped Louisiana from scouring any touchdowns and gave up one field goal. The score at half time was 21 to 10.

The talk in the locker room as intense and the overall consensuses was they needed more points and wanted Sonny to do it. Sonny was relaxed and would do the best he could if the offensive line would protect him that is what he needed the most. The second half was no piece of cake with Sonny running to the left as easy as running to the right and he put on a display of passing that had the fans up on their feet every time he had the ball. By this time Jeff was on the sidelines with crutches and was cheering Sonny on like everyone else. There weren't any touchdowns scored by either team. The Gators had two field goals. A chant started with the fans, Sonny, Sonny, Sonny and Sonny knew what they wanted, they wanted him to score a touchdown. With only five minutes to play Sonny wanted to please them so he went into a no huddle and started throwing short passes and completed nine straight and with the ball on the twenty seven yard line Sonny could see that the defense was beginning to let the long pass go unprotected. So now Sonny was going to go long, He looked short again and pump faked and hit his end in the end zone all by himself. The fans went crazy, Sonny gave them what they wanted he was becoming very popular, his biggest fan was Marie and that was all he wanted.

The players didn't like the Idea that Sonny got all the glory and they go nothing. The coach called for an early practice and told Sonny not to show up until after 3: o'clock he had something to go over with the players. The coach asked who has any complaint about Sonny's popularity and there were about three line men that became very vocal and were mad that Sonny was the only one on the team that got his name all over the sports page. Coach Shaw told the men that Sonny didn't have to do what the press writes about him, all he wants to do is to play football and graduate. Sonny has never given an interview with a news reporter so you can't blame him for the press he's getting. So now they started bitching about his scholarship and the coach stopped them and told them they agreed to theirs scholarship and he agreed to his. He told them if they want to renegotiate their scholarship then go to the administration office and do so. But let's not ever bring up this childish thing again. He told them Sonny did his own negotiating all by himself and let me assure you he is as good at that as he is in playing football. Please don't let you defending him on the field deteriorate and if we start to see him getting hit a lot more. Then he will kick off the team any player that let's Sonny get hit because you're not doing your best to block these defensive players away from Sonny. We film everything and we will see everything. Please read over your scholarship and know where you stand. He said that there was one more thing he wanted to say about all this and that is if they don't like Sonny's achievements or their scholarship then he would expect them to quit the team and pack their bags and get off this campus by sundown.

The coach had a towel around his neck and took it off and threw it at the player that was bitching the most. It was now perfectly clear that if anyone doesn't like the players on the team or their scholarship, there was no doubt now where they stood with him. The meeting broke up and everyone met on the field for some intensive practice. Sonny tried hard at every session and would talk to his ends and running backs about fooling the defense by playing at three quarters speed and mislead them and all the sudden call on that extra burst of speed that will put them in the clear. It's a lot better playing the game then it is to talk about it but when Sonny is on the field it's not boring.

The final game is coming up and with all the TV people in town and the reporters had all the hotel rooms. There wasn't a room in Gainesville to be had. Tail gaiting was up over a 100% there was plenty of food being cooked on the barbeque and plenty of liquor to go around. Anyone that was anyone was out tail gaiting. This was the final game and they had a good chance to go to the orange bowl with this undefeated season. Sonny and Marie were doing real good with their studies; they both knew that the better they did in school the better chance they had in landing a good job. Sonny knew that if he wasn't picked to play professional football then he better have learned something at school. He was hoping to major in marketing that he is well suited for. Marie wanted that as well and they were inseparable and would work well together.

It was announced on the TV and radio that the Gators are going to the orange bowls In Miami and was hoping for a big showing. They practiced hard as long as they could because they just found out that they were playing Syracuse who was not going to be a push over. All bowl games can go either way a penalty or a turnover can change a game very quickly. The pressure *on the school and Coach Shaw for an interview with Sonny who was the best player that they have ever seen and Sonny told the coach again that he doesn't give interviews. Coach Shaw told him that he might have to give in and at least have a news conference, like a one shot deal. Sonny just rolled his eyes and walked away; Coach Shaw knew how Sonny felt about them and wouldn't push the issue.*

The Orange bowl gets plenty of publicity and Sonny was getting his share. The players could see that Sonny wasn't looking for it and they were ok with that now. It was the press and not Sonny that was stirring things up. It's been a long rollercoaster ride for him and no one knows it just him and Marie. He will never get over Pat from the home telling him that he was so displaced as a child that he didn't even have a birth certificate and what she went through to get him one. He owes a lot to her perseverance in doing that for him. They stay in touch, not as much as he would like to. He wasn't regimented enough to follow a schedule and write her a note at least twice a month. She was in his heart and missed her guidance in his life. Marie and Sonny were making new roads into growing up and doing things on their own, by making their own decisions right or wrong. Sonny found that when he regimented himself things were less hectic.

The gators won the toss and received the football on the one yard line and ran it back to the 38th yard line. Now it was Sonny's turn to perform and perform he did he mixed up his plays and could hide the ball like no other and scored on their first possession with a left handed pass to the opposite side and scored easy. Syracuse wasn't about to let this touchdown go unchallenged and were able to tie the score by half time. In the locker room the coach reminded the players that Sonny has never seen his parents and he's knows that he is playing his heart out to win this one for them and wouldn't it be great if we dedicate this second half to his parents, that he has never seen and are watching all of us from above today. Well the players all crowded around Sonny and told him he could count on them to win this one for them.

Coach Shaw knew that he touched their hearts and gave them the boost they would need to go out and win this game, Sonny's game. The gators had to kick off and they exploded on the player carrying the ball so hard that he fumbled and the gators recovered it on the twenty one yard line. The lined up and the ball was hiked to the running back to the right of Sonny and he went through a hole so big in the line that a trailer could have gone through. He took the ball all the way down to the two yard line. With no huddle Sonny called out "Mommy wants it." That meant that he was going to take it in.

With the few fakes that he would need to pull this off they opened a nice hole for him to scoot into the end zone standing

There was no stopping them now, so by the end of the game the Gators had beaten Syracuse by the score of 31 to 10. There was pandemonium the students have emptied onto the field and there wasn't anything moving down there. Sonny and Marie had made plans for a quick getaway and Marie was waiting for Sonny in the same parking place alongside the gym. Coach Shaw knew when he couldn't find Sonny anywhere that he had snuck off with his girlfriend for a very private week end. They would drive far enough away not to be noticed by anyone, they would fit in no matter where they went. Sonny knew to win the Orange bowl game was big. He was sticking to his guns with no interviews.

When they returned there was a note stuck on Sonny's door to contact Coach Shaw in the morning. When he did the Coach told Sonny that there is so much hell being raised to the school by the press that you're not giving interviews will cause some of the coverage they have been enjoying to drop off and eventually cause a decrease in revenue. The school is doing all they can for you and they want you to do the same.

"What do they want me to do?"

"They want you to do a press conference with all the reporters that write about you and don't have an opportunity to interview you."

"I have had press interviews and they all end the same way, they get insulting and ask non related questions that are rude and so on."

"How about if I 'am there with you and lay down the rules of questioning that we would consider fair and noninvasive. Like no personal questions about your past, or scholarship, or your relationship with Marie. I will tell them that and if they should cross those lines of hands off we will walk out of the conference."

"Ok Coach mark my words these blood thirsty reporters will not listen to the restrictions that you have laid out for them to follow and will get downright nasty."

"I will also tell them that if Sonny walks out of this interview he will never grant another one again. I will also tell them that your only here because I promised him you would follow the guide lines."

"Look coach I know you're under pressure to get me there but when you see what they try to do to me you will walk off with me. Each one of these blood thirsty liberal reporters wants to make their career out of one interview

and that means it will fail like all of their other interviews. I didn't get this no interviews attitude out of nowhere, it comes from experience. Please pass my words on to the powers to be that from my experience it will fail."

"By doing this Sonny no one can criticize you for not giving interviews while you were at the Uni. of Fl. I am sure some of the school higher ups will be in attendance somewhere watching this whole interview, right now this is very touchy so let's get through it, do it for me."

"When is all this going to take place, I'll get back to you as soon as I know."

IT wasn't long before the interview was set up; it was on a Saturday at 9: am in the gym. Sonny was told that there would be fifty reporters going to be present and all the TV news stations. Sonny was told that the reporters were given the area's not to ask questions about or you would walk out. They think you're thin skinned and probably looking for something to go wrong and walk out.

"I am not the one asking the questions, I am the one they will be questioning."

The morning of the interview Sonny and Marie had breakfast in the cafeteria, there were some photographers taking pictures of them sitting at the table holding hands. Marie knows what could come of this and was not happy for Sonny. The photographers finally left them alone and they only had a few moments left before Sonny had to report to the gym for the interview. They walked out of the cafeteria together and Sonny asked Marie if she would mind not going because he knew it would get ugly. She told him she fully understood and went to her room and waited for him to return and go for a ride and hit some golf balls. Sonny and Marie were going to start practicing their golf and go out for their teams.

Sonny got to the gym and his Coach took him back stage and told Sonny they could walk out together without any introduction, it probably would be less formal. It was 9: o'clock sharp and Sonny and Coach Shaw walked onto the stage and took a seat at the table in the center of the stage set up for them. The coach made an opening statement about what was expected of them and told them that sonny is only a young man having fun playing football that he dearly loves. So if you would like to begin then please do so. There were two microphone stands set up in the center of the reporters to walk to and ask a question. The first question went to the coach.

Q. *"Coach why didn't you start Sonny instead of Jeff Pabst?"*

A. *"Jeff had the experience and Sonny had the ability. I wanted to see if Jeff could do the job and before we had the answer Jeff was hurt."*

Q. *"Sonny did you agree with that answer?"*

A. *Yes I do, I believed in the coach and what he needed to know."*

Q. *"Sonny you just had a great season and no one knows you."*

A. *"I don't give interviews because I've been hurt in the past."*

Q. *"Sonny why did you run the score up on your opening game against the Citadel team after Jeff was hurt?"*

A. *"That's a good question; I was taken out of the game at the end of the third Quarter. Jeff getting hurt had nothing to do with the score we had a good game and we went right to their weaknesses and were able to score some touch downs."*

Q. *"Are you saying that it wasn't a grudge game?"*

A. *"It wasn't a grudge game played by us. I never heard anyone talk about anything except winning."*

Q. *"It was more than a win it was a slaughter."*

Sonny knew from experience not to carry on such a conversation because they would only stand up their big hitters and it would get ugly.

Q. *"Do you know that you have one of the best football scholarships in all of America?"*

A. *"I didn't know that, thank you for that info."*

Q. *"Is that all you can say about that?"*

A. *"You might want to redirect your Question to Coach Shaw."*

Q. *"Coach Shaw why does Sonny have such an expensive scholarship?"*

A. *"To be honest with you he negotiated it in a room with his friend and got what he wanted, it's that simple."*

Q. *"No young man has that much experience to negotiate such a contract at the age of eighteen."*

A. *"If I wasn't there to see it I would have not believed it either."*

Q. *"Look I understand that this scholarship cannot be revoked, is that true?"*

A. *"yes that's true and no more scholarship questions, shall I send Sonny home if that's all you want to do is ask questions about his scholarship. You wanted this interview to ask him questions about football. Let's ask questions about Sonny and his football career. He's here waiting for some questions."*

Q. *"Have you always been able to throw the football with either hand with the same accuracy?"*

A. *"Yes as long as I can remember I have done so."*

Q. *"Is it true that you were raised in a home for children with no parents. I admire your being able to live through that and be where you are today."*

A. *"Yes I was raised by the state of Maryland in a home and was shown all the love anyone would ever need to make my stay their best anyone could ever need."*

Q. *"Didn't you ever get lonely?"*

A. *No because I only knew the home and they were my family. Those women that took care of us loved us like their own and weren't afraid to show it."*

Q. *"You were the Maryland State Junior golf champion for two years, will you play on the University golf team as well."*

A. *"If I am lucky enough to make the team I will play."*

Q. *"Did you know that you are not allowed to be given a car as part of your scholarship to play football for the Fl. Gators?"*

A. *"Yes I am aware of that, if you are referring to the mustang that the school lets me use, that is not my car, the school owns it not me. I brought the registration here with me in anticipation to you asking me that question. I have it in my hand for any of you to see if you wish. We can even make copies of it if you wish."*

Q. *"Do you drink liquor or smoke at all?"*

A. *"No I do not."*

Q. *"I was one of the photographers that took your picture in the cafeteria this morning, that girl you were with was very pretty. Was she your girlfriend?"*

A. *"Yes she was."*

Q. *"Is she part of your scholarship?"*

A. *"No she has her own scholarship for golf."*

Q. *"What do you think about your not elected for the Hizeman award?"*

A. *"To be honest with you I have never given it a thought. I was too busy trying to win a game."*

Q. *"Do you think you should have been nominated and won?"*

A. *"Again I don't know about who should have won and who should have nominated. This is out of my control and rightfully so."*

Q. *"What are your plans after college."*

A. *"I am studying marketing and I hope to enter that field and work it like I do football."*

Q. *"What do you like to do besides football?"*

A. *"I like to play golf and go the photo lab on campus and work on my photo developing skills. It's fun and challenging for me. Four years is a long time to go before I graduate, so I want to stay busy and not sit around."*

Q. *"Do you have any plans for the summer?"*

A. *"I would like to work at something, not in the golf field because that would make me a pro if I would get paid for my services."*

Q. *"I have tried to talk to Pat at the home where you grew up and she wouldn't talk to me, can you get me an interview."*

A. *"If she won't talk to you I better not ask her to talk to you if she doesn't want to. The answer to your question is no."*

Q. *"Sonny you were instrumental in winning the cotton bowl game. How do you feel about that win?"*

A. *"It was a great team win; we all played out hearts out and came out the winner. Someone had to win, it's almost impossible to tie."*

Q. *"How do you manage to live with a car and no job to earn an income from?"*

A. *"I do have a job in the administration offices doing janitorial work at nights or some Saturdays."*

Q. *"How much money do you earn?"*

A. *"I earn around $200.00 a week."*

Q. *"Wow that's a lot of money."*

A. *"I was hoping for a pay raise."*

The coach broke in and told the reporters that Sonny's scholarship can be looked at in the administrative bldg. between the hours of 9 to 5. You are welcome to read it in its entirety.

Q. *"Sonny how old are you."*

A. *"I am just nineteen years old."*

Q. *"I looked at your birth certificate that is on record as yours and it is only a copy. Where is the original?"*

A. *"I don't know, the lady at the home got it for me."*

Q. *"Are you sure you're nineteen and not twenty?"*

A. *"My birth certificate states my name and date of birth and that is final. If you know something else then let's hear it now. It sounds like to me that you're not stating your hidden motive about all this interest. I can play football if I am sixteen or thirty six, why ruin this day with nothing going nowhere."*

The coach asked the reporters if they had any more questions for Sonny about football or the school, if not lets pack it in and go for another time and everyone leaves here with a chance to come back. Sonny will make himself available to any reporter that doesn't try to hurt him. Maybe he will start to give interviews. He could tell that the questions were very easy and non-intrusive in fact it was dull he thought. He figured that the newspapers reporters will be the hardest on Sonny; we'll just have to wait and see.

Football season was over and all the pressure that goes with it was over as well. Marie and Sonny decided to start practicing golf because Marie had a golf scholarship and Sonny wanted to make the team as a freshman. It wasn't a requirement for him to make the golf team but they felt that Marie should make the team just so she could hold her head up. She would have some stiff competition not like in high school; A lot of these girls were state or club champions just like she was. Everyone that she will play with will be the best from their schools. She could get a few months of practice in before they would meet and compete. Sonny had the same thing for him to overcome except the boys will be a lot more aggressive. Whatever the two wanted they were assured they would get it, all they had to do was to ask.

They both were very excited to be now playing a lady's and gentlemen's game and not have to worry who was going to tear your head off. Winning gave the same enjoyment or as the coach would say "climax." Florida had the best weather and some of the other schools were still digging out of their snowy winters. To Sonny's and Marie's thinking was there wouldn't be any excuse for not being ready and fit for competition in a few months.

There was a club out on the edge of town that would let the university golf team members use the course after three o'clock, Mondays through Fridays, no carts and they had to carry their own bags. It wasn't that long of a course but challenging. They would go as often as they could and that was five days a week. They would practice till dark and stop somewhere and get something to eat. The University would close the dorms for the summer break so for now it was all free until school let out.

Marie talked to Sonny about where they would go for the summer, they couldn't stay on campus so they had to find a job. If they worked in golf and were paid they couldn't play on the golf team because they would be considered a professional. They had saved all of their weekly money they *earned at the adm. Office. Together that would be over $14,000. They put in for a job with the athletic dept. for their summer camp program for all the sports offered by the Uni. They lucked out and were both hired for $300.00 a week and keep their rooms and cafeteria privileges. That was really a stroke of luck, Sonny was placed with the football players and Marie was put with the girls cheerleading and no golf for pay. They asked her if she could help out with the golf, no pay. She told them it would be alright with her. First Marie had to make the golf team and Sonny didn't have to but he wanted to as a goal real bad. It was lucky for them that they put their names in early; they heard those summer jobs go fast.*

It was good that they had to tryout at the course they were practicing at every day. The course was Gainesville Country Club and not that far from campus. Marie was better than ever and looked like she would have a good chance to make the team. This year they were going to have eight players and six alternates. The men's team would have twelve players and six alternates.

After a while the course was loaded with students that were going to try out for the team so Sonny had to be at his best. One day the golf coach showed up and started taking names and when he got to Sonny he told him if he played golf like he played football they would have a great year. They both smiled and agreed to come Monday for a three day tryout. Eighteen holed each day and the cards would be totaled and the low twelve scores would make the team and the next six would be alternates.

The same was happening with Marie she wanted to make the team because of her scholarship and be proud of it. Marie shot par every round and finished with a three day score of 213. The low round was 209 and Marie's score put her in fourth place and on the team as a member. There were two other girls that shot a 213 so it was a close tryout. Marie's coach's name was patsy Horan and Sonny's coach's name was Dick Wood. They both worked for some big name sporting goods company and found their way to Gainesville.

Both coaches were very nice and left everything up to the team members how they wanted to practice and keep their position on the team. Patsy told the girls that she was the coach and not their mothers. Having never been married she doesn't think that she would be a good mother. There were times that I was called a mother it just didn't fit me. She told the girls that she likes a good cold beer and if there are some of you that like a good cold beer but for them not to drink and play golf for this university. Drink after your match. There is a zero tolerance for anyone on any drug in any event. Before you can play for the Gators you have to pass a simple drug test. If there is anyone among you that might have taken any drugs of any kind that might show up in a blood test please see me after the meeting I need to talk to you. If we should find drugs in your blood test and you weren't honest enough to tell us by coming forward, you are automatically off the team. Those of you that have scholarships don't get any special favors. She read everyone's name off that made the team and Marie was fourth and all smiles, and thought all that hard work with Sonny has paid off. She was hoping that Sonny made his team as well. He really wanted to play college golf.

Dick Wood called all the students that wanted to make the team together and there were about thirty of them they sat on the hill where the big oak tree was and he put it to them the only way he knew how. He told them that after three grueling days of competition that he had the names of the players that made the team He read off the # 1 player and went down the line he got to Sonny's name #10. His three day score was 211 he heard hid name called out as a new member that just gave Sonny the goose pimples all over. He thought he was going to play golf for the gators golf team what an accomplishment. With all that out of the way he excused the students that didn't make the team and told them to practice harder and longer.

Now Dick Wood wanted the team to hear him loud and clear when he told them how hard it was to make the team and how easy it will be to get kicked off the team. He told them he wouldn't tolerate any drugs in their systems or any alcohol drinking before any match. They would have to agree to a blood test, they will be looking for drugs, so if there is anyone that might have drugs in their systems that will show up on the blood test please see him after the meeting so we can iron out this issue. If anyone should have drugs show up in their blood test and didn't come forward and tell me they are off the team. He had mentioned this earlier and went on to say that this is a fun game, not a game for druggies it's a gentlemen game; you need to be relaxed to play this game. Not to single out Sonny but if he used his football energy trying out for the team he would have failed. He brought his calm and relaxed game and made the team easily for a freshman. He told them if anyone needed balls, or shoes or gloves or anything else he would get it for them. There are about three golf shirts that will be furnished to you for your matches he said that they would be responsible for the condition of the shirt when you walk on that first tee today you will be given a list what shirt to wear in each match.

Sonny couldn't wait to get back to Marie and tell her the news. She was sitting in a chair by the window and could hear him coming, he pushed the door open and she could tell by the look on his face that he made the team. Marie ran to Sonny and told him that they both made the team and we will be hard to beat in match play. She had played enough with Sonny to know that playing with the girls was easy. Sonny hit the ball further and he could reach some of the par fives in two. They couldn't wait to see their new golf shirts. They had to wear khaki pants and white shoes. They were issued white gloves.

Both coaches would have them play each other in matches and keep track of who would win and who would be down and come back and win. The coaches would look at everything and decide who would play who when it was time to tee it up for real. He knew that Sonny was tough to beat and would always give his all right down to the last putt. Yet he wasn't the best golfer but was the hardest one to beat.

Sonny and Marie tried their best to get away somewhere on the weekends they liked being alone together and Marie always wanted to please Sonny and being alone was the best time to do it. The part they liked the most was that no one knew them and they could go anywhere and do anything. That was priceless to them, they would often stroll the different beaches and go to the movies and relax by the pool if they had one where they were staying.

They had good grades and were lucky enough that their grades didn't affect their scholarship. They have come a long way since the home, when they left their they didn't have any experience doing anything. They caught on quickly and were able to move on to any level they needed to be on. In a way it was easier not having any family because they didn't have to answer to anyone but themselves. When they saw people hugging their parents and going home for the holidays that hurt a little and that does take some time getting used to, if ever. The people involved with Sonny knows that when Sonny says something that is just about it. He meant what he says and definitely he says what he means. He's a perfect gentleman all the time and being a super star hasn't affected him at all. The school car that they use is great and gets good gas mileage. They don't take it on long trips and are not piling the miles on it; they have to take it in for an inspection every three months. It was just another way that had to keep an eye on their investment.

The girls didn't have as many matches as the guys did and Marie played in all of her matches, her team in general lost every match but Marie played very good the team lost but Marie won every one of her matches except two and then she only lost in extra holes. Patsy was very proud of her and her ability to come through for a win for the team. They had a big formal dance at the end of the season where Patsy awarded Marie a trophy as rookie of the year. Sonny stood and cheered her all the way up to receive it and all the way back to the table.

Now Sonny had a much harder schedule and the team had only won four out of twelve matches, whereas Sonny won eight out of his twelve matches, not bad for a walk on. When it was all over His coach Dick Wood asked him if he would play again next year. They had a big formal dance as well. Sonny looked very happy, probably happier than they expected they would be. They both were accepted by everyone who made campus life very nice.

They both passed their finals with flying colors and now they would soon be working for the university in their summer program. They both were given schedules to follow for football and cheerleading they would read them together and laugh about all the little things they expected Marie and Sonny to do. It looked like a fun time and they had the weekends off for their trips to go on. They really looked forward to them they were very close and were always with each other, night and day. That would be to close for most couples but not Sonny and Marie, there was a strong bond there and nothing could break it.

There was only ten days left before school started and they planned on a short get away to Sarasota for three days and Sonny had to report back for football practice.

The next two years were like a fairy tale they both were given great write ups for their sports ability and Sonny was given the team's most valuable player. He just missed out on the Hizeman award. His coach Jim Shaw told Sonny he would be a shoe in for the Hizeman in his senior year, make no bones about it.

Sonny took his team to an undefeated season and he was always going to a banquette every night with Marie at his side and at his table.

19

Jenny felt it was time to really impress upon Chris that she would be expected to go to College and get a degree in something that she would be able to use for the rest of her life. Chris always wanted to go to college and get a degree in marketing because she loved to watch the advertisements on TV and caught on to how to present a product. Jenny couldn't agree more and told her that was a good choice and falls right into what interest her most. Jenny met with her guidance counselor Mrs. Kline and assured Jenny that she had Chris's interest in mind also. She told Jenny when she has to call on these executives and they melt when she smiles at them she will win them over very easily. Jenny told Mrs. Kline that she will have to back it up with some good market strategies. She went on to tell Jenny that she was watching her now for a couple of years and likes what she sees and her career choice.

Chris went out in her junior year at St. Mary's for the High School golf team and made it easily. Jenny was ecstatic about it and made sure she had all the equipment she would need to be successful. The coach did have them buy some school golf shirts so they would all look the same for their golf matches. They only had eight teams to play against and they would need some volunteer drivers to help out with getting the girls to the different golf courses around the state. Jenny volunteered with no problem and the Coach Miss Simpson took a liking to Chris and Jenny right away.

Chris had a tremendous love to compete and it fit right into her golf game. Not too much killer instinct but enough to keep her concentrating. She was very relaxed in her matches and won every one even the ones they didn't think she would win. Her school was always in the paper about the different games they would be involved in. If you followed high school golf then you would see Chris's name in the school team results. Chris went on to win her letter in golf and cheerleading.

It's been almost twenty four years since Jenny left her home to be on her own and no one has tried to get in contact with her except her mother once and Jenny put an end to that once and for all. Thanks to her parents not wanting her to be at home with her new baby she was able to meet Mrs. Topkis who left her a sizeable amount of money that she could live on the interest for the rest of her life. Jenny was away from her family long enough that the love has worn off and she was happy that they are out of her life. She knew that it wasn't an accident that they never got together it had to be planned.

We know from what happened to Jenny that she loved boys and trusted them to do the right thing. She had to instill her knowledge of them into Chris without Chris wanting to know how long she has been a man hater. Jenny took it easy with Chris and fed her things about men slow and easy so as not to turn her into a man hater. Jenny saw that with her looks the phone is going to ring off the hook for dates and Chris had to make up her mind which call was sincere and which call was to get her in the back seat looking at the dome lights. Chris would only go to dances and sporting events when she wasn't cheering. She was almost a double of Jessica Simpson and maturing more every day.

In her senior year, the other cheerleaders voted her the caption, the class president and the home coming queen. She was popular and the best part was that she was handling it very good and not walking around with airs that would turn every one off. She was the opposite of that and just considered herself as one of the girls on the team. The whole football team had her picture on their locker doors, it was perfectly clear that she wasn't going out with any football jocks. She knows from listening to the other cheerleaders that they only want girls that put out and then they cast them aside for another player to take his chances with the next one. She wanted something to do on her honeymoon besides get drunk and not have anything to look forward to.

Chris wants to be head over heels in love with her man that is going somewhere in life and going away to college out of state for four years. She plans to be a virgin on her wedding night. She likes that song, "We don't have to take our clothes off to have a good time." Is there a boy that can sweep her off her feet and not pressure her in to have sex that seems to be the big question that faces Chris? Boys have a tendency to move on when they can't get their way. Jenny was proud of her and let her know it when it was suitable. Chris knew she could always count on her mother for support in anything.

As a member in her senior year on the golf team was great. Chris won all her matches again and was invited to play in the state junior ladies golf championship. She practiced a lot and finished third, far better than she expected to do. Jenny went to all of her matches and walked every hole with her for support. She got a nice write up in the newspaper and a very flattering picture of her hitting her tee shot from the treacherous 10th hole at Louviers. They were also interviewing some of the girls that finished in the top three and Chris came over big time on color television. There were a lot of offers for her to pose for a professional photo album to help her in a modeling career. Jenny turned down all request and asked them not to pursue them anymore about this for them to own all of the pictures that she would pose for.

It was time to graduate and that night there must have been a thousand people cheering the students in as they came in the gym single file to their seats. It was just Jenny out there for her but she was very popular and drew the loudest cheers from the crown. She was given an honorable mention as to be the female student most likely to succeed in her class. Now we all know how that could fall apart in a thousand ways so in order for that to happen Chris would have to win something big, go in the movies, something that would gain her some national recognition. I guess getting married as a virgin wouldn't fit in to that prediction.

Jenny hasn't been with a man for so long she could be considered a virgin as well, at least that's what I hear about women that don't have sex for a long time, the man that gets her is in for a big evening. Jenny isn't giving anything up to anyone either. Once burnt twice shy, if you get my drift.

Chris didn't get a scholarship at the U of D that was where her mother wanted her to go and just be a student there that will change when they get a good look at her. She might try out for the cheerleading squad just for the fun of it and see what it was all about. A post card came in the mail to Chris asking her if she was interested in trying out for the varsity cheerleaders, all female students got the same card. It wasn't a special invitation it was just an FYI note, no one can say they weren't told of the tryouts times and dates. Jenny told her to go and see if it is legit and they really are looking for fresh blood. Chris had a nice tan from the summer and she looked professional.

Now that Chris has graduated from St. Mary's and going to the Uni. Of De. Jenny has taken a job with a local investment firm in Wilmington with good commissions and some telephone work and some appointments at the office. She got her degree and passed the licensing tests to sell stocks and Mutual Funds. The firm was glad to have her and she was right in her prime *as far as her looks go and they are looking forward to her getting them new clients and having the clients assigned to her buying what she offers them.*

The stock market is hard to break into but once you break the code the income just keeps going up making six figures isn't any problem. It might take a year or so but Jenny should cash in with her sales skills and good looks. She can relax now that Chris is at the U of D the first year she has to live on campus that isn't that far away from her home. She would always come home for the weekends and work heavy on her subjects so come Monday she is much more advanced than the rest of her class. The professors could see this and gave her good grades for her efforts. Some days she had two classes and some days she had three and some days she had four. Either way she had to roll with the schedule and meet at the gym with the cheerleaders to practice their routines. She did make the team and now has all the uniforms for home games and away games the cheerleaders never travel with the team, always separate. There is never a problem with this procedure and where they stay when they are out of town is as far away from where the players are staying that they couldn't find them with an AAA road map. The girls are forbidden to tell anyone where they are staying.

Jenny felt real comfortable with those arrangements and didn't have to go to the away games. She would always meet Chris in the school parking lot where the bus would bring them in from the airport or the game. Chris was very happy with what she was doing at the university and felt secure about her home only being a few miles away. Chris has made a good name for herself among the other girls because she is consistent and reliable and an all-around nice person. When she was out on the field cheering she would draw a crowd. A few times she was asked for an autograph; she handled it real well and considered it an honor to give out an autograph. The coach would see how she handled herself and was very impressed. There are a lot of girls that couldn't handle that. She didn't belong to any sorority and now she is being smothered with request. She prefers not to be tied into an organization; that didn't mix with other students just their hand full of members. She wanted the freedom of being on her own.

The work that she was assigned to learn would keep her busy at home when Chris was away. Jenny wanted her clients to trust her and in return she would never lie to them and only steer them in the direction that was good for them and not necessarily the company. This way of thinking would make her successful someday.

One day when Jenny was at the mall she heard someone call out her name and when she turned that person asked her if she was Jenny Moore and she said she was and at first glance she knew who it was. He told her that it was Dave, the father of your kid. She told him that he denied that it was his and if she can remember correctly you so much as called me a whore that night, he apologized for that and said he had grown up a lot since then.

"It sounds like to me that you have screwed over some other women."

"I have and I am truly sorry for it, I know it's too late but I am sorry."

"I can appreciate how you feel but you threw me aside when I needed you the most and for that I can't accept your apology and do not wish to have anything to do with you. You had me for the rest of your life and threw me away like you would discard a used Kleenex."

"Your right and I don't blame you for feeling that way; it must have been hard on you. Oh by the way how is our child doing?"

"You denied it was your child I was having and didn't want any parts of it. I told you that a woman knows who the father is. So you'll forgive me if I tell you none of your business you have lost out on something that would have made your life a lot richer then it appears you have done for yourself."

With that Jenny walked away from him hoping that she would never see him again. After seeing what he now looks like, he looked like his best friend was a bottle of Jack. Jenny wasn't going to tell him anything especially about Rome and what happened to him.

20

It was finally here their senior year, looking back the time has flown by. Sonny was still looking forward to working in marketing, but Coach Shaw seems to think that Sonny was going to be taken in the draft in the pros. He was definitely in the running for the Hizeman trophy. Marie has already told Sonny that she would go anywhere with him. She wants to get married and have his babies. Sonny wanted the same and each day they waited made it harder to hold back. They were both studying marketing and planned on working together as a team for some company that wanted two very successful free thinkers planning their strategies to win over the buyers.

Marie and Sonny planned another secret weekend in Sarasota they were planning their future and having babies when a huge 18 wheeler came through an intersection at the foot of an off ramp on interstate 75 and hit the passenger side smashing Marie so hard up against Sonny crushing her. He was thrown from the car over a hundred feet from the impact. Marie had to be cut out of the car that took almost forty five minutes. At one time they didn't see anyone in the car that's how crumbled up it was. When they got her out on a gurney and her body was all broken up with deep lacerations all over her upper body.

Sonny was lying in the street motionless and moaning a little, he was bleeding from his head and his right arm was broken and both of his ankles were broken. Needless to say he was in bad shape but better than Marie was doing. They were both med-o-vac out by helicopter to the closest hospital about twelve miles away and when they got there they made the decision that Marie was dead and Sonny had a chance to survive if they can get him some attention right away.

Marie lay there in the emergency room still uncovered her bloody body just lying there and no one to claim her or cry for her looking about as bad as anyone could possibly look that has just been crushed to death by one of the heaviest vehicles allowed on our highways. They were searching through Sonny's clothes and found a card that read Gators football and Coach Shaw's phone number. They called and let it ring for hours and no one answered. It was the phone in Coach Shaw's office in the gym and no one was there. They decided to call back Monday to see if this person named Sonny Brown was known by this Mr. Shaw.

In the meantime the hospital had to make the decision how they were going to treat Sonny. Not knowing where to start they gave him complete x-rays from head to toe. He had quite a few broken bones and the worst being his head. His skull was crushed and they decided after a long conference to put a steel plate in his head, another hit there would kill him. The team putting on all the casts worked for hours while the team of surgeons worked on his skull to keep him alive. Most of his face was black and blue and his eyes were swollen shut. He's been in a coma since they brought him into the hospital. He lay there in the operating room with his head completely shaved and almost a complete circle of staples holding his scalp on his head. They put a full white sock over his head to keep him warm; they knew that with no hair he would feel cold.

Behind the scenes early Monday morning the girl in admittance started calling Coach Shaw's office and decided to let it ring until someone answered. It rang for an hour and a half when finally someone answered and said, "Coach Shaw's office."

"I would like to speak to Coach Shaw please."

"I am sorry I don't see him."

"Look I am calling from the hospital in Sarasota about a very serious accident that has happen almost two days ago."

"How is the coach connected?"

"We found a business card in one of the accident victim pockets."

"What is the name of the victim?"

"His driver's license identifies him as Sonny Brown."

"Did you say Sonny Brown holy shit oh my God?"

"Yes I did."

"Do you know him?"

"Yes he was our star quarterback on our football team and he is very famous."

"He was involved in a very serious automobile accident here in our city. His car was demolished by a very large eighteen wheeler."

"Will he be ok?"

"*We are not sure.*"

"*I don't know if you know it or not but he is very famous and has just won the Hizeman trophy.*"

"*O my god I know who you're talking about.*"

"*Where is Mr. Shaw, please stay on the line I am going to find him. Please hold on.*"

"*The girl calling from the hospital could hear the girl screaming out Coach Shaw has anyone seen Coach Shaw.*"

Finally the phone was picked up and the person now on the phone said I am Mr. Shaw.

"*Mr. Shaw I am calling you from the hospital in Sarasota about an accident victim with the Name of Sonny brown. Do you know this person?*"

"*I do, where is he now?*"

"*He's here at the hospital in a coma with only a slim chance of him living through the night.*"

He wrote down the girls name and the name of the hospital you said it was the memorial hospital. He asked if they had a helicopter pad and told her he was on his way. He called the helicopter service company down the road and they came fast. He told them where he had to go and he had to get there fast. The pilot had been there before and said he could get him there in forty five minutes. The Coach nodded and away they went.

There were so many things going through the Coaches mind he couldn't think straight. He never thought to ask about Marie. He hoped she was all right. The Coach knew that Sonny and Marie didn't have any family, nothing. He did remember seeing a woman's name that Sonny put down as someone to contact if it became necessary. He needed to get there first and size up the situation before calling anyone. The pilot told him they were about five minutes away and they know were coming.

When that chopper touched the ground the Coach was off and running to the only person waiting. It was Ann the girl he spoke to on the phone.

"*Can I see Sonny now?*"

"*I need to talk to you now before we see anyone.*"

"*Please talk to me, tell me what I need to know.*"

"*We really should be talking to his next of kin.*"

"*Sonny doesn't have any family, no one; he was an orphan and brought up in a home in Baltimore Md.*"

"*Let me discuss this with a hospital official and I'll be right back.*"

It seemed like an hour but it was less than ten minutes when Ann came back with a very distinguished person with a nice white coat on. He introduced himself as Dr. Levy and asked The Coach what is his involvement with Sonny Brown.

"I was his football coach for four years. If you follow college football he was just named this year's Hizeman award winner. I can assure you Coach he will never play football again or any other sport. Right now he is in intensive care with two broken ankles his right leg is broken in three parts, he has two broken ribs and one cracked rib he has a broken shoulder and left arm and worst of all he has had a very serious head injury that required a steel plate be put in his head to protect him from any other hits he might have to his head.

"Tell me Doctor, how is his friend Marie doing?"

"He looked at the Coach and said she didn't make it, she was killed instantly from the truck practically running over the top of them with the speed he was going at impact. It's only a miracle that Sonny is alive. He was thrown out of the car over a hundred feet away. He must be a tough cookie."

"He was a star football player in the best condition that we can say just might pull him through."

"Where is Marie now?"

"We have her in our hospital morgue; maybe you can identify her for us."

"I'll do my best."

"Dr. Levy took him down to the morgue and had the attendant pull back the sheet and there she was Sonny's love of his life and the Coach said out loud crying how is anyone ever going to tell Sonny that his girl is dead."

"Do you think there is going to be a problem?"

"A problem, these two have never been apart for the last sixteen years."

"Dr. Levy this news will probably kill Sonny that is how much they loved each other."

"We can keep the body in our morgue until he is able to decide on what to do with the body."

"I think that would be a great idea and would help Sonny with some closure.

"Now Coach I am going to take you to Sonny in a private room just off the intensive care room. He's not going to be anyone you would recognize. I am sure his features have been totally altered and he will take months before he can ever look like somebody you recognize."

The Coach couldn't stop thinking about Marie and how Sonny and her were in separable and now she lay there all alone with no love one to be with her. It really tore the coach up to see this first hand. He kept thinking that this is unfair and with the life she must have had at the home with Sonny no family, not one single relative that could be notified of this tragedy. He thought that she was a displaced person in a very congested world.

Dr Levy put his arm out for the Coach to stop and said he would leave him alone with Sonny and let us know if he needs anything. He walked in the room slowly and saw this figure lying there with more tubes in him then you could count. He couldn't help himself he broke down again and asked how this could happen too nice people like Marie and Sonny. He took some Kleenex from the box and just stood there looking at a young man that will never play sports and marry his longtime girlfriend, this was not going to be an easy transition. Sonny would have to overcome his physical injuries and overcome his mental anguish of the loss of the only person that he ever loved.

The Coach called the school and got a hold of someone in administration and told them what happened and to pull Sonny's file and get in touch with the woman from the home where they came from. They told him they would get on it right away and have her call him at the hospital as fast as they can. It didn't take long when his phone rang and a voice identified herself as Pat from the county home in Baltimore Maryland. She asked him what happened and he told her that what he knew him and his girlfriend Marie were driving their car on their way to Sarasota FL for the weekend when a eighteen wheeler slammed in to the passenger side of their car crushing Marie and throwing Sonny over a hundred feet down the road bouncing off of anything that was around for him to hit after being thrown from the car.

Pat wanted to know because of how the Coach told her how Marie was and he said, "She didn't have any chance for survival she died almost instantly." The Coach could hear Pat on the other end sobbing and finally she just let it out and screamed no not them, I loved them like they were my children.

"Did Sonny die too?"

"No but he is hanging on by a very thin thread. If you want to see him he's at the Memorial Hospital in Sarasota, FL Room 402 and here is my ph# to call me I want to assist you in anything you want to do."

"I don't know what to do except to get approval to came out there and spend some time with Sonny and try to comfort him."

"Right now he's in a coma, so there isn't anything you can do until he comes out of his coma."

"What about Marie?"

"*Right now she is in the morgue here at the hospital and can stay here until Sonny is released, which won't be for a while.*"

"*I think on this end here at the home I will have to get some permission to travel down there when it will be a good time to come.*"

"*That sounds like a plan to me, I feel better now that I have found you the only person he had in this whole world that he wanted to be notified in the event of something happening just like this. You are the only family he has. Sonny and I got close but not like you.*"

Pat thanked him and hung up and immediately started calling people about the accident and what she could do through the county about burying Marie and the funds that were needed to go to Sarasota and things like that. The home was the only home they knew and Pat was going to make sure they were going to be taken care of if need be.

The Coach stayed with Sonny for three days and after talking to the doctors they told the Coach that he might as well go back to Gainesville he was close enough to call if they would need him. Pat contacted the hospital and added the Coach on as a living will interested party that they could consult with if they need permission to do something. The Coach told the nurses and doctor that he was going back to Gainesville and let the healing process continue and he wanted to be called if and when Sonny would come out of his coma. They agreed with his plans and told him they would be in touch if there would be any change in his condition.

The Coach would see Sonny lying there and have all kind of flashbacks about his ability to play football and how bright of a future he was going to have. When he got back the Hizeman people wanted to know from the Coach who was going to receive the award for Sonny at the sports banquet. The Coach told them he would receive it for Sonny just tell him where he needs to be and what time. The night of the banquet the room was solemn and everyone was talking to the Coach about Sonny and his chances of coming through this. He told them that Sonny's playing days are over.

Now it was time to receive the Hizeman award and the Coach was required to say something. With tears in his eyes and a lot of crying the Coach told the people in the room that sonny was holding on to life by a very thin thread. He told them that he has been seriously injured to a point that he has a steel plate in his head. There wasn't a dry eye in the room, the women present in the room were bawling like babies and some men were doing the same. He finished by telling the reporters that Sonny was in a coma and will in time come out of it. The Coach held the trophy in the air and said go Gators and went back to his table. Some reporters were asking for some exclusive interviews and The Coach turned everyone down and said he was having a hard time getting anything done not knowing whether or not Sonny was able to pull through this nightmare.

The driver of the truck and was finally charged not keeping a proper log and having traces of a sleep blocking drug in his blood. He was going to be charged with vehicle man slaughter and dui causing the death of Marie. He could go to prison for twenty years. The trucking lawyers were saying that sonny ran a red light but witnesses told a different story. The trucking company Ins. Co. knew they were going to have to pay out millions of dollars to Sonny when the smoke lifts and their lawyers were just trying to keep the numbers down. The trucking co lawyer's son played football with Sonny in his junior year. The lawyer heard from his son how much of a straight shooter Sonny was. He told the trucking company that he knew Sonny through his son and would they want him to step down. There reply was no we are going to lose no matter who our lawyer is.

Sonny is still in a coma and is showing signs of coming out of it. He did moan to one of the nurses but he still hasn't opened his eyes because of the swelling but that would be a very good starter. It wasn't a few days later that Sonny did finally wake up and is not able to talk but he is alert as best he could. The head nurse called the Coach to tell him the good news and he said he would fly up the next morning. The chopper notified the hospital that they were about five minutes away and they were waiting for him to land. He jumped out of the chopper and ran to the door way where they were waiting and he asked how he was doing? They said, "He was awake and falling in and out of a coma which means to us that he will be totally out soon if not now."

The Coach was definitely nervous and anxious to see Sonny not knowing what could transpire between him and Sonny. He walked in the room and saw Sonny laying there with his eyes open, not wide open just little slits because they were still swollen. The Coaches first impression was that he was very hurt and has a long way to go before he could go home back to the campus where he lives. Now that the Coach can see how Sonny is doing he put a fast phone call to Pat at the home to come as fast as she can. He fears that Sonny is going to start asking questions about Marie and he could use the help that she can provide only in this case they will need a lot of help in breaking the news to Sonny about Marie.

Pat told the coach that she would come right away she should be there very early in the morning. The Coach told her he would stay. The Coach asked Sonny if he could get him something to eat or drink and he quietly said no thank you. He faintly heard him ask where Marie was and he purposely pretended he didn't hear him. Sonny fell off to sleep again and the Coach sat in the contoured chair and read the newspaper and he too fell asleep. The nurse came in the room early and started doing things to Sonny and giving him an infant's bath being very gentle and putting skin cream on his face because it was peeling as if he were sun burned. It was the result of dry skin and the dry room condition.

The nurse held a cup up to Sonny and asked him if he would like some cool apple juice. He nodded he would and the nurse put the straw in his mouth and he took a little sip. She was happy that he did that. Another nurse came in the room and asked the Coach to come with her; she took him into a conference room where he was introduced to Pat from the home. He shook her hand and said he was glad she could come.

"How is he doing?"

"I think that this morning is his best one so far. He seems to have come out of his coma now and is trying to speak. I think he is going to push us to tell him where Marie is. We will need some advice from some of these doctors whether we should tell him if he asks where Marie is."

"I agree with you, my biggest concern is what will he do when he knows that Marie is deceased."

They had an interview with the resident Physiatrist about if Sonny should know about his girlfriend's status. Will he try to get out of bed, hurt himself all those things that we can think of that he might do. The Physiatrist told them if he asks where Marie is tell him the best way you know how. She is with God to heaven, to be with God something like that. Show him that you're strong and hopefully it will wear off on him. He knows how hurt he is then he must have a feeling how hurt she is. If he wants to know then he knows the worst he can hear.

They went back to the room and when Sonny saw Pat he just let it go he cried and cried until he wasn't strong enough to keep crying anymore and he fell asleep while Pat held his hand. She was also overcome with emotion and never in her wildest thought would she see him in the condition she has just seen him in. She had a lot of concerns about his head and would he have any permanent brain damage from his skull split open. The white stocking that covers his head and hides that awful scar has a ring of blood stains around it that should be changed to a new cap. It was only a few minutes later that they changed the cap to a new one. He looked better now. He sleeps for hours and Pat was given a chair to sit in because she couldn't let go of his hand and didn't want to either.

Sonny woke up and Pat told Sonny that she loved him and the both of them started crying again. This time he looked at Pat and asked where Marie was? She looked at him for the longest time and finally told him that she is with God in heaven. He squeezed Pat's hand and the river of tears were flowing down his face and sobbing for the longest time and fell asleep again. They thought to themselves that it was better than they expected. The Coach told Pat that he wasn't strong enough to really show some sorrow. He is exhausted and will probably sleep through the night. The Coach told Pat that he was going back in the morning. They both slept in the room and Pat held Sonny's hand and leaned forward and placed her head on his bed and fell asleep that way.

When the morning came Pat was sore as hell from being crouched over all night so she got up and walked it off in the hall way, it took about ten minutes but she was starting to feel better. Sonny was in the hospital now almost two weeks and has made some improvement but had a long way to go before he could check out. The Coach left and Pat had the truck ins. Co. claim rep come by and introduced himself and said, "He would pay all the hospital bills and any other expenses for Marie and Sonny." Pat told him that is what would be expected for them to do. She took his card and told him until Sonny is on his feet out of the hospital they are not to speak to Sonny without her being present. He said, "He under understood." She told him she was from Balti. Md.

Pat came back in the room and Sonny was trying to drink through a straw while Pat held it for him. He seemed more relaxed that Pat was there. He tried to talk a little with her and said that he missed Marie and cried a little just saying that. She told him that she didn't suffer and went on peacefully. He asked Pat where she was and she told him that she is in safe keeping until he and her can give Marie a good burial. He told Pat that he wanted her buried back in Balti. Md. and Pat said she was hoping he would want that. She asked him if he was in any pain and he said no, none at all. She told him she would have to leave in a few days so let me see some improvement before I leave.

The request from the newspapers that wanted some pictures of Sonny were so numerous they had to assign a person in admittance to give them a briefing on his injuries and how long his stay would be at the hospital. They just didn't know and didn't want to guess at something like that. They were given a full briefing and there wasn't anything more they could do for them. Thank God they didn't know anything about Pat or she would have had them sitting on her lap on her flight home. It was time for Pat to go and she hugged Sonny for the longest time and whispered in his ear that she loved him. He cried at that and Pat left the room in tears herself. This was not something that Pat was used to but came through in flying colors. She really did love those two and had to make sure that she didn't show any favoritism at the home.

Sonny was all by himself now and all he could do is to just lay there and think and watch a little TV. It was the thinking that hurt the most. Dr Levy came in with a gentleman from the life ins. company where he and Marie bought a million dollar life ins. policy on each other that also paid double for an accidental death. The proceeds were for $2 Mil. He wanted to give it to Sonny rather than hold it and he not get the benefit of getting some interest. He showed the Doctor the deposit slip and the receipt for the money that was put in a money market account that the ins. co has all of its funds. Dr. Levy took the envelope and told the ins. claim rep that he would like to check it out and will be right back, Dr. Levy was back in five minutes and said everything was as he said and that he would keep the envelope in a safe at the hospital.

It was probably safe to say that he didn't fully understand what the claim rep said but did get the jest of it. Sonny was improving with a greater speed and he had to be x-rayed to see how he was healing and make a decision when they can start removing some of the cast. This was happening around the twenty forth day he was in the hospital and he was told that he was being moved to a private room next door because he has graduated out of intensive care. He couldn't show it that much but he was very happy to hear that. He was starting to watch some cooking shows and he thought he could do some cooking on his own someday.

The nurse came in one day and told him that the casts were coming off in two days because he was getting better fast. They cut the cast off right in the room and cleaned him up pretty good. He still had his catheter in and it would have to stay in until he can get out of bed and stand unassisted and have the strength to return on his own. He really could use a shower but was afraid of falling down so he practiced putting his feet on the ground and standing where the nurse could keep him from falling. He would do this a few dozen times a day until he got it right.

They made the decision to take out his catheter and see if he could stand with a walker for five minutes. His broken bones had healed real good and nothing hurt him. He took his first shower in almost a month and didn't want to get out but he knew he could collapse on the floor without any notice. The coach was calling him almost every day and was thrilled to hear about him taking a shower on his own, even though there was an attendant standing outside the shower curtain. It was for his own good. Pat would call him as well and never hung up without her telling him that she loved him. This last time Sonny told her that he loved her also. Pat cried like a baby after she hung up when she heard that from him.

He was wheeled down to therapy twice a day and he loved it he would tell the nurses that it was just like going out for football. He has just completed his sixth week at the hospital and one day Dr Levy came to see him and told him that he could go home very soon and the doctor asked him where home was and Sonny told him that it was on the campus of the Uni. of Fl. The doctor looked at him and said that's right you still live on campus. You will have to have a visiting nurse see you twice a week until she releases you out of her care own your own. Sonny told him he agrees with him. He told Sonny that he would set it up with the school.

The day that Sonny was to be discharged Coach Shaw had a helicopter running out on the pad ready to take him home. Sonny had to have crutches and would transfer to a cane and then not need any assistance to safely walk. There were a lot of nurses that came to the lobby to say goodbye as well as Dr Levy who was carrying his envelope from the life ins. co. and the $2 mil deposit that they made for him. He saw the bill that the hospital was charging the trucking co. and it was around a half million dollars and the trucking co. had to pay. Marie's body was being transferred to a mortuary in Gainesville and when Sonny is well enough to travel he can take her home to Maryland for burial. He would work with Pat on it and she can help him out with all the arrangements.

21

Sonny's farewell was sad, he wanted to thank everyone that was there that helped him and said, "He would never forget them." Dr. Levy walked out with him and shook his hand and told him to be very careful with his money. He went on to tell him that if someone has an investment that is too good to be true then it is and walked away. Sonny thought about that and said to himself that he would use that as his guide to live from. The Coach had to help Sonny on the helicopter and when he was strapped in they took off for Gainesville. The Coach didn't tell Sonny anything that was going on at the school when they got there. The chopper got near the field and started hovering around until he found a safe spot to land.

A couple of golf carts came out to meet the chopper and helped Sonny on and be seated. The coach was in the other Cart and went ahead of Sonny and into the stadium with some deafening cheers that caused Sonny some alarm. It got real quiet and his cart started through the tunnel when he heard someone introducing him and the place went crazy. His driver kept up his slow pace and told Sonny to wave to them. He could see this large stage off in a distance and there were a lot of people standing on it.

The first person that ran to him was Pat she hugged him and helped him up the steps for him to meet all the dignitaries from the state senator down to the governor to any one that could get something out of being there to greet Sonny. Sonny was taken to the front of the stage and he waived to everyone that started the cheering all over again. The Coach put up his hand and asked the students to quiet down and they did.

He told them that Sonny to this moment didn't know that he had won the Hizeman award. He lay in that hospital for two months and didn't know it. Sonny stood by the Coach while he presented Sonny with the most prestigious award a football player can receive. He knew he couldn't hold it but he did touch it and smile with his approval. The flashes were going *off continuously throughout the presentation. The Coach handed Sonny the microphone and asked Sonny to say something. The Coach stepped back three or four pacer leaving Sonny all alone with the microphone.*

He thanked everyone for coming and was sorry that Marie wasn't here. He went on to tell them that he missed her very much and still looks for her to come in a room or step from behind a corner or be in an elevator when the door opens. I guess I won't let go. Usually the Hizeman winner plays professional football and everyone wants to see how he does in professional sports. He told them that he will never play football again not with a steel plate in his head. He wants to donate the trophy to the school that gave him the opportunity to win this trophy, as far as he was concerned it belongs to all of you for being on my side and coming to every game faithfully rain or shine. He told them it's yours and I am sure they will find a place for you all to see it every day. He thanked everyone again and turned around to hand the microphone back to The Coach and walked back to Pat and held her hand until it was over.

Sonny asked The Coach if Pat could sleep in Marie's room and he said, "She could and he would have it open for her when she gets there." That was a relief for Sonny that Pat could have a safe place to sleep in this evening. It wasn't long before the stadium was empty and he and Pat were all alone and it was only 4:30 in the afternoon and the both of them were starving. The Coach spotted them leaving the stadium alone and asked them if they wanted to catch a bite to eat just off campus. They both said yes and he drove them to a small Italian restaurant where the food was first class it was called Mom's Place. Sonny couldn't eat much so he just had their wedding soup. He said that was plenty for him. Pat and Coach Shaw did the whole works from calamari to the Italian shrimp. Sonny just couldn't eat that much yet.

Pat was dropped off at the dorm where Marie bunked and said good night to them both; Sonny told Pat that he would see her in the morning outside at 8 o'clock. She said goodnight and walked away. Coach Shaw drove Sonny to his room and told him he was proud of him winning the Hizeman award and was happy about his recovery. After breakfast Pat told Sonny that she had to leave and would start the burial arrangements for Sonny as soon as he would tell her he was coming with Marie.

Coach Shaw got up with Sonny in a few days and asked Sonny to meet him at his office in the gym at 10 o'clock. Sonny tapped gently on his door and the Coach told him in and asked him to be seated. He told Sonny that the university has made almost $ 200 Million dollars from Sonny's popularity and the viewers that would watch the games on TV. He told him that his draw has come to an end now that football season is over and you will graduate. They had a small fund set aside and it appears that there is $3.8 mil. left and the board met and is awarding the money to you because you can't play professional football and earn the big bucks. He opened his draw and took out an envelope and handed Sonny an envelope with the check in it for $3.8 mil. He told Sonny that he would drive Sonny to the bank and deposit it right away in a money market or something

Sonny was not getting around that well so the Coach drove him to the bank where Sonny and Marie had their checking account and went in with him to deposit the check and kinda looked at things from a arms distance just to back him up. Everything went well and they were back on campus in no time. He informed them that Marie was deceased and her name should be removed from the account. They told him they would need a death certificate and Sonny told them that he wanted to open a money market account. They took the check and gave him the necessary papers to sign and temporary check book to use until a better one arrives in the mail. Sonny opened up a student checking account and withdrew all of the money in the account except ten dollars and placed it in the new student checking account. He told the girl that he wanted new checks as well.

When they got outside the Coach told Sonny he liked how he moved his money around. Sonny had to sign a lot of papers relieving the University of any and all Claims that he might bring from the money made by the university from his playing football on TV.

Sonny met with his professors and they all were glad to see him back and with the short time left before the finals that told him that they were going to test him and if he passes they will pass him for his degree in marketing. They told him what to study and he passed all of his finals with no problem and was going to graduate with his class next Saturday and he informed the funeral parlor that he wanted Marie to be shipped to Mealeys funeral home where Pat had made all the arrangements knowing when Sonny was flying in to Baltimore. Sonny stood with his class and walked slowly to the stage when they called out his name the place went wild and it gave Sonny goose bumps everyone was shaking his hand and it was over as fast as it started. Soon he would just be another graduate from the University of Fl. He made sure he thanked everyone in the adm. Office and all of his professors and caught the morning flight out of Miami to BWI that would take 2 hrs. 20 min. He threw away all of his clothes except a small suit case just enough to get by on but he wanted to buy a nice suit for the funeral. He kept some of Marie's things that he could never throw away.

Pat was waiting for him and she had him checked in to the embassy suites in Balti. Where he can stay until he finds a place and a job. The morning of the funeral there were a lot of people there and it was sad to see all the children from the home walking by and touching the closed casket with Maria's picture on the top. Sonny was standing by the casket when he heard this familiar voice tell him he was very sorry about Marie and when he turned around it was Babe their old paper boy. They hugged for the longest time and Babe congratulated Sonny about the Hizeman Award. Sonny told Babe that he might be the only reciperant of the award that will never play the game again. Babe told him that he has made a name for himself and that should open a few doors for him down the road. Babe asked him if he had any plans and he said that he was going to look around for something here and dig in to.

The grave side ceremony was real bad for Sonny and Pat had to prop him up more than once he finally had to sit in a chair to get the feeling back in his legs. He told Pat that he was really going to miss her, especially at nights when he starts thinking of her. He knows that he wants to rent a penthouse on the top floor of a nice place with a view and find work in Balti. if he could be so lucky. He also wants to buy a nice car because he has to be able to get around on his own and not need anyone to taxi him around. He can afford it.

He purchased a nice mid-size car an Acura and he found a penthouse with a view in downtown Balti for $1,600. a month and hired a person at the furniture store to furnish it for no more than $15,000. They had all the furniture there and unpacked in three days while Sonny was out buying some clothes. He did have all the money that was in the checking account that amounted to $49,748.00 he can live off that for a while and add to it when he gets his job.

Let there be no mistake, Sonny is still recovering from his accident and will be for a long time. He did hire a lawyer to take over his case and get a settlement against the trucking co Ins company he wasn't going to negotiate a settlement, he didn't have the time or the stomach for it. He signed a contract that they would take thirty percent. Sonny agreed and left it up to them. They told him that it would take a while if they don't choose to settle the policy limits as a gesture of good faith. Because if they should lose the case in the court system and didn't offer the policy limits then they would have to pay punitive damages. They explained it all to Sonny and said, "He hopes they *will see that there isn't any way out for them." They got up with Sonny a week later and told him that the policy limits were $50 mil.*

Sonny landed a job with DuPont marketing dept. and worked out of their Baltimore office in their Corian dept. and they trained him about the product and showed him all the advertisements they had over the last ten years. He loved it and was put on a six man team with four men and two women and they would bounce ideas off each other and come up with some great ideas. Every now and then he had to go to the DuPont bldg. in Wilm and sit in on some advertisement meetings and get the feel of how they were thinking. He would go back to Balti and come up with some good ways to show their product like they haven't done before. The adventure was so successful he was promoted to the N Y office to take on the Scratch resistant frying pan coating process that should be doing better than it is. It wasn't long before they asked him to transfer over to sales and dig into their polyurethane film dept. and show those people how to present their product differently.

They put him up in a house they owned in Manhattan and only charged him for the utilities. That was a bargain for him and it put him at ease. Every one that he came in touch with knew he had won the Hizeman award and loved to do business with him. They couldn't believe how he doesn't miss football and not understanding him when he tells them that if he can't play it then he won't let himself miss it. He was extremely popular and was always getting letters sent to the company praising him and his work ethic. They actually were having people from the company calling out to these people to see how legit these letters were. They soon found out that these people were very impressed with someone like him that didn't have a selfish bone in his body and was so honest he would show them the good and the not so good of their product. They loved it and the sales after the first three months were almost double He would always take someone that hasn't been with him out on a call so the customer would associate them with him so they could have the customer trust them like they do Sonny.

Finally after eight months he was called back to Wilm and was asked if he would like a VP position in the sales dept. and prepare himself for the top spot in that dept. someday they would pay him $200,000 a year with a $35,000. min bonus each year. He would do some traveling but mostly talk to the supervisors of each sales locations that he would bring to Wilm and show them the road to success. He told the person in HR that he would like the position and would accept the offer. Now he had to give up his penthouse and move everything to Wilm with the DuPont co paying for everything.

He found another penthouse with a view of the De. River and NJ and his furniture fit perfect. The rent was about the same as Balti. with his salary he had no problem with the rent or the living in Wilm.

His law firm got a hold of him and told him that they want to go to court and test the jurors out that Sonny ran a red light even though there weren't any witnesses that came forward in the extensive accident report. His lawyers told Sonny that this ins. co was making a horrible mistake. All they are doing is bringing themselves into a frivolous situation and could bankrupt that co. They told Sonny they want to get so deposition from him. So he was told that he might have to spend a day telling them what happened that day almost two yrs ago. It wasn't long before Sonny was in deposition starting at 10 o'clock and ran four straight hours that were a complete waste of time and Sonny's team were hoping that they will want to go to court.

Sonny want back to work and loved his sales position and was good at it, all the women in the sales dept. were head over heels in love with him. When he would go out for lunch in any of the favorite restaurants around town he was always having a big fuss made over him and his cohorts loved being with him and watching him take all of this attention he was getting in stride and not let it change him to a look at me, look how popular I am kind of a guy. He was just the opposite. The women knew he was single and they wanted him to see them and show him there best side. Everyone noticed the women dressing real up scale in the building it was almost a fashion show being put on for Sonny to see and choose one of them to be Mrs. Brown.

Chris just graduated with honors and Jenny couldn't be any happier for her. She has an interview with a GM in marketing and she is all excited about that. She knows that they get their orders from home office in Michigan. She knows that it's only an interview and just another obstacle to get over to finally get an offer from them. Chrysler also wants an interview with her so now she can play one against the other. Their marketing departments are huge and she will just be a small ripple in the ocean of sales. The Uni. Adm. Office will also pass along any inquiries if any should come in as well as interviews that might come from other companies. She will be very good in interviews that should put her over the top.

Unbeknownst to him his step sister has just been hired on in the marketing dept. after she has graduated from the U of D with her degree in marketing. They were on different floors and might never meet up. There were some connection with the sales dept. and the marketing dept. They both were doing real good and the company liked them both. Jenny has never told Chris that she had a brother that was kidnapped around twenty years ago and given up for dead. Chris would play some golf at their country club and from time to time she would see this guy on the driving range hitting balls. They would always say hello and Chris would hit her balls and leave. Sonny liked the way she looked and wondered if she was single. He was too busy getting his game back where it was before the accident.

Sonny's lawyers called and told him that he would have to come to Baltimore for his trial. He would need at least one week. Sonny took a vacation and booked a room in Balti at the Embassy Suits for the long haul. His appearance in court couldn't be better, his legal team questioned all of their witnesses and proved to the jury that they weren't witnesses it was all here say. Sonny's lawyers couldn't understand why they were going on. The judge called both sides back to his office and he asked the ins co lawyers if they had anything solid that could use to take this trial out of its frivolous mode because he was going to instruct the jury about frivolous and it looks like you have shot yourself in the foot on this one.

They left the judge's chambers and the case was ended and the jury was told what was expected of them and they were given a folder explaining what frivolous meant in a trial and what the punishment was for being frivolous. The jury left the room and the Judge told them to stick around for a couple of hours this might not take long. The ins co lawyers asked sonny's lawyers if they wanted to settle for the policy limits and they flatly refused. It was close to 9 o'clock when they were called back in to the court room for the decision. It took a few minutes for the bailiff to get them settled down and have the juror assigned as the head juror to read their decision to the court.

The juror stood up with his papers and put on his reading glasses. He paused for a short second and said, "That the jury all twelve of them have unanimously awarded Sonny Brown the sum of $50 Million dollars the policy limits and because of the frivolous charge that was put against them we all agree to award $75 mil dollars in punitive damages. The judge asked the jurors how they found the defense guilty of being frivolous and they all answered that the defense never had any creditable witnesses and put the plaintiff through unnecessary heart ache. They completely ignored the parameters in presenting their case, the told the judge that they were reckless.

The judge told the ins co lawyers to get busy and get your check to the plaintiffs lawyers in five days or I will fine you 10% every day you're late and the day ends at 3 pm. The defense lawyer said they were going to appeal and the judge told them that an appeal was frivolous as well and if you should *be turned down and the sentence be held up I will tack on more money for wasting the courts time. He told them that they didn't have a case and you still knowingly wasted the courts time and there for you request for an appeal is turned down and you have 5 days to settle this claim or you will owe the plaintiff $12.5 mil a day for every day you're late. He told the judge that this was grossly unfair of him to do this. He leaned forward and told the lawyer that he was grossly unfair to waste the money of his employer on such a strong case the plaintiff has presented and you evidently didn't tell the ins co how strong this case was.*

Sonny just sat there and wondered why this lawyer would put them through such a misery in the name of money and his fee. He felt washed out and his legs felt like leaded pipes, he was hoping that when he stood he could walk and not fall down. The judge dismissed the lawyers and Sonny was able to walk away and the more he walked the better he felt. His lawyers took Sonny into a conference room and told him that they couldn't see how the ins co would risk a fine of $12.5 mil a day when they were the ones that took this to this ending. They all shook hands and they told Sonny that they would call him as soon as they know something.

Sonny went back to work and buried himself into the job and was doing something that he liked. The national news on TV and the radio was continuous showing news clips of Sonny playing football winning the Hizeman award and not being able to plat professional ball and how he was just awarded $ 125 Mil against an ins company that tried to present their case with no evidence just hear say. Chris couldn't help but to see it on TV and all over the radio and didn't realize how rich this suit was going to make him. She hoped it would keep him around and not quit.

On the fourth day the ins co paid his law firm the $ 125. Million dollars and they kept their word and called Sonny right away to give him the news. Sonny was relieved and was eager to have closure and now move on. Of course everyone knows his business but he hopes that they will live up to the public's reputation that the public has a five day memory. Even if they don't remember the number they will know that he would have millions. His share of all this is $87,500,000.00 and he would give every penny back just to have Marie back again. So far of all the money he has he really hasn't spent any money on himself such as a house and expensive sports cars. He's not going to do anything until it is clear what he wants to do.

Meanwhile Chris is still going to the driving range and not seeing Sonny now for almost two weeks and finally he shows up and Chris was looking gorgeous and he finally came over to her and said, "She has a nice golf swing, would she like to play a round with him this afternoon." She said, "That sounds like fun but don't expect any strokes. He burst out laughing and he put her clubs on his cart and headed for the first tee. There was hardly anyone on the course and they both hit the ball real good. Sonny just broke eighty and Chris shot an eighty three. It was almost 7 o'clock and he asked her if she wanted to get a bite to eat in the club house. She liked that and they had to sit in the bar there were a couple of tables and felt more comfortable sitting there because they were dressed to casual, Sonny didn't have a suit jacket on that was required to eat in the dining room.

Chris liked Sonny's humor and laughed until her cheeks hurt. They left each other saying they should do it again. Chris couldn't wait to get home and tell her mother who she has just spent the day with. She reminded her mom that he was the guy that just won that big lawsuit; it was all over the television. He also won the Hizeman award and is in the DuPont sales department. Jenny was real happy for her that the club is exposing her to these kinds of people. She told Chris that she has spent the day studying some work procedures that she had to have right. It's the stock market you know and there cannot be any room for error.

Chris went to work the next day and she heard some people talking about Sonny and his office is only one floor up. Chris didn't want to bother him; he probably knows where she works and is leaving her alone as well. She was curious to know if Sonny knew how popular he was in the building among all of these women. She thought that he kept himself together and wasn't chasing anyone that she knows of. She saw him again on the driving range and she asked him to look at her swing and see if there can be any improvement. He put down his club and came up behind her and put his arms around her and moved her arms and fixed her grip. She could hardly stand up when he finished touching her all over. Chris thought that this was the only time a guy has ever put their hands and arms around her.

He stepped back and asked her to step back and address the ball again for a split second she thought her legs were going to give way and she was going to fall down. She took a towel and wiped her face and had gotten composure back and was ready to hit the ball. She told Sonny that she felt like she was hitting the ball more solid and knows if she practices what he showed her she will improve. He asked her if she could play nine holes and she told him it would be a good time to try out her new swing. She did very well and he seems to be comfortable with her. When they finished he asked her if she

197

would like to take in a movie that is only going to be around for another few days. She asked him what is the name of it and he said, *The Winslow Boy*, it has a 3 out of 4 star rating. It's about a fourteen year old boy that was expelled from the British Osborne naval college for something he didn't do. He didn't want to spoil it for her if she wanted to go. She told him that it sounds very entertaining. It was all that and Chris loved it and it will stay with her a long time.

They drove back to the Country Club parking lot and Sonny could hear Chris's stomach growling all the way there. He pulled into the lot and pulled into a parking spot and told her that he was going to get her something to eat like they did a few weeks ago. She said that he probably heard her stomach growling and knew she needed something to eat. They had a nice dinner and they finally exchanged phone numbers and promised to do it again. She couldn't wait to get home and tell her where she was and who she was out with again. Jenny was real happy for her and told her that it sounds like you have finally found someone that you feel comfortable with. She told her mom that he was a dream come true. She went to bed and could hardly sleep he had her so excited. Sunday Chris and her mother went out to the club for a round of golf and Sonny wasn't to be found. Chris asked the cart boy if he has seen Sonny and his reply was he's not here today. They played eighteen holes and left for the Italian restaurant at Prices Corner. Jenny could see that Chris was sad and she could see that it has to do with Sonny.

Jenny took a hold of Chris's hand and told her that he has her # and he will call you. A few days later he called Chris and asked her if she wanted to play nine holes again. She had to control herself and told sonny that she could meet him at the club at one o'clock he said he would be there. This time when they met he gave her a hug and said he missed her. She never thought she would ever hear that from the most popular man in the country. She told him that she missed him too. They had a great day and dinner again and Chris was so happy being with him and laughing all the time. He walked her to her car and when she turned to thank him his face was only inches from hers and they couldn't do anything but kiss and she melted in his arms. He stepped back and said, "He would wait for her to start her car and drive away." She cried all the way home and was a wreck when she came out in the kitchen where her mother was sitting having a nice cup of tea.

Chris started crying again and told her mother that he kissed her and was a perfect gentleman and let her go without any further advancement.

"Mom he is so nice I have never met anyone like him in my life."

"Tell me all about him Chris."

"You know come to think of it he looks a lot like you. He has your face in a manly way. Mom he is so gorgeous I want to be with him for the rest of my life. He kissed me in the parking lot when he walked me to my car and I almost passed out."

"Well Chris you have really been bitten by the love bug."

"Mom he's funny as hell and makes me laughs all the time."

"What does he do for a living?"

"Mom he's the VP in charge of sales for the DuPont Co and just in case you missed it he was just awarded $125 mil in a law suit stemming from an automobile accident three yrs. ago. His girlfriend was killed instantly and he only just survived. He was two months in intensive care. He can't play football anymore because he has a steel plate in his head and can't take another hit." Mom he has the cutest little heart shaped birth mark behind his right ear. Just then Jenny staggered to the chair at the table walking back from the sink. She turned white and started to break out into a cold sweat. Chris not paying much attention to what she was saying and what affect it was having on her mother she went on to say that he grew up in a home for motherless children in Baltimore since he was six years old. Jenny thought that was about the time her Rome was kidnapped. Jenny thought that it has to be her son Rome it just all adds up to be him and now my daughter has fallen in love with her brother. Jenny looked up at Chris in a shaky voice and told her that she wanted to meet him, please bring him home.

The End